SEAS THREATEN

The DCI Tom Tallis stories

SEAS THREATEN
UNHOLY WAR
LIDYA

SEAS
THREATEN

John Malyon

First published 2021 by John Waldram
Copyright © John Ryder Waldram 2021
Cover photo © Dan Towers
The author's moral rights have been asserted
All rights reserved
ISBN 978-1-7399165-0-3
Computer typeset in Palatino
Printed and distributed by KDP

FOR LEE

Suffered a sea-change

The corpse hadn't drifted far. A bubble of air in its waterproof jacket held it face-upwards—an inapt description, for most of the face was missing. Blood oozing from the mangled skull made a brown fog in the rolling Atlantic swells, and arrow worms were busy about the partly detached flesh.

*

Thirty miles to its south a forty-four foot ketch wallowed in corresponding aimlessness. At the moment of her owner's departure she had been looking after herself, hove-to and facing north-west aslant the northerly wind, her main and mizzen furled, the big jib hauled aback, her wheel lashed to starboard. After a few hours, however, the sheet had shaken out of the jam cleat. The jib, freed, had begun to flog in the strengthening breeze. Slowly, she had come to a standstill, her head had fallen away downwind, and she'd wandered off south-west across the swell, alone. Gradually, as the days had gone by, her jib had shredded itself. Now the wind had eased, but her two masts still jerked uneasily at their stays.

*

On June 28th, a miniscule dot, creeping slowly across the Atlantic chart, approached the ketch's almost fixed dot. *HMS Leicester*, homeward-bound after a spell of showing the flag in Bermuda, was running steadily eastwards in murky weather. The two dots coalesced and *Leicester*'s radar operator sent a laconic report to the bridge. Her commander ordered half-speed, and a few moments later the ketch floated out of a rainsquall into the circular view of his binoculars. He noted her disintegrated jib and wandering course, stopped his ship neatly nearby, and sent over an inflatable to investigate.

Her Majesty's frigates are not yacht-nannies, so a tow was not appropriate. But he had on board a couple of young sailing enthusiasts, and a spot of salvage work might, perhaps, double as useful exercise in practical navigation. So Lieutenant Peter Grainger and Sub-Lieutenant Adam Bough found themselves collecting what spare navigational equipment and wet-weather clothing they could find, and getting pleasurably damp in the inflatable. They checked out the ketch's radio, found some winch handles, hoisted a bit of sail, and set their course for Plymouth.

*

The ketch's lonely proprietor, however, now even less recognisable and a little higher in the water, continued to rotate as inexorably and aimlessly as before. A swarm of nuzzling copepods had joined the bloated arrow worms.

To present business

'Dad! Supper!' yelled Miranda.

A powerful whiff of pasta sauce drifted through to the living room. 'Cider?' Tom called.

'Something better here.' She stuck her head round the kitchen door and pushed a Sainsbury's bag onto the sideboard. Tom hauled himself up, peered inside, fetched two glasses and a corkscrew.

She brought full plates through from the kitchen and dumped them onto the table. They settled themselves, poured the wine, smothered her sauce in grated Parmesan, and for a while it was rotating forks and no conversation. Tom savoured the chestnut mushrooms, the strong cooking onions, the virgin oil. The Chianti went down well, too.

At last she said, 'Jack rang.'

'Ah.'

'Home as soon as term finishes, he said.'

'When's that?'

'After you're off. Thursday week.'

'I'll be at sea by then!' Tom could feel a surreptitious grin creeping onto his face: for several weeks now his forty-eight years' maturity had been trying in vain to repress boyish anticipation. 'Oh, and by the way,' he added. 'I may have to leave early.'

'Why?'

'New investigation.'

She looked at him and waited.

'One of the OSTAR yachts was found abandoned.'

Miranda nodded. 'Was in the *Western Morning News*,' she said. She scattered more Parmesan, and stirred. 'The *Cas A*.'

'Not Mike's, thank goodness. The Navy brought it in yesterday.'

'Charles somebody? Swept overboard, they said.'

'West. Charles West.'

Miranda opened her eyes wide and gave a little shiver. 'Single-hander's worst nightmare,' she said. 'Out in the ocean, watching your boat sail away from you. What's it got to do with leaving early?'

'The Navy think something dodgy may have happened.'

'Meaning?'

'Can't tell you!'

Miranda frowned. 'And?'

'I have to question the other competitors.'

'In Newport? As they arrive?'

'That's the idea.'

She smiled to herself and asked no more.

They had farmhouse cheese and granary bread. She made coffee and Tom poured. Then he washed up, neatly. His linen shirt and black chinos were neat too, but his greying fair hair was tousled.

The luminous summer sky faded. When he returned to the sitting-room Miranda was reading. In autumn colours today, he observed: trousers dark, top buff, a scarf dramatic in browns and oranges twisted round her slender neck. Leaving Plymouth in two days to visit friends, he remembered with a pang. He turned up the radiator, switched on the reading lights and found his own book.

At last he said: 'Jack's doing well, isn't he?'

'He's bright,' said Miranda.

'Yes,' with a wry smile. 'A lot cleverer than I was at his age.'

Miranda sniffed. 'Don't give me that, Dad!' she said, and read on.

He looked at her and thought: keeping me in line— she wouldn't have said that last year.

What foul play?

The following day was hot. Tom, in working kit of trousers and checked shirt, opened the sun-roof of his old Corolla and rolled down from Crownhill to Police Headquarters in Hampton Street. He re-read the Navy's report on *Cas A* twice, and called the OSTAR Millenium race office to get a first sense of what they knew about Charles West. Then he drove over to the dockyard.

Peter Grainger was waiting to meet him at the checkpoint, uniformed and tanned. They shook hands, parked Tom's car, and walked in bright sun to the basin by the Hamoaze where *Cas A* lay moored.

Tom examined her rigging and hull as Peter watched him silently. Everything seemed in remarkably good shape. 'Well, Lieutenant,' Tom said at last, 'shall we sit down?' They settled on the cockpit seats. The breeze off the river lifted Tom's hair. 'You made a quick passage, didn't you? The competitors are all still at sea, they tell me.'

'Favourable wind.'

'I can understand why you called us in... But a bit tenuous, don't you think?'

Peter raised one eyebrow.

Tom dug out his filofax, settling to the routine, conscious of being scruffier than his witness. 'So...' he said. '*Cas A* shows up on your radar?'

'Murky day. Yacht wandering about with her jib

torn to bits. James—Commander Johnson, my skipper—says we should investigate. Sends me over with two seamen for a look-see.'

'First impressions?

'Nobody at home!'

'What else?'

'Very tidy. Wheel lashed to starboard. Main and mizzen furled and secured.' Peter, his arms folded, seemed determined to be exact, his voice clipped Dartmouth. 'Like he'd been hove-to on starboard, and the jib sheet had shaken loose after he'd gone. And he didn't fall overboard because something gave way—the stanchions and side-wires were all OK.'

'No signs of an accident, then?'

'Nope.'

'Personal safety kit?'

'Safety harness in the companion locker.'

'Why wasn't he wearing it? First commandment for single-handers, isn't it?'

Peter raised his eyebrow again. 'Maybe he'd come on deck just for a moment: didn't bother.'

'Or perhaps the one you found was a spare?'

'Could be. Maybe he *was* wearing a harness, but never clipped it on.'

'Lifejacket?'

'Couldn't find one. There was an old buoyancy-aid in a cabin drawer.'

'They told me single-handers don't like them—once overboard you've had it, and there's no point in prolonging the agony. But he was supposed to carry one.' Tom scribbled for a while.

Peter Grainger leaned back against the cockpit coaming, observing the scene around the basin. In the sunlight two black-headed gulls were tugging at a scrap of pizza.

'Now,' said Tom at last. 'He wouldn't want to waste time hove-to without a reason.'

Peter hesitated. 'Nothing damaged and needing repair, and using his number-one jib—the wind can't have been that strong.'

'Any sign he'd been working the sails?'

'No winch handles left in the cockpit. Full set in a rack below, by the companion ladder.'

'Signal halyards rigged? Could he have been contacting another boat to come alongside?'

'*Flag* signalling? He had a perfectly good VHF.'

'Right.'

'The long-wave radio fixed up for the race was working too.'

'How difficult would it be, coming alongside at sea?'

Peter unfolded his arms and laid one forearm along the tiller. 'Good question! Bloody hard for a single-hander. And who, for Christ's sake, in the middle of the Atlantic?'

Also a good question, reflected Tom. 'Any sign his inflatable had been used?'

'Hard to be sure. Stowed.'

'Liferaft?'

'In its deck container. Sealed and unused.'

More black-headed gulls were swooping onto the quay-side competition. Tom took a final look around the deck. 'Let's get the lie of the land below.'

Peter led the way down the companion ladder. Tom followed and settled onto a settee berth, writing more notes at the cabin table. Peter removed his uniform cap and jacket, produced a pipe and lit it. Whiffs of Kendal Kentucky floated around the cabin.

'Now,' said Tom at last. 'This rifle?'

Peter nodded, twisted round and pointed at a vertical rack to the left of the companion ladder. 'Extraordinary, we thought.'

Wondering whether there was any point, Tom opened his equipment case and pulled on thin cotton gloves. 'World war two Lee–Enfield three-oh-three. Good padlock. Where's the key?'

'We couldn't find one.'

'We'll do a proper search tomorrow.'

Peter nodded. 'As I said, we found later it was loaded, with the safety catch off. To be honest, we came damn near pulling the trigger by accident—in the rack, before we realised.'

That was a more engaged reply, thought Tom. They'd been intrigued by the gun—and stuck their fingerprints all over it. 'How did you work out it was loaded?'

'You can't operate the bolt without unlocking that padlock, but you can take out the magazine.'

Tom did so. 'Looks like he loaded two clips of five, and loosed off just one. Your report said it had been fired?'

'If you twist your head round, you can see the rim of a spent cartridge in the breech.'

'Found any other ammunition?'

'No. We looked.'

'OK.' Tom made more notes. 'Navigation kit?'

'Built-in GPS, here, and a calculator set up for navigational work. Sextant and digital clock, but he didn't use them—no records of sun sights or calculations. Two hand-bearing compasses, RDF. Built-in log and echo sounder, like most people.'

'You said his Atlantic chart was missing?'

'That was the other strange thing... *Nobody* crosses an ocean without a big chart, ever. You need to plot your fixes. Even if you do everything by calculator, you need to *read* things: ice-pack limits, steamship routes, weather ships. Plot your competitors' positions.'

'Mm.'

'We had to fetch one from *Leicester*. The other sheets were all there. Channel Approaches, for instance—he'd been plotting himself and competitors on it after he left Plymouth.'

Tom looked and nodded. 'Log book?'

'Here.' Peter extracted a slim volume bound in red leather from the chart drawer. 'Well kept. The entries just stop after 24th June.'

'His last reported position was for noon that day.'

'He went through some heavy weather around the 20th, but no record of any trouble. Kept a separate notebook for hand bearings and GPS fixes. Here.'

'Thanks. I'll take the log and notebook... Now, we need to make a quick search of the whole boat. Just to see if there's anything else obviously missing. I've got the list of equipment the race rules specified.'

Peter rolled up the white sleeves of his shirt, tucked out of harm's way the loose ends of his black uniform tie, and they went to work.

When they reached the fore-cabin, Peter said: 'Another odd thing. My colleague Adam used the big locker under this bunk for his kit. It's a useful locker, but we found it completely empty, apart from this.' He held out a rubber foot-pump.

'Clean, looks unused. For blowing up inflatables?'

'Probably.'

Tom scratched his head, and the search went on. 'That's everything now except the kedge anchor,' he announced eventually.

'Kedge?' Peter's forearms were greasy from feeling around below the engine. 'Heavy, should be low down.'

'Below the heads, maybe?'

Peter found a screwdriver in *Cas A*'s tool box, faced into the tiny WC compartment, and levered up the hatch in the floor.

'Oho!' said Tom, sitting on his heels.

'Now why ever would he need that?' said Peter. He'd uncovered an empty set of chocks with three corded lashings. They'd been slashed at with a knife as though someone had wrenched out the spare anchor in a tearing hurry.

Tom was peering into the turn of the bilge, below the cut lashings. He fetched a torch, donned his gloves again, and pulled out a flat-sided bottle. It bore a label marked *J's Jamaica*, showing an island, a palm tree and a schooner. Attached to the label was a neat foil sticker with the legend *OSTAR Millenium 2000*. The bottle had been opened, but was still nearly full. Tom knelt inspecting the cut lashing for some time. He raised his eyebrows at Peter, but made no comment.

'Well,' he said at last, 'that's it... Nothing else you noticed? Just those two things made you wonder, the fired rifle and the missing chart?'

'Plus the stowed safety harness and empty locker, I suppose. And now this.'

'Not a lot to go on.' He looked thoughtfully at Peter. 'But whiffy, definitely.'

Peter was smiling now. 'Want to talk to Adam?'

'Not yet. But we do need a proper search. I'll send two detectives in the morning.'

'OK.' Peter was scrubbing his arm with kitchen wipe from the galley.

'Keep your mouths shut in the wardroom, please.'

They tidied themselves in silence, walked silently back to the guard-house barrier, and shook hands once again.

17

Tom drove thoughtfully back to his office, and arranged for DS Howe and DC Cullis to tackle the search. Then he followed the slow lunchtime traffic home to Crownhill, and disappeared into the bedroom he used as an office while Miranda got on with her packing.

*

Next day, Tom left the house at eight. Miranda saw nothing of him till lunchtime, when he dashed in and offered to cook them both an omelette. This she upstaged by announcing she'd already made a paella as a departing feast, to be followed by bananas in brandy, 'and some decent coffee, Dad.'

After the bananas, Miranda remarked: 'If you *really* won't tell me about it, we shan't have had any intelligible conversation for *two whole days!*'

'Can't give my family crucial details of investigations.'

'No, Dad.'

'And we don't have much time… Still, perhaps… Let's have that coffee, and then, if you persist, I might mention a few of the oddest things… You can exert your womanly intuition.'

'*Intelligence.*'

Tom grinned. 'Womanly intelligence. I'll do the coffee.' He clattered around in the kitchen, brought it on a tray, and said: 'Might be hardish not telling your course mates about this one?'

'I won't do that, Dad.'

'Well, let's see…' He gave her an exaggerated frown. 'First off: would anyone in their senses cross the Atlantic without a chart?'

'No,' said Miranda, with a half smile and sparkling

eyes.

'And could you just *lose* a big chart like that?'

'He might have brought it on deck and let it blow away. But why bring it on deck at all? Not like sailing along the Devon coast trying to recognise headlands.'

'Well, if it wasn't lost, what happened to it?'

'He must have got rid of it on purpose... But, even if he had good reason, why do it in the middle of the race, when he'd be needing it?'

'He could just as easily have done it later?'

Miranda nodded.

Tom looked at her quizzically. 'OK,' he said, and thought for a while. 'Next, why should a nearly full bottle of rum have been left in the bilges under the WC floor?'

'A big bottle?'

'No, a small flat one. *J's Jamaica*. Advertising goody. All the competitors were given one.'

'Sounds like fortifying himself. Had he been doing something there?'

'Getting out his kedge, it seems. In a tearing hurry.'

'Why would he need to fortify himself, getting out an anchor?'

'Well, that depends... What uses can you think of for a kedge, in the middle of the Atlantic?'

'None! Sounds crazy.'

'None at all?'

'As a weight, perhaps? Can't think of much else.'

Tom beamed at her. 'Good girl! Super intuition—super intelligence!'

'Thank you!'

Again, Tom thought for a moment. 'Now, if a compulsively tidy man kept a rifle on his boat, why padlock it into its rack loaded, with a spent cartridge in the breech, and the safety catch off?'

'He kept a *rifle* on the boat?'

'Seems so.'

Miranda asked him to repeat the question. 'That sounds crazy too,' she said. 'I'm not sure about leaving it loaded: I suppose he must have had a reason. But if he *wanted* to keep it loaded, he'd have ejected the spent cartridge, wouldn't he? And if it had been fired, he'd want to clean and oil the barrel.'

Tom was surprised she knew so much about rifles. 'Someone *did* clean the outside. The only fingerprints on it were the Navy's.'

Miranda raised her eyebrows.

Tom smiled back. 'Now the last... Why was the big locker under the bunk in the fore cabin completely empty apart from a rubber foot-pump?'

'That's odd, too,' said Miranda thoughtfully. The sunlight had worked its way round to one of her mother's paintings, and the sitting room had come alive with colour. 'There's never enough storage space in boats. Any reasonably organised person will spread things out between the lockers.'

The clock caught Tom's eye. 'Hey,' he said. 'I'm driving you to the station. Time's running on. I'll wash up later... If you have any more bright ideas, call me from Edinburgh.'

She grinned happily back. 'I might,' she said.

Tom ran upstairs to fetch her suitcase.

Ride the curled clouds

July 9th, and Tom was slumped in a window seat. Flight BA 215 to Boston, no longer sitting on her tail, had settled to the metallic growl of a jumbo at cruising height. The thin young man to his right had been reading, but after twenty minutes he'd stretched, got up, and ambled forward into club class. After a considerable time he reappeared in the opposite aisle, walked slowly past Tom towards the back of the plane, and disappeared again. Early leg cramp, Tom decided.

The browns of Wales passed, giving way to the vivid green of Ireland and then the turquoise of the distantly furrowed ocean. The great circle route would be taking them north of the race competitors below. But he couldn't have picked them out anyway: even supertankers would be minuscule and lacking in contrast. It wasn't the ghostly sea but the fretted minarets of the clouds, hard-edged, that gave structure to the scenery up here.

*

'Better come up,' the Super had said, three days earlier. New to Plymouth, he'd installed a pair of deep leather chairs by his office window, with airy views over the city centre.

'Sit down Tom, good… I've studied your summary.'
Tom settled himself.

'Basically, I agree.'

Tom smiled. The Super was four years his junior, but they got on well.

'Got a few issues, though... You want to hop over to Rhode Island?'

'Yes.'

'Cheaper to ask the locals, don't you think?'

'That's the point, Sir—it won't cost us. I'm going to Newport anyway.'

'You are?'

'Got a friend in the race, I'm taking leave to help him sail his boat home.'

'Ah yes... And suppose your friend proved to be the villain?' It was the Super's turn to smile.

'Unlikely,' said Tom, raising his eyebrows. 'Old police colleague.'

'Do I know him?'

'I wouldn't think so... Mike Guerdon—left Plymouth five years ago.'

'A sailing plod? How can he afford that?'

'Left the force and went into business.'

The Super looked down his nose at Tom's summary. 'Time and money, then?'

'Paying my expenses.'

'He must like you!'

And I like him, thought Tom. 'He used to be on my team.'

'Where's he live now?'

'In Essex, where he grew up... And we're not talking about million dollar racing machines. This OSTAR race is for amateurs, what they call a Corinthian event.'

'Ah,' said the Super, 'I remember now: back to the original spirit.'

Tom nodded.

The Super looked thoughtfully at him. 'So it

wouldn't cost us... Thought about jurisdiction?' he asked.

'We're OK for anything that happened on board the yacht. She's British.'

'Off our patch, though. Need Home Office app-roval... And questioning witnesses in the US? Our American friends won't like that.'

'The race sponsors want it sorted, Sir—I can do it under their auspices, unofficially, gives me a bit of cover.'

'Well, maybe. But we'd still need to clear it ...'

'... I was hoping, Sir ...'

'... It's OK,' the Super smiled again. 'I'll see what can be done. Intriguing case.'

And the organisational side of things had worked out far more smoothly than Tom had feared. The Rhode Island State Police had been squared through Interpol. The Super's secretary had even rebooked Tom's air ticket.

*

Two stewardesses with fixed smiles were hauling a drinks trolley up the aisle, one short, pink and round-ed, the other dark, gangly and of uncertain age. Tom asked for a latté. His neighbour had left his book face down on the seat. Stretching over it for his plastic mug, Tom recognised *Childhood's End*. He sipped his caffeine fix, found and opened his filofax, and settled down to work—in seven hours' time the Newport City Police Chief would be demanding detail.

The first page allocated to the case was headed:

Forensics to date

He ran his eye rapidly down the notes jotted below.

The official search, he reminded himself, hadn't found the padlock key. But Sergeant Howe had discovered an ammunition box and clips in a coffee tin in the galley. As he'd mildly put it: 'perhaps Lieutenant Grainger dan't drink real coffee, Sir.' Ballistics had identified the rounds as Federal Power-Shock deer-hunting ammunition, high-velocity and soft-nosed: an American product that made an ugly and massive exit wound in the quarry, not a neat round hole.

The lab had tested the empty locker in the fore-cabin for traces of drugs, but found nothing.

The rum bottle, unlike the rifle, had carried prints, but too smeared to be useful.

The Met Office had quoted the wind at *Cas A*'s position on 24th June as a gentle Force 3 northwesterly.

Victim's background

The next sheet carried more detail, and Tom mulled it over for some time.

Cas A was an F&C 44, a German Frers design built in Buenos Aires in 1981. West had been racing her since June 1997 and kept her on a Southampton marina. The Race Commodore had described him to Sergeant Howe and Constable Cullis as: 'meticulous, stand-offish, too bloody critical of our organisation'. His secretary had put it rather differently: 'cool clothes, tanned, straw hair and ice-blue eyes, a loner. Didn't like him. One of those who'd rev you up and drop you like a hot penny.' She had his address on file, a flat in Salisbury.

Howe and Cullis had rushed up to Wiltshire and, with the help of the local force, discovered that West had been renting the place since 1996. The neighbours hardly knew him, and he wasn't on the Electoral Roll. After a spot of bother obtaining a warrant, a search of his two rooms turned up membership papers for the Salisbury Rifle Club, and the club vice-captain told them West had joined in October '97. He'd bought the rifle, properly licensed, from a retired club member, and was fussy about it. The club didn't stock deer-hunting ammunition.

And that was about it.

Tom had called the two detectives in. 'Not enough, where's his *roots*?' he demanded.

'None apparent,' said Howe, scowling.

'None at all, Sergeant?'

'No papers, no address book, no job, no tax, no National Insurance.'

'No *job*? What about a car?'

'White Golf GTi. On the street outside. Nothing in it.'

'Bank?'

'Nat West. Salisbury. Opened in '97 with two grand in cash. No regular income, no BACS transfers. Only one cheque deposit ever, and that was just a refund of overcharged marina fees. Periodical big cash deposits, which he paid in himself.'

'In Salisbury?'

'City branches in London... Didn't want to be traced, this one.'

'What's this, then? Drugs?'

'Could be. But the flat and car were clean.'

'Correspondence?'

'Zilch! Had a powerful desktop, though, a Power Mac G4. And a pile of technical printout.'

'I showed it to the university computing department, Sir,' said Cullis, young and keen to make progress.

'And?'

'They said it was heavy maths. Like he was a professional programmer.'

'A *programmer*? Who the hell for?'

Cullis shook his head.

'What about his hard drive? Letters, e-mails?'

'Nothing. Didn't use the mailer, hadn't even got Word.'

'Any apps at all?'

'Just the standard Mac ones, plus a Fortran compiler for the programming, and QuarkXPress.'

'What's that?'

'Desk-top publisher.'

'Any book layouts he'd done?'

'Not that we could find.'

'Odd… Internet service provider?'

'Telewest.'

'So what'd he been browsing?'

'The Safari cache was empty,' said Howe gloomily. 'And not just empty—securely wiped. Knew what he was doing, this one.'

'Damn!' said Tom.

The background sheet left a lot to be desired.

*

The coffee had left Tom needing to visit the loo, and realising that his neighbour had reappeared and was about to sit down, he jumped up and set off. On his return the thin young man had abandoned Arthur C. Clarke and was deep in something with a purple cover, but stood up to let him past. Tom found his miniature airline pillow, arranged it behind his neck—and glancing sideways was able to decipher the new title: *Monthly Notices of the Royal Astronomical Society*. He raised his eyebrows, tipped his seat back, and turned to his best-thumbed section:

Key issues

At the time of Tom's promotion to DCI, three years earlier, his colleague Iain Gemmill had been passed over. But that hadn't disturbed Iain's Kilmarnock, son-of-the-manse comradeship, and the whole of this section, which ran to several pages, had been chewed over with him several times.

'Face it, man,' Iain had said at last, 'it's still perfectly *possible* the guy just tripped and fell overboard.' This was in Tom's office at a chilly 8 am. Iain had fastened all the buttons of his tweed jacket, thrust his fists deep into its pockets, and was perched on Tom's radiator.

'OK,' agreed Tom. 'So what are our *strongest* reasons for thinking otherwise?'

'The gun, the chart and the anchor.'

'Right. The gun. Seems that West was a tidy man who was fussy about his rifle…'

'…so you'd think,' ran on Iain, 'he'd have been careful to eject the spent cartridge and clean the barrel before he locked it back in the rack…'

'…suggesting it was *someone else* who put it away. Which is a bloody peculiar conclusion.'

'Alternatively,' said Iain, 'it's possible he himself put it in the rack, but hurriedly, just before he left the boat, so he never had time to deal with it.'

'But that would suggest the gun was fired just before he disappeared…'

'… which would in turn suggest there was someone else there,' said Iain. 'That's your second point.'

'Third, he can't have been alone and gone overboard through some freak accident with the gun, because that would have left no one behind to lock it up,' said Tom firmly.

'That's clear enough. And your fourth point is…'

'… someone wiped the outside of the rifle, pretty

thoroughly. Who wouldn't have been West...'

'... because *he*'d have no reason to wipe his own prints. So whichever way we look at it, we reckon there *must* have been someone else on board!'

'Yup,' said Tom sombrely, 'we do.'

'Who knew about prints, but not about guns?'

'That's about it.'

'Right. The chart?'

'Not so strong, but similar. If he lost it innocently much before he disappeared, he'd surely have said so in his log. And he'd have set up a sketch chart, or something, to record progress. And if he was really on his own, having some private reason to destroy the chart, he'd have waited till later, when he didn't need it for navigation. *Therefore* he can't have been alone.'

'He *might* have fallen overboard holding it—but we think that'd be too much of a coincidence.'

'But if there was someone else around, *they* might well have ditched the chart, to destroy evidence,' said Tom.

'Like evidence of West being somewhere other than he'd reported, for instance.' The thermally challenged headquarters central heating was at last beginning to take effect, and Iain, still on the radiator, had cautiously unfastened his top button. 'And the kedge anchor?' he queried.

'By itself, less suspicious. But a heavy awkward object, lifted from its chocks in a hurry—the rum bottle means panic, someone scared and fortifying themselves.'

'You yachties say there's no *sailing* reason to dismount that anchor far from land. But it's hard to think of any *non*-sailing use that would make it disappear from the boat, other than weighting something to make it sink. Such as a body!'

'That's it. … Not a bad set of arguments, Iain.'

'Put them to the Super now, man.'

And the Super had been sufficiently convinced to agree that investigation was required. Tom mulled over the arguments slowly and carefully yet again. They still looked pretty solid to him.

*

At last he spied the lunch trolley on its way, pushed by a bronzed male steward this time, the tall thin stewardess in attendance. She asked Tom what main course he wanted, and his neighbour passed the tray over. 'Smells good!' he said, in a cordial New England accent. Tom did his best to enjoy the packaged food, washed his scrap of mature cheddar down with the last of his minuscule bottle of Beaujolais, and brushed crumbs of water biscuit from his groin. Once the plastic tray and utensils had been removed he settled to work again.

What really occurred?

This section was all rows of dots and question marks.

'So what do you reckon *did* happen?' Tom had asked Iain, when at last, late in the afternoon, they'd found time to think further. The radiator was now thundering and the office over-warm, though dim because it was raining outside.

'Well,' said Iain, sitting this time on Tom's desk. He forced his hands up through his ginger hair. 'We have to ask, why the rifle? And why that particular ammunition? That guy was either *bringing* big trouble to someone, or *expecting* big trouble.'

'He was pretty open about it,' said Tom. 'Perhaps

he wanted to show he was armed.'

'Drug smuggling?'

'Seems possible.'

'But a handover out in mid-ocean doesn't sound right,' said Iain, 'and forensics found nothing.'

'No. And he was travelling in the wrong direction.'

'If not drugs, what *was* stored in the fore-cabin?' Their conversation had rattled this way and that.

'Does it have to involve another boat?' Iain had asked, this time dragging his fingers down over his cheeks.

'I think it does. West *might* have had a stowaway, but if he did, how did the stowaway leave *Cas A*, if not by some other vessel?'

'They could have gone overboard together. In a struggle.'

'Even more of a coincidence!'

'Or maybe West shipped a second life raft. Stored in that empty locker.'

'Come off it Iain! No one *plans* to leave a yacht in mid-Atlantic by raft!'

'Perhaps he made a rendezvous at sea, left his boat, and deliberately set up this evidence to puzzle us!'

'That *is* possible. Dramatic planned disappearance. Been done before.'

No, thought Tom. This sheet is a waste of time, pure speculation... The video screen in front of him was showing BA 215's progress on a moving map. They were now further west than Iceland: level with where it all happened. His neighbour had dropped off to sleep.

Opportunity

There'd been no time to discuss the next sheet with Iain. But who had been in a position to board *Cas A*?

Being hove-to in quiet weather suggested some sort of meeting at sea. Brisk work with the Navy and Lloyds of London had shown there were probably no large ships near on June 24th. But there were several competitors within 150 miles, who must be his initial suspects. Before leaving Plymouth, with the help of Race Headquarters, Tom had sketched out a chart showing their noon positions from 19th to 24th June. He extracted it from his briefcase. [See next page]

It showed two groups of three boats. In the northern group were *Cas A* herself, and two twenty-year old American-owned Contessa 35s, *Flying Cloud* and *St Louis Blues.* These three seemed evenly matched and had steered similar courses, being at times as little as ten miles apart. They should surely have sighted each other from time to time.

The southern group of three had been more dispersed, and the northernmost of them, *Ugly Duckling,* a British OOD 34, had reported herself within 100 miles of the northern group on the 24th. The other two were a British Rival 38, *Ariel,* and a more recent custom built 36-foot cruiser-racer from Waterford called *Shamrock.*

Tom had marked the wind directions on his sketch. The boats were sailing against the wind: until about noon on the 21st it had been west of south-west, forcing them to sail close-hauled a little north of the ideal course. At that point a cold front had passed over the fleet from the north and the wind had veered to north-west, allowing them all to tack, turning left to lay a course passing south of the Grand Banks, still some 800 miles ahead.

Under these conditions none of them would be doing more than 6 knots, say 150 miles a day. Tom stared at his chart for a long time, trying to work out which of the skippers, while slightly misreporting their

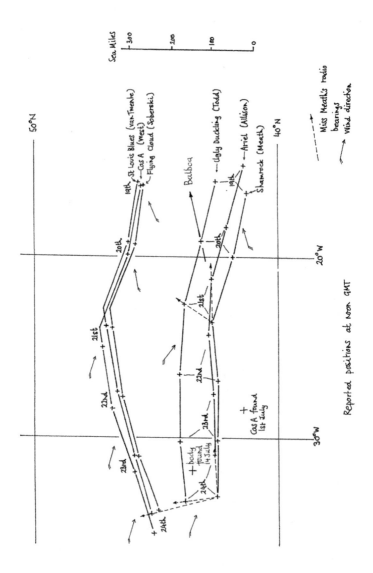

Reported positions at noon GMT

Sea Miles
— 300
— 200
— 100
— 0

50°N

19th ⟶ St Louis Blues (van-Tweate)
+ ⟶ Cas A (West)
⟵ Flying Cloud (Soberski)

Balboa

⟵ Ugly Duckling (Todd)
19th
+ ⟵ Ariel (Allison)
Shamrock (Meath)

40°N

20th

21st

22nd

23rd

24th

20th

21st

22nd

23rd

+ body
found
14 July

24th

+ Cas A found
1st July

Miss Meath's radio
bearings
Wind direction

30°W   20°W

32

position, could have surreptitiously closed with *Cas A* on 24th June. But he found this a pointless exercise: *any* of them might have managed the manoeuvre if they'd started it early enough. What he had to hope was that they'd seen each other, which would provide a few cross-checks on the reported positions.

He changed his approach, and began settling in his mind lines of questioning for each of the five suspect skippers. But he knew from experience and training that such rational plans were not always successful. The most effective angle was often best found by observation, watching for that almost imperceptible shrinking or fractionally deeper breathing, and its subsequent dissolution, anxiety melting into watchful unease and then re-establishing itself as the questioner sniffed his way around the factual landscape. The over-dry cabin air made his head stuffy. His neighbour was still asleep. Tom, after an exhausting two days, and unconvinced of the value of his work, let his attention droop and dozed over his chart.

*

He woke suddenly an hour later, opening his eyes without moving his body; but nothing much was happening. The cloud palaces on his left had jumped into new shapes, and his neighbour was upright and awake. Hurriedly folding his chart and squinting sideways, Tom saw that *Monthly Notices* had morphed into a *Loaded* centrefold. The young man saw Tom was awake, gave him a gentle grin, and tidied away his generously rounded sylph. After a moment, however, he nodded towards the folded chart, and enquired rather firmly:

'The OSTAR Millenium?'

Tom considered his options rapidly. 'You a sailor then?' he countered.

'Only very occasional... But I'm a bit of a groupie—been following on the website... You involved somehow? Know any of the competitors?'

'I know one,' said Tom judiciously. 'I'm coming over to sail home with him.'

The young man looked sharply at him. 'Lucky you!'

There was a pause. But after a while the young man nodded a second time at the sketch chart, and added,

'*Cas A*'s the one where that poor guy went overboard?'

Tom's instincts for caution jerked back into action. 'That's right,' he said.

'Funny choice of name for a boat.'

'*Cas A*?'

'Yes.'

'Why funny?'

'It's a *star*.' The young man nodded. 'I'm an astronomer, you see,' he added.

Tom thought some more. 'Is it an unusual star?' he asked.

'You could say so. *Cassiopeia A*. It's a supernova remnant.'

'So why did you think it a funny choice?'

'If I owned a boat, I'd choose some *bright* star, one folks would have heard of: *Polaris* or *Sirius* or *Arcturus*. Then they'd understand what I was on about.'

'And they wouldn't have heard of *Cas A*?'

'Most likely not. It's an *astronomer's* star. Can't be seen with the naked eye. You need a long-exposure photograph in a big telescope, and even then it's just a little bubble of brightness... Calling it *Cas A* is astronomer speak.'

'An amateur would have called it *Cassiopeia A*?'

'I reckon. But the puzzle is, that guy, Charles West, he *isn't* a professional. Not that I've heard of.'

'And you'd be sure to know?' asked Tom.

'Maybe not.'

'I suppose even an amateur might have come across the shortened name?'

'Well, sure. Anyone might know *something* about it. It's in the coffee-table books. But it still seems a funny choice for a boat… That's how I see it, anyway.'

Tom was inclined to agree. He thought at some length, but wasn't sure how far it was wise to pursue the conversation. At last, the young man opened his brief case and extracted *Monthly Notices* again; he turned to a page marked with a paper clip and started to read with close attention.

Tom turned to the final page in his notebook, angling it away from his neighbour. It read:

Unsolved minor puzzles

(i)   If two single-handers meet in mid-ocean, is it possible for one of them to get onto the other's boat?

(ii)   Where did West get the money to buy Cas A?

(iii) Why was the forward locker empty?

(iv)   Why the rifle, and why that particularly vicious ammunition?

(v)   What does the name Cas A signify?

The fifth of these being now happily solved, Tom let his imagination run on the others, and sensed that a few useful ideas were hazily forming at the edge of his unconscious.

Brave new world

After a further half-hour, BA 215 began its descent. Passengers came to life, filled in customs forms, queued for the loos. Ears popping, Tom collected his things together. The plane rumbled onto the runway twenty minutes late; the Captain apologised, told them the temperature was 72 F outside, welcomed them to Logan International Airport, and thanked them all for flying British Airways. As they finally jolted to rest, everyone stood up; the thin young man briskly hoisted the strap of his cabin bag onto one shoulder, and pushed off down the gangway. Tom followed in more leisurely fashion.

Some time later, however, they met again at the baggage carousel. The young man grinned, though he was jigging about anxiously and looking at his watch.

'Here for a conference?' Tom asked.

The young man nodded. 'But there'll be the odd day off. Maybe I'll get myself down to Newport, see the boats… Know where I'd find them?'

'There's a welcoming yacht club—the Point Judith YC.'

'Point Judith?'

'That's it.'

'Maybe we'll meet again… Hey! There's mine.' The young man pointed at the carousel, waited as it trundled around, leaned down to yank up a bulging rucksack, and slung it over one shoulder. He grinned again, looked at his watch and disappeared at a run towards the US customs.

Tom stared thoughtfully after him.

*

The Point Judith Association had its headquarters on an old landed estate towards the south end of Conanicut Island, facing Newport across Rhode Island Sound. The porticoed facade and lawns of the great house overlooked the water imperiously. Behind it, to the west of a brick-walled garden, white clapboard buildings housed the offices, washrooms and restaurants; to the south lay the marina with its beacon and sky-blue control tower.

In these patrician surroundings, Police Chief Patrick Slieve of the Newport City Police Department looked even more out of place than Tom did, though not in the least disconcerted—ex New York, thickset, fortyish and freckled in uniform and gunbelt.

'*Officially*, Chief Inspector,' he said as he twitched Tom's suitcase from the trunk of his navy and white police cruiser, 'ain't that much I can do for you. Goddam sailboat's right outside my jurisdiction… So, unless it turns out some US citizen was guilty of crime… or crime was committed on some US vessel… which we've no evidence of so far…' He dusted his hands slowly. '*Unofficially*, sure, mighty pleased to assist—intelligence, whatever, cutting out hassle. Care to swap ideas over a bourbon, just give me a buzz, my pleasure… Figure out what this guy was after, with his antiquated rifle and his hunting slugs, sure.' An appraising pause. 'Best of luck then, Tom!'

One powerful handshake, a big grin at the sunny sky, and he was off.

The building might be grand and the club members

well-heeled, but Tom's welcome was warm enough. The Commodore, grizzled in a well-cut blazer, swept him into the bar for a martini, then out again, for appropriation by a beaming acolyte.   A pleasant gravelly voice said brightly, 'Hi! I'm Della!' A curly head bobbed. 'A pleasure to meet you, Inspector Tallis.'

A fussy tug, she convoyed Tom away to the old house. A lavish visitor suite had been carved out of a vast bedroom. Tom dumped his very small suitcase onto the king-sized bed and admired the view.

'What's your role here, Della?'

'Me, Mr Tallis? Do-it-all lady!' She laughed. 'House mom… Secretary to the Committee.'

'And you know why I'm here?'

She smiled winningly at him and nodded.

Typed the emails and took in all the finer points, thought Tom. 'This questioning of competitors…'

'…in the library.' Without a pause, she grasped his elbow and propelled him out through the door again and towards the stairs, heels clicking busily on the parquet.

The reading room on the ground floor had an Edwardian air, and housed a collection of yachting books and exhibits. There were reading tables and chairs.

'This is fine.'

'The competitors get to hand in their logs to me, Mr Tallis. Will you be wanting photocopies?'

'Some of them, yes please.' Tom yawned. It was the end of a jet-lagged day. 'What happens when they arrive?'

She'd noticed the yawn. 'We give them a meal, let them sleep. Then the Commodore welcomes them, in the bar after breakfast most often. And Ed checks out their boats.'

'Ed?'

'Our coxswain.'

'What's he checking for?'

'They kept the rules.'

'Ah!' said Tom. 'I might ask him to look for a few other things at the same time... So when do *I* get to see them?'

'After the Commodore?'

'Sounds good. I'll tell you which I want. Will you bring them here?'

'Yessir!'

'Tell them it's about Charles West's disappearance—make out there are life insurance issues. Don't let on I'm police.'

Della nodded. 'The big handicap boats mostly arrived already,' she added. 'But the ones you're after will be slower, right?'

'That's correct,' said Tom, attacked by another yawn.

Della smiled, tactfully walked him back to his bedroom, clicking all the way, and withdrew.

Tom dug an apple and Granola bar out of his brief case and munched thoughtfully. It was still only 6.30, but he needed to sleep off his jet-lag and tumbled quickly into the huge bed

Give us particulars

Tom began his interviews on the Monday morning, meaning to concentrate on the skippers of the five boats on his sketch chart, plus the French woman Laurel Delon in the ketch *Bon Appetit,* whose last position had been recorded on 17th June. This was so early in the race that she could have been anywhere by the 24th, but her first few fixes suggested that she too had been following the northern route. He'd arrived only just in time: *Flying Cloud* and *St Louis Blues* had been welcomed in the previous evening.

Flying Cloud's skipper Dan Soberski appeared on time, a tall, softly spoken Marylander of about thirty who said 'Hi!' firmly as Della introduced him, and remained standing politely as she disappeared. His pullover was cashmere-casual, and his white sneakers had certainly not just been worn for four weeks at sea. The Millenium might be a Corinthian event, Tom reflected, but he must still expect all of his suspects to stand—like Mike—distinctly above himself in the income pecking order.

'Do sit down,' he said. 'As you know, I've been asked to sort out what happened to Charles West, if that's possible.'

Dan nodded.

Tom showed him the sketch chart. 'His last reported position was at noon on 24th June, about 35 miles west of you. But it looked as though *Cas A* had been left hove-to. If she stood still for long, or if one of your positions was a few miles in error, you might well have seen her.'

Dan considered. 'I used GPS,' he said, 'so my positions should be accurate, but his might have been wrong, sure.' He thought for a moment. 'I knew from his noon positions he must be near. I didn't see him on the 24th—the visibility wasn't good, and his sails would have been edge-on. But the day before, I *did* see something in the right direction, a long way ahead, one time when the sun broke through: I guess I wrote that in my log.'

'Did you see him earlier in the race at all?'

'At the start, tracking out to the Eddystone. Hassle getting up his mizzen. And then I saw him very close on the 19th. I was neck-and-neck with *St Louis Blues* that day—only twelve miles apart. He overhauled us slowly, and passed between us a little after noon. He came within half a mile, almost like he wanted to speak.'

'And did he?'

'I called him up on the VHF, but no response.'

'Sure it was him?'

'I could read the name on his spray dodger through binoculars. Anyway, that ketch is pretty distinctive, and I'd been plotting all the positions—no one else it could have been.'

'And he just drew ahead and disappeared?'

'That's correct. He was moving faster than us, but not pointing as well, getting pushed up north. Too much sail up, I reckoned. Could still see him on the 20th, just about. After that, except for the sails on the 23rd—which I'm not sure about—I can't prove he was where he said he was. His radio reports came in strongly, though.'

'Was he on deck when he passed?'

'Yeah, at the wheel.'

'You didn't see anyone else in the cockpit?'

Dan stared. 'No,' he said after a pause, 'but it was a long way off, and I wasn't expecting to, naturally.'

'Between then and the 24th, what other boats did you see?'

'None, except for *St Louis* and that doubtful sail on the 23rd.'

'Why were you so near *St Louis?*'

'Hard to say. We finished up close after the blow on the 17th and we were following similar courses. From the 19th to the 23rd we stayed more or less within sight. Gave me something to measure my performance against—same class of boat.'

'Contessa 35?'

'Old but good.'

'*St Louis* is Dale van Twente, isn't he? Know him from the class association?'

'I didn't at the start. Feel I do now.'

'Weren't you afraid of colliding in the dark?'

'Yeah! But Dale heard my VHF message to *Cas A* and called me back. After that we traded news and kept listening watch for each other. We arranged to sleep at different times, and switched on our navigation lights.'

'But then you separated?'

'On the 23rd I decided to sail a little freer, and gradually moved off from him. By the 24th, we were out of sight, but we kept up the VHF chat for three more days—till the next storm.'

'So on the 24th and 25th, you couldn't see *St Louis*, but exchanged news. When? What did you talk about?'

'The first day, the 24th, he was fixing up to do some baking. Sucker for new bread. That was about 1500

GMT. I called him up at 1700 to find how it had gone and what was for dinner. Fresh rolls, he said, franks and tinned apricots.'

'Hm! And after that?'

'Not certain. We didn't fix up anything for that night, we were far enough apart to be safe. I called him up the next day too, but what did I say? Oh, sure—second-guessing tactics. I needled him: "Hey, Dale, why aren't you off down south with me? Two to one in dollars this breeze veers ten degrees by lunchtime!" —that kind of stuff.'

'How did he reply?'

'Said he was too busy to talk—if I wanted to know his tactics I'd better listen to his next position. I did that, and afterwards we spoke again. I ribbed him about still not changing course, and he said he'd been baking again. We noticed Charles West didn't report that day, but we didn't pay much attention. Reckoned his radio must be taking a vacation.'

'Did you know West at all?'

'I met him once or twice before the start, chewing up the Race Management, wearing those massive Ray-Bans. Knew he was British and had lived in the US. I didn't drink with him, or visit his boat. He wasn't liked.'

'Mm... Why not?'

'Too cold. Threw his weight about too much.'

'But not with you?'

'I could see how people reacted.'

'Yes... You used GPS. Did you take sun sights too?'

Dan smiled. 'Lost the habit. I have a nice sextant—but I never got to renew my almanac this year.'

'Were you given a bag of goodies by the race organisers with a bottle of rum in it?'

Dan frowned, then nodded.

'Do you still have the bottle?'

He grinned. 'No—my target was to cross in thirty days, and I rationed my rum that way, to punish myself if I got late. I finished up the bottle two days ago and pitched it overboard with the rest of the trash.'

Tom closed his notebook. '*Flying Cloud*—famous ship-name isn't it?'

Dan smiled and leant back in his chair. 'My great-grandpop was a Boston shipowner, there's tea-clipper money went into my boat. Seemed like a natural choice.'

'Shipowning stay in the family?'

'Nope. My pa's an engineer and I'm busy getting a small microwave outfit off the ground. My wife tells me I waste too much time sailing.'

Tom smiled and checked through his notes. 'I think that's all just now, Dan,' he said. 'Thank you. For your help and your time.'

'You're welcome,' said Dan, and stood up. He paused. 'You're *investigating*,' he said slowly, eyes on the floor. 'Seems like somebody reckons it wasn't just a poor guy fell overboard?' He raised his gaze and peered at Tom.

Tom considered. 'Not necessarily,' he said. 'I have to find the facts as far as they can be found—and maybe they can't.'

'Well, I sure hope you *do* find them,' said Dan. He loped slowly away.

*

Dale van Twente also turned up on time. About the same age as Dan, smaller, muscled, neat, but rather less crisp, wearing a white T-shirt with a small Contessa logo and his boat's name in blue. Tom began

44

as he had with Dan.

Dale looked sharply at him and narrowed his eyes. 'Hey!' he said, then stopped and frowned. 'So this guy goes OB. I'm sorry. But why the hell are you questioning *me*?'

'Because,' said Tom slowly, 'there were some slightly suspicious things about his boat when it was found and his insurers want to know why.'

'Not just an accident?' Eyes wide. Another long pause. 'Like I said, why me?'

'Your boat was one of those near,' said Tom, and showed him the sketch chart.

Dale put his chin on his thumbs and took a long breath through his teeth. 'Chief suspect in the hot seat?'

Tom shook his head. 'Suspect for *what*?' he said. 'Look, my job is to find the facts as best I can. How would you go about it?'

Dale kept his fingers curled over his mouth and peered at Tom. 'OK,' he said, after a while.

So Tom worked through his queries as he had with Dan. The answers came tensely but straightforwardly. At first, little new emerged, and no obvious inconsistencies. Dale had been too far away on the 19th to read *Cas A*'s name as she passed between them, but, like Dan, he'd already deduced who it must be, and recognised the ketch. He'd seen no distant sails on the 23rd. He had indeed baked rolls on the 24th, had got hot and irritated below decks, and found little opportunity for observing distant sails after 1400 GMT. He gave essentially the same account as Dan of their VHF chatter on the 25th. He'd seen no other boats that day, but had again been baking and unobservant from about 1500 GMT.

He hadn't known Dan before meeting him at sea.

He, too, was married, and worked for IBM in New York State as an electronic engineer. Like Dan, he navigated by GPS. He didn't drink, and had given his rum to his landlady in Plymouth. However, when Tom asked whether he knew Charles West, he replied:

'I met him before the start… And he did something stuck in my gut.'

Tom raised his eyebrows.

'Goddammit!' The tension broke a little. Dale seemed to gather himself. 'You'll most likely tell me there was nothing to it.'

Tom waited.

'Well, I'm in the clubhouse bar with this young English guy, Sam Deeds, and Charles joins us. Dislike him straight off, in his huge Ray-Bans. But Sam seems to know him, invites us both to supper. So I drive over in my hire car, doing my best to keep up with Charles in his flashy white GT. Big brick house, over the river… Sam's kid sister was there—she's nine, I guess—and she was all upset because the family cat just had kittens.'

'Upset?'

'Sam's pa had laid it down they should keep only one. And in that family they drowned unwanted kittens, which I didn't much like the sound of. Sam said it got to be done straight off, before the mother cat learned to count them.

'The parents were away?'

'In Amsterdam… The little girl understood they'd got to do it, but she'd seen the little blind things. So Sam needed to calm her down, and he couldn't be doing the drowning at the same time.

'Suddenly, Charles says he'll handle it. So we get this big plastic bag, the little girl distracts the mother cat, and Charles gets the three smallest kittens into the bag. He says "Get Jilly out the way," so Sam and I take her into the back room.

'Then we heard nothing for a long time, and at last I went to look. He was standing by the kitchen door. His cheeks were tight, eyes shining. He said: "All done. I'm off." "Why?" I said. "Jilly's not going to want me to supper," he said. "Not after what I just did." He jammed on those horrible Ray-Bans, and off he drove.

'I didn't like it. Something about him I couldn't make out, aroused, but chilling too. Or maybe it was just those goddam shades and that shiny white car. I thought, that's all fine and dandy, but where's he put the bodies? I looked in the trashcan.

'Know what I found? Three plastic bags, tied up with metal twists. One had three kittens' heads in it. One had the top halves of three bodies, with two legs, and one had the bottom halves, with the other two legs and the little tails and some blood.

'I thought, Jesus, *why*? And where the hell did he do it? The kitchen was all neat and clean, but the bowl was wet, and draining in it was a chopping board and a knife. I felt sick. I thought, they mustn't know how he did it; and, hell, they mustn't use that goddam board. I stuck the board and knife down at the bottom of the trashcan. Then I thought, that's not good enough, so I stuck everything in the trunk of my hire car. Trashed it all later.

'It wasn't easy helping Sam cheer the little girl up after that, or eating with him, when he kept looking for that chopping board… You think I'm paranoid?'

Tom narrowed his eyes and shook his head gently.

'Beheading the little things was quick? No worse than drowning them, maybe? If something made him slice them in threes and stick them in three bags, does

47

it matter? Maybe he just defused a difficult situation. But, goddam it, *I* think there was something sick in his mind.'

Tom thought he might well be right.

*

Tom's remaining three interviewees had not yet arrived, though the news board showed that *Ugly Duckling* and *Ariel* had both been sighted: *Ugly Duckling* should be in the marina by late afternoon. So at lunchtime he took the opportunity of finding Mike. The arrival of his old colleague's boat had been listed the day before, but anxiety over presuming too much on Mike's generosity had made Tom hesitate a little.

He found Mike sitting in the cockpit of his boat, wearing a three-piece suit and eating an enormous pizza. He looked up irritatedly as Tom's shadow fell across him, but the scowl melted with recognition.

'Hey, *Tom*!' he said. 'Come aboard! Wasn't expecting you for two days yet!'

Tom found himself smiling equally broadly, but said nothing, and, rather carefully, clambered over the boat's side, shook hands, and found himself a seat, warm in the sun.

'How long?' asked Mike.

Tom laughed. 'Four years,' he said, 'but the grey hairs haven't been sprouting *too* fast!'

Mike leaned forward to take a look. 'Don't you worry!' he said. 'Business lunches sow the damn things a sight faster than honest police work... I dreamed of you last night.'

'Me?'

'You and Miranda, tramping on the moor... Now *that* young lady will be something to lighten the eye, by now! Boy friends, I suppose?'

'Nothing established,' said Tom judiciously.

'Jack, too?'

'Girlfriends? No. But Miranda and I are feeling rather proud: he got a first last year.'

Mike shook his head and adopted a severe admonitory frown. Tom was disconcerted.

Mike leant forward and placed one hand over Tom's on the cockpit seat. 'Teasing,' he said. 'Now the problem is,' looking at his watch, 'in three minutes' time there's a damn great limo arriving. To whisk me into Boston for a business conference I could wish in Hades... I'd best leave you the keys, you can settle in on your own.'

'But I haven't explained,' said Tom. 'They've given me a room up in the old house. I'm here on duty.'

'On duty *here*?'

'Unofficial, like.'

Mike looked at him sharply. 'Investigating what?'

Tom hesitated.

'Not Charles West?'

'Yes, actually.'

Mike whistled. 'Now why ever,' he said, 'would the dear old Devon & Cornwall be involved in *that*?'

Again Tom paused.

'Now don't go bloody inscrutable on me, Tom! ... Oh hell, here's my monstrous panjandrum.' He fetched a set of keys from the cabin. 'Back tomorrow evening—and gagging to wheedle the lot of it out of you then! In the meantime, take a look round... Drop them into the marina office when you're done.'

For a confident man, it was quite a shy smile he gave Tom. Then he jumped up, grabbed a briefcase and white gabardine lying ready on his chart table, and strode off along the walkway to the sleek black

49

machine waiting on the service road. He waved as he clambered into the back, and was driven away.

Tom pocketed the keys and relaxed in the sunshine. It was OK; the warmth of friendship was going to survive his little jealousy of Mike's enhanced affluence, and the age gap between them hadn't widened. After a while he went and made himself a cup of coffee in Mike's galley. He washed it up and then took advantage of the skipper's absence to identify all the ropes and winches, and memorise their positions. He found and examined Mike's sextant, and the sun-sight tables in his almanac. He lay down for a while in the cabin and dipped into a few of Mike's books, listening to the water lapping and chuckling under the boat and the ropes tapping on the mast. The sun, reflected in the water outside, sent ripples of light chasing each other across the cabin roof. Later, he made a cup of tea, and watched *Ugly Duckling* being towed into the next arm of the marina.

By the time he'd locked up and wandered over to the clubhouse to find some supper, he felt he knew Mike's boat quite well, and the challenge of their joint enterprise had become by some definite measure less anxious and more boyishly anticipatable. Before going to bed, he walked quietly down the lawns to the water and saw red and green navigation lights moving slowly in the dark. Perhaps *Ariel*, too, was being brought in. Back to police work in the morning, he reflected—but long-anticipated adventure was on its way too.

Strangeness of your story

Next morning, as he settled down to work, the prospect of sailing was still distracting Tom. Land's apron strings irked him: he felt lured by the deep, impatient to navigate by sun and stars. And the two suspects interviewed so far had seemed ridiculously innocent.

Della clicked into the library brightly, accompanied by *Ugly Duckling's* skipper.

'Good morning, Mr Todd,' said Tom, still sorting files as she disappeared. 'Please sit down.'

'Dr Todd.'

Tom looked up. His new witness was bronzed and heavy, with penetrating watery-blue eyes in a powerful face. He seemed to be about Tom's age.

'As Della will have explained, Dr Todd, I'm investigating the disappearance of Charles West... Your boat wasn't far from his at the time. I hope you'll allow me to ask you a few questions?'

'Not far, for your purposes?' Steady stare. 'A hundred miles? What are your purposes?'

'West's insurers have some issues.'

Dr Todd didn't blink. 'Loss adjuster? I don't think so...'

Tom looked at him.

'Police, aren't you?'

Tom hesitated. 'You're British, I believe,' he said at last. 'Yes, I'm a UK policeman.'

Dr Todd leaned back, breathed in noisily through

twisted nostrils, and put both hands behind his head. 'So you've no jurisdiction here?'

'That's correct,' said Tom evenly. 'But *Cas A* is a British yacht, and the Devon and Cornwall force has an investigation in train.'

Dr Todd looked down at his feet and then back at Tom. He gave another snort. 'Fire away,' he said.

Tom showed him the sketch chart. Dr Todd asserted firmly that during the important period between 21st and 25th June, he'd seen no other boats of any sort. He knew from the radio that his nearest neighbours had been *Ariel* and *Shamrock*. 'Bloody women,' he added.

He also confirmed what he'd noted in his log, that just after noon on 20th June he'd sighted a small Panamanian trader, and spoken to her skipper on VHF. She was the *Balboa,* on passage from Trinidad to Cardiff.

Tom was writing. 'It appears to be possible', he said quietly, 'that some other boat interfered with *Cas A*.'

'Not *Ugly Duckling*, however.'

'But in theory, let's say, you were sufficiently near, after your meeting with the *Balboa,* to rendezvous with West on 24th June. Supposing you'd wanted to.'

'While falsifying my reported positions?' Dr Todd's lips pushed forward into something resembling a smile. 'So you'd like to see my bloody sun sights?' He felt in his breast pocket and produced a little plastic-bound notebook. 'Guessed you might... There you are, all nicely salt-stained.'

Tom took the notebook and leafed through the pages. They appeared to contain a complete series of raw sights running all the way from the Channel to the Nantucket Light Vessel, in sequence.

'Thank you,' he said. 'You'll have it back this after-noon... Did you use GPS as well?'

'Imbecile to rely on electronics.'

'But did you possess one?'

'Hand-held Garmin. Didn't use it.'

'I see… Did you know Charles West personally?'

'Of course.'

Tom straightened up. 'You *did*? How was that?'

'You didn't know?' Dr Todd looked grimly amused.

'No.'

'I employed him.'

Tom's eyebrows shot up. '*Employed* him!' he said. 'I'm sorry… His disappearance must be distressing for you.'

Dr Todd remained impassive.

'What did you employ him to do?'

'Computer programming. Molecular orbital calculations.'

'Chemistry?'

'Yes.'

'Where?'

'University of Southampton.'

'I see. How did you come to take him on?'

'Advertised.'

'When?'

'September '96.'

'Where did he come from?'

'He didn't tell me.'

'And you *really* have no idea?'

'No, Sir, I do not!'

'Surely, you got references?'

'No!'

'You must realise this sounds extremely odd?'

Dr Todd shrugged.

'Mm… Did he know how to do these calculations when he arrived?'

'No. But he knew Fortran. And he was a lot faster

and cleverer than the scatterbrained woman I had before.'

'And socially?' Tom was still upright, impassive, pencil poised.

'Don't mix work and play.'

'Just so, but what was he like? A pleasant man?'

'What the hell's that got to do with it?' The blue eyes were disdainful. 'Bloody good programmer. Paid him over the odds.'

'How did you pay him?'

'Into a girobank account, I believe.' Dr Todd was leaning back now with a satisfied smile. 'Self-employed.'

'Did he ever mention family? Activities?'

'Not to me.'

'Did he make friends in your research group?'

'No. Insular character. Rolls-Royce nerd.'

Tom allowed himself a small nod. 'And did you know him as a sailor?'

'Certainly not. *Extremely* surprised to find him in the race.'

'Really? A totally unexplained and unexpected coincidence?'

'Exactly so.'

'Could the sort of money he got from you as a pro-grammer have bought that boat of his?'

Dr Todd laughed. 'No!'

'How did *you* buy *Ugly Duckling*?'

Dr Todd cleared his throat. 'Didn't… She belongs to a syndicate.'

'What sort of syndicate?'

'Damn good—all chemists!'

Tom was busy writing again. He finished and looked up. 'Have you still got the rum bottle marked "J's Jamaica" that the race organisers handed out?'

Again Dr Todd put his large hands behind his head, and peered at Tom. 'No,' he said after a pause, 'finished it in the first week and pitched the bottle overboard.'

'How long have you been sailing?'

'Three years. This is my first year single-handing.'

That seemed to Tom a very short apprenticeship. He pursed his lips, and decided suddenly that there were far too many oddities in this interview. He needed time to think:

'Thank you, Dr Todd,' he said, frowning. 'I may have more questions later.'

*

Ariel's skipper didn't turn up at the appointed time. Tom rang through to Della, who explained that Miss Allison had rushed into town to visit someone, and wouldn't be available till after dinner. *Shamrock* had arrived in the marina during his morning's interview, but Tom couldn't reasonably interview her skipper till the next day, so he had time on his hands again.

He looked closely at Dr Todd's sun sight booklet, but could detect no signs of forgery. He got Della to photocopy the pages for 19th to 24th June, and took the copies down to Mike's boat, where, with the help of the sun tables in the nautical almanac, he recalculated the fixes. Once he'd eliminated several errors of his own, they all agreed with Dr Todd's reported positions. Discouraged, he wandered back to the administrative building. As he opened the heavy entrance door, he saw Della peering at him through the plate glass of her office; she was beckoning violently and holding a phone to her ear.

'Yes, yes, he's coming now!' she was insisting

piercingly as he pushed open her door. And more quietly, with her free hand over the mouthpiece, 'England caller—and frantic about the cost of the call, for godsake!' She handed over the receiver.

Iain Gemmill's concerned breathing floated over the satellite link. 'Tom? Thank God. Iain here. Listen… It's murder, man!'

'Why?'

'Found the body! Nimrod pilot saw it from the air— must have incredible eyesight. Destroyer picked it up and they rushed it back here by helicopter… He'd been shot all right: a lot of the face was blown away.'

'Had a look yourself?'

'Threw up, to be honest…'

'Ah.'

'And a rope tied round his middle. Thick, nothing like anyone would use for a safety line—the Navy thought somebody tied a weight on it that worked loose and fell off… Now listen: *third*, he had in his pocket another of those J's Jamaica bottles.'

'Marked OSTAR Millenium 2000?'

'Aye.'

'That's bloody important, Iain.'

'And why d'you think I'm making this extravagent call to you, Tom? Fourth, his face and jacket were stained reddish-brown down the front. Pathologist reckons it might be algae, because those parts of the man were facing upwards and more exposed to the air, you see.'

'Mm. When did they find him, Iain, and where?'

'Two days ago. A hundred and eighty miles south-east of his last reported position.'

Tom scribbled and read back the facts for confirmation. 'OK, I've got all that… Any other news from your end?'

'No, man. We still can't find a single ruddy thing before 1996. No social life, no women. No record. Nothing like him on the police computer. Just came in out of the blue, paid £2000 into that brand new bank account, rented his flat, and took up sailing... He didn't buy that boat out of any account I can trace, and he didn't buy it from a British broker. And he didn't have it direct from the builder in Argentina, either.'

'Iain, two new things at this end may help... First off, he did have a job.'

'He *did*?'

'Computer programmer... Working for another of the competitors, would you believe it?'

'Which?'

'Dr P. N. Todd, academic chemist. Southampton University. Can you check him out?'

'Sure.'

'Self-employed contract—no PAYE or National Insurance. And, unbelievably, Dr Todd didn't seem to have the slightest idea where he came from.'

'Hm... This fellow sure doesn't want to be traced.'

'Big-time crime?' asked Tom.

'You might think so. But we've heard no whispers. No mystery contacts in Salisbury. He doesn't mean anything to the Met, or Interpol—I checked, naturally.'

'Well, my second discovery may help—the name of his boat.'

'*Cas A*?'

'Turns out, it's the name of a star.'

'A *star*?'

'And a star that probably only a professional astronomer would know about. West's evidently not an astronomer now, but could have been earlier, which should be traceable. Can you give it a go?'

'But equally well he could be just about anyone who

happened to read about the star and liked the idea?' said Iain with a sigh.

'Oh sure. But it's worth a try... Oh, and Iain, can you track down a Panamanian ship, the *Balboa,* bound from Trinidad to Cardiff, spoke to Dr Todd's yacht, *Ugly Duckling,* on 20th June, and confirm the position with her captain?'

'Sure: *Balboa.* Bound for Cardiff, you said? *Ugly Duckling.* And Dr P.N. Todd, Southampton University. I've got all that... Now, shouldn't we be winding up this ridiculously expensive call? Bye then, Tom!' and before Tom had time to say more the phone clicked.

Tom returned it to its cradle. Della was watching with a conspiratorial smile. He told her to keep the news about West to herself.

The damage to the man's face suggested one of his own hunting bullets. And the second rum bottle! That came near to *proving* there'd been an intruder on board *Cas A,* who was also a competitor. Even their guess about the kedge anchor had confirmation. He and Iain were entitled to a mite of self-satisfaction.

Cold porridge

After lunch, Tom returned to the library; the sun was bright, and a breeze off the water was stirring the maples encircling the old house. The finding of the body was sure to be in the news bulletins within a day or two. He must aim to finish his interviews tomorrow.

He mulled over those completed. Dan and Dale seemed harmless enough and had given each other partial alibis. But if Dr Todd had been near to *Cas A* on June 24th he'd disguised the fact, and his professed lack of interest in West's background was ridiculous. None of the interviews had suggested any link with astronomy. Tom turned the day's developments over in his mind for some time, but eventually, making no progress, decided to take a break, and hunted round the library for something to relax with.

He found himself a volume on the Nantucket clippers, and spent the rest of the afternoon reminding himself about the original *Flying Cloud,* built by Donald McKay in 1851. Only 221 feet long and 1098 tons net, she'd immediately shown unparalleled speed in the California via Cape Horn trade. In 1860, however, she'd entered the China tea trade with her spars sadly reduced, and was sold to T. M. MacKay of London in 1862, before finally going aground and breaking her back off Newfoundland in 1874. He was amusing himself with paper and pencil, trying to get clear how these old square-riggers had been sailed against the wind, when the phone rang.

'London call for you,' said Della.

He waited.

'Tom?'

'*Mike!*'

'Don't be too amazed.'

'You're back *in England*?'

'It's bad, mate... Hostile bid.'

'For your firm?'

'Yes—Consolidated Amory buggers... Hold on.' His voice trailed off, and Tom could hear a female voice pressing for a signature. There was quite a long pause. 'Blast her, blast! No dammit, she's doing what I told her... Tom, I'm *devastated*. The long and short of it is, we can't sail home together. We *can't*. I'm so mad. And *sorry*. What can I say? Look, I *know* how hungry you were for it... Angela dear, they won't be in the office now!'

'Mike!' shouted Tom. 'Cut that out! Don't *apologise*! I can take it. You pitch in there. Come for a tramp on the moor when it's blown over. For *God's* sake don't be miserable about me—it'll cramp your style! Chin up!'

'Tom! Thanks mate...   Oh damn, here's my other angel now! Look, I'm *really* grateful, you not minding. No, that's not right, you must be ruddy spitting teeth! I'll be in touch the *moment* this tsunami's subsided, I will... Godammit, got to cut you off now...' The phone went dead.

And so too, with an inaudible whimper, did something inside Tom.

He remained for ten minutes slumped in his chair. Then he forced himself to wander over to the administrative building, to look for post. He found Della, looked straight through her, focused and smiled distantly, and drifted back towards his room, the post forgotten.

Even at forty-eight, anguish could still strike hard when something delectable was snatched away. He attached to Consolidated Amory a number of words that didn't usually venture beyond his subconscious, and felt slightly better. He berated himself for being stupidly boyish and smiled wanly in the mirror... And how would he get home? What would *that* cost? Another wave of staccato imprecation welled up.

Eventually, he made a face, washed, combed his hair, and went in search of supper in the cafeteria. He limited it to clam chowder, French bread, a liqueur, and sweet comforting coffee.

As he was downing the third cup, Della wandered up to his table. She had with her Jane Allison, *Ariel's* skipper, returned at last from Newport. Tom did his best to wrench himself back to his investigation.

'Oh, Miss Allison,' he said. 'I hope this is a convenient time... Excuse me while I slurp this down... There. Perhaps we could walk over to the big house?'

She followed without a word, and at once he felt irritated by the clicking of her heels. There was something unsatisfactory about a slender, wiry yachtswoman wearing black court shoes. In the library, she sat silently once he'd found her a chair, and watched as he dug out his files.

'I'm half asleep,' she said at last, shaking her head and attempting a smile. 'I got horribly tired towards the end, haven't worked back to normal yet...' When Tom didn't reply, she added hesitantly, with the ghost of a smile: 'Perhaps it's been a long day for you, too?'

He glanced up. She was in her early thirties, and apparently composed, but her narrow face was drawn.

'Thank you for coming,' said Tom. He opened his notebook. 'As Della will have told you, I'm investigating the disappearance of Charles West... One of the things I have to do is to establish where everyone was at the time.'

She shut her eyes, and opened them again, as if with an effort. 'I'm not too clear *why* you're investigating,' she said. 'Are you a British policeman, or something?' The hands in her lap were grasped tightly together.

Some instinct prompted Tom not to dissemble. 'Yes,' he said, 'I am. From Plymouth... There are one or two things that look a little odd, and I've been asked to look into them... So far as you're concerned, I'm interested most in what you saw of the other competitors during the race. You were some distance away from *Cas A*, I think?'

'Oh!' she said. The neat skirt and dark blouse she wore were spoilt for Tom by a large floppy silk bow pinned at the neck in the American style. '... All right, fire away!'

But little of use emerged. She'd sighted no boats at all between 19th and 25th June, but had worked out from the radio reports that *Ugly Duckling* and *Shamrock* were her nearest neighbours. Both of them had consistently come in strongly on her HF radio. She didn't know Charles West, and hadn't seen his boat during the race, or at Plymouth beforehand. She did, however, know both the other women suspects, Eileen Meath on *Shamrock* and Laurel Delon on *Bon Appetit*.

'Both very nice,' she volunteered.

Tom looked up.

'Kind to me, too. And what a contrast!' she added.

She told him that *Ariel*'s performance had been disappointing at first, but her days' runs had gradually improved, and she was pleased with her race, overall.

She'd finished her rum, and thought the empty bottle was in her medicine box.

She was a doctor, a GP in a large practice at Maldon. She'd been sailing her Rival 38 out of the Blackwater for years; it was a comfortable boat, and docile at sea. No expert at deep-sea navigation, she'd never equipped *Ariel* with a GPS receiver, and stuck to what she knew, cribbing from Mary Blewitt's *Celestial Navigation for Yachtsmen*. She used a digital watch as chronometer and limited herself to sun sights.

Tom asked whether he could examine them.

'My observations?' she said. 'They're on *Ariel*. Would it be OK to leave them with Della for you in the morning?'

'Yes, thank you, ' said Tom. 'I won't keep them long.' At the end of a trying day, and after a minimal supper, his head was throbbing. 'I think that's all.' He did his best to look unintimidating.

She closed her eyes again for a moment and he saw her tightly grasped hands relax. She got slowly to her feet. He glanced down at the files on his table, then up again, and caught, to his surprise, the tail-end of another cautious smile. Then she was gone.

Tom sought his too-palatial room. He must *not* let this horrible disappointment get to him; and tomorrow he must grit his teeth and get his interviews finished before tackling the problem of getting home. He hadn't the heart for anything from the library. Instead, he switched on network TV and watched its jumpy outpourings until 12.45, took a sleeping tablet, clambered into the huge bed without washing, and fell promptly but uneasily asleep.

More such shapes

Tom awoke with a blocked nose and a thick head. He shaved, and forced himself to plan his day. *Shamrock's* skipper was due at eleven, which would allow him time to talk to Ed. He ate and drank his way through an alien breakfast, washing down rye biscuits and blueberry preserve with big cups of weak coffee. Then he faced the practicalities of getting home. Moodily, he called his bank in Plymouth to fix up a credit line in Newport and asked Della if she could explore the possibilities of cheap flights.

The powerful sun and sparkling water softened his mood a little as he strode down to the marina. The coxwain's office, dim and musty, lay behind the chandlery.

'Morning, Ed!'

'Hi, Tom.' Ed's eyes had materialised glittering from the gloom. He dumped the spreading folds of a red-tanned sail onto his workbench, and tucked a reel of matching twine into the pocket of his dungarees. A sailmaker's needle was jammed into a circle of cork on his workbench.

'How's it going? How were the engines?'

'Not a thing.'

'Seals intact?'

'Yup. Figure none of 'em been touched.'

'Tanks full?'

'Yeah. Your five got reserve cans, three–four gallons… All untouched.'

'No fuel used then?'

Ed pushed his full lips forward, doubtfully. 'Could've set out with more, and ditched the empties.'

'Of course. Any strong fuel smells?'

'Always smells in bilges.'

'Not in the cabins?'

'Nope.'

'So nothing there,' said Tom. 'Dodgy sun sights?'

'I look out for second sets, or charts with peculiar plots on them,' said Ed, nodding to himself. 'Not a thing. None of 'em got a second Atlantic chart. No marks of positions plotted and rubbed out. They all got working notebooks: courses, clearing bearings, times at buoys. No second versions of logs.'

'Nothing for me to look at, then?'

Ed grinned broadly up at Tom, a stray sunbeam from the dusty window shining through his thick brown curls. 'Was a diary.'

'Oh… Whose?'

'You want to read that, you best ask Miss Meath *very* nice.'

Tom raised his eyebrows.

'I put it back on the wrong shelf.' Ed pulled a face.

'And she noticed?'

'Boy, did she!'

Tom grinned. 'Ah! … Missing equipment?'

'Flares,' said Ed. 'Two of 'em use up a white flare. *Ariel,* fired hers from a Very pistol, crossing the bows of a steamship coming out of the English Channel she said—and *Ugly Duckling,* he used a hand-held flare off Sable Island… All still got their dinghies and life rafts. Unpacked all the inflatables and repacked them: took a month and a half! No blood nor nothing… *St Louis Blues* lost his Dan buoy. Swept overboard one night.

Line not properly secured, he said. Sounded weird to me, Tom—need a wave five feet over deck-level to unship that buoy.'

'Mm.'

'*Ugly Duckling,* his radar reflector was gone: hoist chafed through, gone overboard while he was asleep.'

Tom was scribbling all this down. 'Signs of violence?' he asked.

'Not a scrap,' said Ed. 'No blood, inside nor outside. No firearms damage, no busted gear. No gore, nor hair on winch handles and such.'

'J's Jamaica rum?'

'Miss Allison's was in her medicine chest. Miss Meath's with her cooking stores. No others. Dr Todd, he had other brands.'

'That agrees with what Allison and Todd told me,' said Tom. '… That's everything on my list, isn't it? Anything else you noticed?'

'Nope,' said Ed thoughtfully. 'But might've seen something dain't register at the time. Starts tinkling little bells, I'm back to you.'

'I'm very grateful, ' said Tom, nodding. 'Learnt a lot.'

'You're welcome,' said Ed, and allowed himself a gentle pleased smile.

*

Tom hurried back to the library. Della met him in the corridor. 'Anxious, I reckon.' He got a broad grin: Eileen Meath was getting no sympathy from Della.

His suspect was seated facing his empty desk, her neck muscles tense. 'Please don't get up, Miss Meath,' he said. He unlocked his filing cabinet and dug out the file. The brightness outside the windows made the room glow, and moving clouds sent luminous patches skating across the polished floor.

She cleared her throat. 'You are a British police-man?' she asked. She was tall, tanned and slightly red-haired, in her early forties, wearing faded jeans and a slate green oiled-wool sweater. Her voice was a little gravelly, with only a hint of an Irish lilt; her arms shapely under the heavy wool, but muscled enough, thought Tom, to cope with a genoa winch.

'That's correct,' he said. His identity must be getting around.

'And investigating Charles West's shooting?'

So the news had spread. 'Yes.'

She looked at him very directly. 'So how am I to assist you?' Her eyes were dark, he couldn't make out the exact colour.

'I need first to work out where everyone was around the time that he disappeared.'

Her eyes seemed to deepen. 'Very well,' she said at last.

So Tom took her slowly through his series of questions. She'd sighted no other boats between 16th and 24th June. She knew Jane Allison, but none of the other suspects. More professional than Jane about her navigation, she used star and moon as well as sun sights, and handed over her sight book to Tom without demur. She thought herself above GPS navigators and had never fitted one. An experienced single-hander, she'd sailed for a number of years from Waterford, where *Shamrock* had been built.

She was the only suspect so far to carry a radio direction-finder. Normally, this would have been useless in mid-ocean where there are no radio beacons. But she'd persuaded a friendly engineer to adapt it to the frequency of the noon position reports, and had amused herself by taking bearings on her competitors at various stages in the race. It hadn't been easy, because the signal was unsteady during a transmission, but she'd been able to get repeatable nulls when the boats were not too far away. During the important period from 19th to 24th June, she'd recorded bearings on 21st June on *Ugly Duckling* and *Ariel*, and again on 24th June itself, on *Ugly Duckling*, *Ariel* and, with difficulty, on *St Louis Blues* (but not on *Flying Cloud* or on *Cas A*, though she could hear their transmissions). Tom plotted her bearings onto his sketch chart as she watched. They were all consistent with the reported positions within three degrees or so.

She owned and ran a house of perfumiers operating from Limerick, with outposts in London and Dublin. Tom could detect no scent now, however. He clasped his hands behind his head and examined the chandelier, dim behind a shaft of sunlight.

'Did you know Charles West?' he asked at last.

'I met the man in Plymouth.'

'What was he like?'

A long hesitation. 'Boorish, I have to say.'

'In what way?'

She reflected. 'In this way, Mr Tallis… At the civic reception he caught my eye, from a distance. And persuaded himself, I suppose, that he'd made some sort of impression. I was afterward in the bar, with a woman friend, when he forced himself upon us. He threw off some few sparks of threadbare wit, and took me, I imagine, for a pair of Irish eyes with little behind them, according me the information, Mr Tallis, that I was to be *bedded* by him, and sooner rather than later!'

'By hints, do you mean?'

'Directly and blatantly.'

Tom raised his eyebrows. 'What did you do?' he

asked.

'I showed the man what I thought of the proposal!'
'You did? How?'

Eileen stretched her arms sideways, and smiled a little at the recollection. She seemed to have lost her tension. 'I'm ashamed to say it, Mr Tallis... I spat!'

Tom pictured it: on bar stools, crushed side by side?
'At his face,' she added. '... But it fell into his drink.'
'Not ladylike,' said Tom with a grin.

'It was not. Angry he was, white with anger. But there was no public altercation. The man took himself away.' She smiled again, at Tom this time.

'Angry enough to make you fearful for your safety?'

There was a long pause. '*I* was angry too, Mr Tallis, very angry... But yes, I was concerned.'

'When he caught your eye, that was the first time you'd seen him?'

'Indeed.' Was the response, perhaps, a fraction too insistent? Tom looked up, but could detect nothing evasive in her face.

He let the point pass, and asked about her bottle of J's Jamaica. She had taken two fingers of it with hot water occasionally, when cold coming off watch. She thought there was a little left, in her food locker.

He went back over his notes. 'Am I right that you kept a personal diary as well as a log?' he asked.

Her eyebrows shot up. 'So!' she said. 'It was you, Mr Tallis, was it, who had Ed search my boat?' The eyes were cold. 'My diary is private.'

Tom pondered for a moment. 'I understand that, Miss Meath,' he said. 'But you will be aware that my enquiry has recently taken a more serious turn. I am investigating a murder...'

She turned her head and looked sideways at the sun on the polished floor for several seconds. 'I see,' she

69

said at last, and looked furiously at Tom. Then she jumped up, and her chair scraped on the floor. Tom scrambled to his feet; she frowned at him silently and walked away without another word.

Fifteen minutes later Della appeared, bringing the diary. Tom thought he should do what he had to do promptly, and read it right through. It told him much about Eileen's thoughts, something about her fantasies and ambitions, and was shot through with a raw poetical sensitivity. It said nothing whatever about who might have got onto *Cas A*, and where it referred to other people, it was only obliquely and in a way that seemed to have no possible bearing on the case. He found Della and asked her to return it.

Fresh springs

Towards the end of the morning clouds had been boiling up, and over lunch the wind rose and the weather broke; rain drummed on the restaurant windows. Through the streaming plate-glass Tom could just make out the boats in the sound churning at their moorings as swell passed under them. Yachtsmen damp from the marina tramped in, leaving a mass of dripping oilskins on the pegs outside.

He needed to get into Newport to fix up his air ticket and Della suggested he might share the cab already ordered for Gus Fletcher, a Canadian who was off to the Greyhound terminal to meet his wife. Tom ran back to his room to find a cagoule and pocket his travellers' cheques. When he returned, he found Gus carrying a multicoloured umbrella. Beside him stood Miss Allison, *Ariel*'s skipper.

'Jane's coming too. OK?' said Gus.

'Just shopping,' she explained. She was wearing orange sea boots, and without the neck bow that had irritated Tom at the interview. She still seemed a little stressed.

The rain stung his face as he eased himself into the taxi. 'Managed to get some proper rest?' he enquired of Jane, once it had swayed away from the yacht club on its soft big-car suspension.

'It doesn't take me long to recover,' she said. 'Are you shopping too? Or is that a professional secret?'

'Fixing up my flight home.'

'Professional?' put in Gus. 'How?'

'Oh,' Jane said. 'Mr Tallis is the British policeman who's looking into what happened to Charles West.'

'Aw,' said Gus and looked curiously at Tom. 'Worrying business.'

'When are you off, Gus?' asked Jane.

'Tuesday.'

'Where to?' asked Tom.

'Nova Scotia... Back home to the Rhode Island Reds.'

'Chicken farmer?'

'Broiler house.'

Jane looked doubtful.

Gus pulled a face. 'You city folks!' he said. 'But if I'm to pay for my boat, that's how it's gotta be.' As the taxi wormed its way along Thames Street to the shopping centre, he announced he'd ride on to meet his wife at the bus terminal and return to the club independently.

'What about you, Miss Allison?' asked Tom. 'How will you be getting back? Should we share a taxi again?'

She seemed a little taken aback, but agreed to rendezvous at Washington Square at 4.30. They clambered out into the rain, waved to Gus, shot into the Brick Market Place for cover, and separated.

Tom first searched for something to treat his stuffed-up nose, and was sold a remedy overfull of potent chemicals in a drug store. Then Citizen's Bank, which was handling his money transfer. His credit line from England still hadn't been established. After squelching past half a mile of small town boutiques, he located the American Express office fixing his reservation. His ticket for the morning flight on the 26th was ready, but until paid for couldn't be confirmed, and if the money wasn't forthcoming in two days the cheap flight would be lost.

Seething at this further hassle, he found a café near Bowen's Wharf whose seats overlooked the harbour and tried to drown his sorrows in a *cappuccino.* The rain beat a steady tattoo on the awning overhead, and big bubbles swam in the gutter at his feet; gauze cinema curtains of wet swept continually over the anchored boats.

'Oh my!' sounded after a while in a deep New England voice. 'We meet again!' Tom looked around: a familiar lanky young man was standing beside him, holding a briefcase and a steaming hot chocolate.

'Why, hello!' said Tom. 'You made it, then!'

The young man grinned and settled himself without more ado at the table. 'Hot off the bus. So, where is this clubhouse?'

'Ah,' said Tom, 'Not here. Over on Conanicut Island.'

'Over the sound? Goddam it, I only have two hours! … *And* there's something I need to tell someone.'

Tom raised his eyebrows.

'I asked around at the conference, but no one had heard of Charles West… then I saw the news—body in the sea, they said, shot dead,'

Tom nodded.

'And the investigators short of information about him. Police will have been at the yacht club, I guess?'

Tom hesitated. 'Yes,' he said.

The young man looked at him anxiously. 'Problem is, I had this idea.'

'What idea?'

'I think West could have been a *radio* astronomer.'

'A *radio* astronomer? Why?'

'This object *Cas A*… Like I told you, in an ordinary optical telescope it doesn't look like anything much, in fact it's hard to see it at all. But then I remembered: in a radio telescope, it just happens to be the brightest thing in the sky. For a *radio* astronomer, you see, *Cas A* is something so bright it blinds you.'

'You think the name might have been a sort of in-joke?'

'A big-headed one: "Look at me," that name says, "I'm *actually* the very brightest thing around—but you poor ordinary suckers just don't know it!" … Don't you reckon?'

'I suppose that's possible… Are there radio astronomers at your conference?'

'Wrong sort of conference… But maybe I shouldn't be hassling the police?'

'Why ever not?' said Tom. 'Might help them.'

'And now I don't even have time to get to the yacht club.'

'You could call them from Boston,' said Tom with a smile. 'Or… I could contact them on your behalf, if you like.'

'Could you?'

'Don't see why not. It's just that one point you want to make—that West could well have been a *radio* astronomer?'

'That's it.'

'Where do you find radio astronomers in Britain?'

'Why?'

'The police might want to know—West was British.'

'Oh, yes… Jodrell Bank Observatory… Cambridge. A few other places in a small way… You'll be sure to tell them, then?'

'I certainly shall.'

'Make me sleep easier.'

'Let me take your phone number so they can contact you.'

'Sure.' The young man obliged.

Tom thought for a moment. 'Would radio astronomers be likely to know about computer programming?' he ventured.

'Computer programming!' echoed the young man. 'Radio astronomy is *all* computer programming—no computing, no radio astronomy...' He smiled. 'Hey, this rain's easing. Now I've got *that* off my chest, shall we go wander down the quay? Sure to be *some* sort of attractive boats there, and you can cut me the dope on how the race finished, which boats had the most intriguing equipment.'

Tom felt both grateful and kindly towards the young man, so he spared more time with him than he should have done, and had to run to make Washington Square by 4.30.

*

'Get your ticket all right?' asked Jane once they were seated side by side in the taxi separated by two glossy store bags—bulging, she explained, with American teenage fashions begged for by a young cousin. He explained his lack of success.

She turned her head towards him, and seemed to be considering. 'Perhaps I shouldn't say this,' she said at last. 'But I know why you needed it: you were planning to sail home with Mike Guerdon originally, weren't you?'

'You know Mike?'

'Yes, I do.'

'How?'

'Same sailing club.'

Of course, thought Tom—Essex, the Blackwater. He had an annoyed sense of friendship invaded.

'Della told me.'

Tom said nothing

She looked questioningly at him. 'She said you were terribly disappointed... My family knew the Guerdons,' she went on. 'My father was their doctor... He was always pontificating about Mike making a good detective.'

Tom hesitated. 'He was quite right,' he said.

Again she seemed to be considering, and smiled. 'I really shouldn't ask this either... Mike knew you in Plymouth, didn't he? Weren't you his team leader?'

He paused again. But her smile seemed to suggest straightforward interest. 'Not any more,' he said.

'No, he's in business now... But he told me. Said you were a good boss.'

Tom was taken aback. Friendly, he thought.

When the taxi had dropped them at the yacht club, she ran with her three shiny bags back to *Ariel* through the rain.

Tom went dripping to the library to collect Eileen's sun sights. Then he collected Mike's boat key from the marina office, splashed down to the pontoons and went aboard. He pulled out Mike's nautical almanac, and settled at the chart table. After an hour's hard work, he found that his sight calculations agreed exactly with Eileen's reported positions, just as they had for Dr Todd. Dan and Dale had navigated by GPS, so there were no calculations to be done for them.

That left Jane Allison's sights, awaiting his attention in Della's office. It was too late to collect them now, and he put them off till the morning. She must be about Mike's age, he thought uneasily.

Drift of my purpose

Next morning was warmer, but rain was still falling in sheets, as Tom could see from the library. A brisk call to Citizen's Bank revealed that the money for his flight in four days' time had still not arrived. He cursed, and punched more buttons.

'Della! Could you very kindly bring me over Miss Allison's sun sights? Plus a nautical almanac? Thanks.'

More button-punches.

'Pat? Tom Tallis here.'

'*Great* to hear you, Tom.'

'Could I come over for a talk?'

'Why not? Later today suit you?'

'Sounds excellent.'

'Got something for you, too. I'll send a cruise car. 4.30 OK?'

'Many thanks.'

A longer sequence of buttons. He waited; and smiled as Iain's anxious breathing floating into his earpiece. 'How's progress?' he enquired.

'I found your ship's captain.'

'And?'

'Let's see…' A long pause, then more breathing. 'He met *Ugly Duckling* at 1420 hours GMT on 20th June.'

'Right. What position?'

'43° 05′ N, 19° 21′ W.'

Tom read the details back. 'Thanks Iain, good. Any

more on West?'

'Not a thing.'

'I picked up a lead here. Seems he may have had a previous existence as a *radio* astronomer.'

'*Radio* astronomy?'

'Try Jodrell Bank Observatory and the University of Cambridge.'

Iain gave an irritated grunt.

'Very likely under a different name... And one of our suspects says he gave his J's Jamaica to his Plymouth landlady. Dale van Twente. Can you check it out?'

'Right, man, Dale van Twente... Anything else?'

'No, that's it.'

'OK, Tom. Cheers for now.'

Tom clumped down the phone, pulled out his sketch chart, and plotted on it the position quoted by the *Balboa*'s captain. It confirmed exactly what Dr Todd had told him.

He groaned. Not a *single* inconsistency, no *hint* of a motive, *all* my suspects damn respectable. It was time, he lectured himself, to be systematic. He laid out his folders in neat piles behind the blotter, switched on his most powerful desk light and settled back into his chair. Guiltily he extracted from his investigation bag a battered pack of Embassy, lit up and found a tin for the ash. A slow column of smoke wound its way up towards the hemlock beams of the library roof.

Means? A man had died, his face blown away. No need to look further than West's own gun and hunting ammunition.

Evidence? That second J's Jamaica bottle on West's body. It *proved*, didn't it, that some other race competi-

78

tor must have been on *Cas A*? *And* it ruled out Miss Meath and Miss Allison, who still had their bottles; Dale too, if his landlady backed him. That seemed to leave only Dan and Dr Todd.

Motive? None so far for Dan and Miss Allison. Miss Meath and Dale had each experienced an unpleasant social contact with West. But no serious motives for them, though he'd seen the slightest possible hint that Miss Meath knew West and was concealing the fact. For Dr Todd there was at least *scope* for a motive: he knew West well; and if drugs were involved, he had the expertise to manufacture or purify them. Tom massaged his Adam's apple.

Behaviour under questioning? Dan merely concerned, Dale anxious. Dr Todd blustering. Miss Allison tense at first, but friendly later. Miss Meath cool. Apart from the one very slight hint from Miss Meath, no lies apparent anywhere, not even from Dr Todd.

There was a knock at the door. Della appeared with the sun sights and almanac.

'Thanks,' said Tom. 'You couldn't send me in some coffee, could you?'

Della sniffed the cigarette haze. She looked pointedly at Tom's makeshift ash-tray and raised one eyebrow. Tom stubbed out his Embassy. She smiled cheerfully. 'I can do that for you, Mr Tallis, no problem!' Having opened one of the library windows she clicked briskly away.

Opportunity? Tom yanked his brain down into third gear: this was the biggie—it had been bobbing through his head for days.

West's radio was undamaged. Whether his reported positions were true or false, Tom couldn't imagine any situation in which West would have chosen not to radio in some position. Which meant that by the calling time on the 25th June he was probably already dead and in the water. It followed that *he must have met another competitor at sea during the twenty-four hours following his calling time on the 24th.* But how?

Scenario 1: *The meeting was pure accident.* On this assumption, everyone would have been racing normally and the reported positions would all be correct up to 24th June. But *Cas A* was at that point the furthest west of all, and travelling as fast as any. If she'd continued westward at her usual speed, there was no way any of the others could have caught her within 24 hours. If West had stopped for some sailing reason, both Dan and Dale would have passed close to him a few hours later—but there was no sign of any problem on *Cas A* that would have forced West to stop racing, and the weather was gentle. Provisionally, Tom ruled this scenario out.

Scenario 2: *West and one of the other competitors made a rendezvous,* with one or both of them falsifying their reported positions. But this scenario seemed crazy: what could they hope to gain from a mid-ocean rendezvous that could not have been achieved with far less effort, either in Plymouth before the start or in Newport after arrival?

Scenario 3: *One of the other competitors intercepted West unilaterally* for some reason, falsifying his own reported positions in the process. Tom buried his head in his hands to think.

In this scenario, there was no reason why West should have stopped racing, and it seemed clear from his talk with Ed that none of the suspects had used their engines.

In the northern group, Dan's and Dale's positions were mutually confirmed up to the 23rd June (unless they were in some sort of conspiracy). And interception of West by either of them thereafter just wasn't physically possible under sail alone: as in Scenario 1, neither of them could have caught him in the time available.

In the southern group, Miss Meath and Miss Allison both still had their J's Jamaica bottles, which left them in the clear; so presumably their positions hadn't been falsified, and this was confirmed by Miss Meath's radio bearings on 21st and the 24th, which agreed with Miss Allison's reported position. Dr Todd's position had been confirmed by the *Balboa* on the 20th, but it would have been easy for him to move northward during the following day, by bearing away from the wind. The breeze had then veered round to the north, which would have stopped him moving much further in that direction. However, it did seem possible that he was further north than he'd admitted, and Miss Meath's radio bearing on the 24th didn't rule this out. On the other hand, her bearing put him no further *west* than he'd reported, so, like Dan and Dale, Dr Todd couldn't have caught up with *Cas A* in the time available.

Like the two others, Scenario 3 simply didn't work.

Tom paced around the library. At this point Della appeared, smiling broadly, bearing a large cafetière of coffee, with cream and a heap of chocolate chip cookies. Tom thanked her and refreshed himself liberally, gathering strength for his final lap.

Scenario 4: *West unilaterally intercepted one of the other competitors*, falsifying his reported positions in the process.

West's true position was established by Dan and Dale on 19th and 20th, and he was *possibly* seen by Dan on 23rd.

He would have had no difficulty thereafter in intercepting either Dan or Dale. If Dan was wrong about seeing West on 23rd, West also had plenty of time after the 20th to turn south and intercept any of the southern group before the reporting time on the 25th. And if Dan was right about seeing him on 23rd, interception of any of the southern group was still just about possible, though much tighter.

At this point Tom remembered something. He consulted his notes and plotted onto his sketch chart the position where West's body had been found. Then he hunted round the library and found a copy of the North Atlantic Pilot, which told him that in the relevant sea area the drift current is variable in direction, but always has an easterly tendency, usually at about 0.2 knots.

So he did a few calculations. He soon discovered that if West's body had entered the water at the reported positions of *St Louis Blues* or *Flying Cloud* on the 24th, it must have drifted roughly south-east at nearly 0.4 knots: fast, but perhaps not impossible if helped by the prevailing wind. From the reported positions of *Ugly Duckling* and *Shamrock,* however, the drift speed would have been 0.2 knots, roughly south-east and north-east respectively: both very plausible. From *Ariel*'s reported position, on the other hand, the speed would have been less than 0.1 knots in a north-

westerly direction and against the prevailing wind—extremely unlikely.

And there was another consideration. If West had been falsifying his position, he would need to do so in such a way that he could rejoin his reported track later without too much difficulty. This would have been possible starting from the reported positions of Dan, Dale, Dr Todd and possibly Miss Meath. But an interception of Miss Allison would have left him so far to the east that he could only rejoin his fictitious track by reporting suspiciously short days' runs for the days following the 24th—if West had intended to intercept Miss Allison, he would surely have kept further east by deliberately sailing more slowly in the days before the 24th.

In this fourth scenario, then, West had opportunity to intercept all five suspects, but it seemed unlikely that he would have planned it this way with Miss Allison. The drift evidence made Dr Todd and Eileen Meath rather more likely than Dan and Dale, and appeared to rule out Miss Allison.

Tom looked up, more satisfied. This fourth scenario seemed much the most plausible—and it made sense for another reason. To be sure of succeeding, any interceptor would need a boat faster than his quarry's, and *Cas A* was the largest and fastest of all those involved. This reflection reminded Tom of Dan's comment that West wasn't sailing *Cas A* very well on the 19th June—perhaps he was deliberately sailing badly so as not to get too far ahead of his quarry. And perhaps he'd intentionally passed close to Dan and Dale on the 19th to validate his reported track before turning away to make his interception.

The cafetière was cold, but Tom poured himself

another cup anyway. He frowned. He seemed to be left with two reasonably firm conclusions:

First, Scenario 4 was much the most plausible: *it looked very much as though it must have been West himself who made the interception.*

Second, on this scenario, *the likeliest suspects in terms of opportunity were Dr Todd, Dale and Dan.* Eileen Meath was possible in terms of opportunity and drift, but ruled out because she still had her rum. Jane Allison was trebly ruled out: she still had her rum, the required drift was extremely implausible, and it seemed unlikely that West would have planned to intercept her from *Cas A*'s known starting position.

But *why* West had made the interception, and how he had subsequently finished up dead, remained totally obscure.

*

Outside the rain had stopped; puddles were beginning to shrivel in strong sunlight. Tom cleared away his files, tidied the coffee tray, lit a final cigarette, then decided he would just have time before lunch to call Miranda, who should now be back from Edinburgh. The phone rang only twice before she picked up.

He explained his disappointment first.

'Oh *Dad*! *Poor you!*'

'I feel gutted.'

'I *bet*. Oh dear. I'm *really* sorry.'

'These things happen. Have to work out how to get home… How was Edinburgh?'

'*Fantastic*, really enjoyed it… How's the case working out?'

He hesitated.

'Dad?'

'… I'm not sure.'

'I saw on the news that West had been found shot.'

'Yup.'

'Meaning murder, I suppose?'

'Oh yes… I've just been working through a very careful analysis.'

'But it's not tumbled out quite as you hoped?'

'I've come to a firm conclusion about the logic. But it doesn't *feel* right…'

'Hm… Any serious suspects?'

'Yes. But I don't *believe* in any of them.'

'Motives?'

'One or two.'

'Anyone who benefits?'

'Not obviously.'

Miranda laughed. 'So what was this logical conclusion?'

'About opportunity. The conclusions all *seem* quite watertight… So what is my instinct telling me? … I'm seeing the local police chief this afternoon.'

'There's an American connection?'

'Not yet, there isn't. But he seems to have something to tell me.'

'Maybe that's where the answer lies.'

'Maybe.'

But Tom didn't find the thought reassuring.

*

After a thoughtful lunch in the club restaurant, he returned to the library to perform his calculations on Miss Allison's sun sights. Opening the almanac, he found the name *Ariel* inscribed on its flyleaf in flourishing calligraphy: Della must have borrowed Jane's copy. Seeing that inscription reminded him sharply of what Jane had told him about Mike. He imagined the two of them moored together at Maldon, alongside the Thames barges with their red sails. The Allisons had liked Mike, listened to him rabbiting on about his work as a policeman in Plymouth... Tom wrinkled his brow and set to work.

After three quarters of an hour, his calculated fixes all agreed exactly with Miss Allison's reported positions. He returned the almanac and sight book to Della, and took a leisurely stroll around the marina with the sun beating on his shoulders, blinking in the harsh light off the sound, as vapour rose steadily from still damp decks and sail covers. At 4 o'clock he broke off to change, collected his notes together, and was waiting in Bermuda shirt and sun hat when Patrolman Kidd in his navy-and-white cruise car squealed to a halt before the old building.

Taste my bottle

Pat's fifth-floor office was humid. The windows were open, a sultry breeze clattered the venetian blinds, and a big fan was revolving above the desk. An ice-machine hummed in one corner, and on Pat's desk stood an open bottle with two heavy cut-glasses. Another man was stretched out in one of the chrome executive chairs, gesturing with a third glass. He looked about thirty, unshaven, in dirty T-shirt and jeans.

'Hi, Tom,' said Pat. 'Sit yourself down. Whiskey? … This is my very good friend Captain Sam Greenbaum.'

'Good to see you, Sir,' said the captain, and leant over to shake hands without getting up. 'US Customs.'

'Sam here's into narcotics,' said Pat. 'And right now, him and me is working together, busting a goddam drug outfit.'

'Got you,' said Tom.

'An' I tell Sam here about your case, Tom,' said Pat. 'How's it making out?'

Tom would have preferred water as well as ice with his whiskey, but was in the mood to relax. He gave a run-down of his interviews. Then he announced the discovery of Charles West's body.

His two listeners looked sharply towards each other.

'Now *that*,' remarked Pat, 'changes things more than a bit… You see Tom, that rifle of yours put me in mind of Sam here's lousy scumbags. So I ask him if your

West's showing up on his radar, by any chance. And, surprise surprise, he was.'

'*Really*?' said Tom.

'Eighteen months back FBI intelligence tells Sam there's a cocaine shipment coming in... Sure enough, local market gets flooded. But there's no small freighter showed up over that time, only goddam sailboats. And there's dozens of them skitting around... One of which was your *Cas A*.'

'Ah.'

'In from Britain. West and another, name of Stacey. Mean anything?'

'No,' said Tom.

Again Sam Greenbaum and Pat exchanged glances.

'So, Tom,' said Sam, taking up the story in friendly style, 'we pull in all the intelligence we can on those goddam yachts... And we find your West purchased *Cas A* from a guy in Florida, and paid for it out of a Colombian bank account. Was all. But enough, we figured.' He looked up questioningly.

Tom said nothing.

'So we touch base with your British customs—and hey, *they* got him on their schedule, too.'

'British customs?'

'Plymouth, England, Customs and Excise... Ain't informed you? There you go... And they warn us West's on his way over. But they swear blind he never shipped anything hot out of Plymouth, Tom. Barring that rifle. They knew about that... So we were waiting for him... And kind of sorry now we hear he won't be making it.'

Pat fetched the bottle and poured a massive second slug of whiskey over the remains of Tom's ice cubes.

'What were you expecting him to do,' asked Tom, 'if he left Plymouth clean?'

'Rendezvous with some punk freighter, pick up a shipment,' said Sam, as Pat did the same office for him. 'Three hundred miles offshore. Too far out to show up on radar. Sail in here with the stuff, or pitch it overboard with a weight and a buoy for some bum clam-boat to collect.'

'Supplying the *American* drug market you mean, not the British?'

'Sure.'

'I get the picture,' said Tom, drawing cautiously at his whiskey. It was almost neat. '… I suppose this means my six suspects are of interest you too?'

'Absolutely.'

'Pat told you about them?'

'He did.'

'D'you have anything on them?'

'No we don't… Your Dr Todd, however—he hired West, and he's a professional chemist.'

'And I reckon he's hiding something… What about the two Americans? Dan and Dale? They *seem* honest enough, but they had good opportunity.' That second slug was getting to Tom now.

'Not a peep on them,' said Pat. 'Sam here checks out all six of your suspects with Interpol: nothing again… I hear that ice a-tinkling.' He stood up and carefully brought all the glasses back to their load lines.

Tom yawned and resolved to drink no more. 'Did any… any cocaine come ashore 'bout the time the race ended?' he asked carefully.

'We figure not.'

Sam was looking closely at him. He tried breathing deeply; it didn't help. 'And has there been… small freighter hanging about?'

'Hell Tom,' said Pat 'they'd know by then West was dead. If they *were* out there, it wasn't to meet him.'

Sam shifted in his chair. 'Something you need to know, Tom,' he said. 'We got access to satellite images.'

'Of the Atlantic?'

'I requisitioned some for your sector, 24th, 25th June... No response yet. Pat here'll tell you.'

'That should be very helpful,' said Tom. He made a herculean effort. 'Before we finish, there's a few arguments about opportunity I wanted to put to Pat. Can I try them out on both of you?'

'Sure, Tom.'

It took some time, but they seemed to agree in the end. He was pleased to find they took seriously his drift calculations and the J's Jamaica evidence. Then things began to deteriorate.

'Not clear where this leaves us,' he said, concentrating hard. 'Time's running out. Flight's Wednesday... Or, maybe...' He felt himself frowning. '... I'm a *very* long way from wrapping this up, Pat...' His face had sagged and he tried desperately to straighten it. 'Maybe we can be phoning... After I'm back in Plymouth... That possible?'

'Sure, fine,' said Pat.

'That Frenchwoman... Delon... Mamselle Delon! ... *She* turns up... *Very* kindly Pat? ... Could *you*?'

'Could I?'

'*Interview* her.'

'Sure.'

' ... By phone?'

Pat looked puzzled.

'*Report* by phone, I mean. To *me*.'

'Sure Tom, make it my pleasure! And you'll keep me in the loop? ... Now, gentlemen, before you hit the trail, one last breath o' life? On my penthouse

90

maybe?'

Flying upwards in the grotty elevator, which smelled of disinfectant, they lolled, each with a glass, Pat carrying the bottle. On the roof, Pat waxed forthright about British police tactics in Derry. Later Tom retained surprisingly sharp memories of the *loudness* of the heated debate, of the sun beating on his head, the dustiness of the breeze fifteen floors up, the tepidity of the glass in his hand in spite of its rapidly melting ice cubes, and the uncertain shimmer of the harbour in the middle distance. The faces of Pat and Sam advanced and receded at times, but at the end they had become closer allies, certainly closer friends.

Eventually, he was returned to the yacht club by Patrolman Kidd, who drove gently and attempted no conversation.

Moon out of her sphere

Next morning, the cafeteria was dark, and steamy with oilskins. At the servery, concentrating hard, Tom negotiated for and placed delicately on his tray a glass of V-8 juice, a little oatmeal cereal, and two mugs of black coffee.

Peering around from the check-out he realised the rain had brought in all five of his interviewees. Carrying his tray, he passed Dan and Dale in loud laughter over grits, bagels and blueberry jelly, and at the far side of the room Eileen Meath was nattering with Jane Allison, their table bright under a wall lamp, a puppet-show of nodding heads and gesturing hands. By contrast, in a shadowed corner behind a glossy-green fatsia, sat Dr Todd hunched over his New York Times, a statement of contact despised.

Sharing an eating place with suspects was a new experience, thought Tom. His mind ran off at a tangent, reviewing the pigeon-holes he liked to keep separate. 'Colleagues': he got on easily with most of them. 'Villains': chatting up criminals was different, but he enjoyed that, too. 'Friends and family'—and that empty hole 'Beth'. Outside, tarpaulins stretched over slender hulls rattled in the wind. He found himself an empty table overlooking the marina.

He guessed Dr Todd had seen him arrive and the women hadn't. But as he was downing his second mug, Jane Allison stood up, glanced in his direction, and walked rather deliberately over to his table.

'Hullo,' he said cautiously, and indicated a spare chair, which she took.

'This isn't about Charles West.' She tilted her head a little to one side. 'I have a suggestion to make.'

Tom looked at her rather sharply.

'It may be out of order... I was thinking about my plans.' She gave a quick, eager smile. 'I knew you'd been disappointed by Mike, and I wondered... whether you might be at all interested in helping me sail *Ariel* home?' Doubt was mixing with encouragement in her face. 'Second-best to going with Mike, of course... But, well, single-handing's tiring on a long trip, it would be a real help for me to have someone to lend a hand. Just a practical arrangement.'

Tom's first reaction was to be very sorely tempted. He felt his face lengthening. There was a pause.

'Oh!' she said. 'I'm sorry... That was a mistake. Not proper, forget it!'

He blinked. 'Of course it's not *improper*,' he said quickly. 'It's a very kind offer. I just wasn't expecting it... But I can't, you know. I'm investigating—I'm police.' He managed a companionable smile before turning it into official disapproval.

Jane gave a little laugh, but looked hard at him nevertheless, then frowned and looked down. 'I was supposing,' she said, 'you'd be off duty after Sunday.' She looked up again questioningly.

Tom hunted for words to ease the situation, but found none.

She waited a moment with her hands on the table, then stood up. 'I'm sorry if I embarrassed you,' she said, and walked slowly back to Eileen Meath. They talked. He saw Jane standing, shaking her head; they both looked serious. After a few minutes Eileen got up, gently touched Jane's elbow, and they left the cafeteria together.

Tom was glad he'd detected no amusement. He thought: what was all *that* about? He sat for several minutes over his empty mugs, returned them to the crockery rack and made his way to the library.

*

He began work by calling Plymouth again; as he waited for Iain to answer, Jane's unexpected invitation played over in his mind.

'Iain Gemmill.'

'Tom here, Iain. A contact in US Customs tells me our Mr West sailed into Newport last September, same time as a big cocaine shipment appeared. And they discovered West purchased *Cas A* using a Columbian bank account.'

'Drugs then?'

'Sounds like it. He had with him a man named Stacey, UK citizen.'

'In *Cas A*?'

'Yup. The Americans contacted Plymouth Customs and Excise, who, it seems, were suspicious of West anyway, and had quietly checked out *Cas A* before the race.'

Iain sniffed sharply. 'Without telling us?'

'You'd better get onto them. I guess we don't know of a Stacey, but check out the name too.'

'Aye.'

'All for now, Iain. I'll be in touch.'

Tom rang off and punched Sam's coastguard number into his phone.

An operator answered, yelled 'Hold, please!' and while Tom waited, he could hear the thrumming of a

94

powerful engine, and a second voice, more distant, shouting over bursts of static. Then 'Yes?' came the operator's voice sharply. Tom asked for Sam.

'Call you back.'

Five minutes later, Sam rang through.

'Can we talk?' said Tom. 'I need some background.'

'I'm on a job right now, Tom… But maybe we could talk while I work, why not? … Front of the Point Judith clubhouse.'

The rain had stopped, and ragged clouds were lifting. Tom collected a plastic raincoat and walked down to the waterfront, where he found Sam seated on a camp stool under the maple trees, behind a huge pair of binoculars on a heavy tripod. He was wearing a blue Jersey and white cotton trousers, and looked so different from the layabout figure in Pat's office, that Tom's curiosity was aroused. The wind was rustling the leaves overhead.

'Surveillance!' half-shouted Sam. 'Hi there.'

'What surveillance?' asked Tom, and threw his raincoat down to sit on.

'Crazy!' Sam laughed. 'Our go-getting new Mayor contracts this dredging outfit by the barge-load—and some kibitzer tells City Hall the guy's a crook, we better count them down the river.' His shoulders were hunched forward. 'My boss is swapping favours, so that's my task for today… Want to take a look?' he added, tapping the binoculars.

Tom took Sam's seat and, peering through the glasses, saw a distant tug with two red barges, and nearer to him raw spray spewing off the waves, crystal-clear in the eyepiece, vivid between patches of sunlight and cloud shadow. He was impressed.

'Fifty-seventies,' Sam explained. 'Real bright.' They changed places again. 'So what's this background you want?'

'My five suspects.'

'Yes?'

'Do they sound like drug couriers?'

'Ah,' said Sam. He paused, and looked up from his binoculars. 'To be honest Tom, no they don't… Mules are chancers, get-rich-quick, anything goes. Some of them's addicts. Some got themselves into debt…' An extra burst of wind was buffetting Sam's hair and rippling the grass under his feet. 'Broads, often enough,' he shouted, 'stupid dumb broads.'

'Pathetic types, you mean?'

'Exactly. Your guys don't fit.'

'Well, if my guys aren't mules, could they be something bigger inside the organisation?'

Sam looked sharply up at Tom and screwed up his eyes. 'Maybe,' he said. '… Here comes my next load.' He lined up his binoculars. 'Ask me again in a couple of days… But yes, big operators, they like to look up-scale, respectable.'

'Like my suspects?'

'That woman doctor, for instance.'

'But she's ruled out on other grounds,' said Tom, and reminded Sam. The wind was getting to him.

Sam listened, interested. He nodded. 'Sure, that rum bottle,' he said. 'You told us.'

'Right,' said Tom. 'Question number two… Last night you assumed West was carrying cocaine into the US, but not into Europe. Why?'

'Just we *knew* stuff was getting in,' said Sam, 'and we figured he might be providing the transportation.'

'Could he be carrying it to Europe, too?'

'Why not?'

'But cocaine for Europe would go direct, not through Newport?'

'Sure,' said Sam. 'But he could collect at sea, *near* Newport, on his way home. Side-operation.'

'So far you've got nothing to link any of my suspects with drugs in the US?'

'That's true. You got links with Europe?'

'Nothing firm. But Dr Todd's chemistry group or Eileen Meath's cosmetics company: both could be covers for making crack.'

'But crack mostly gets manufactured inside Columbia now,' said Sam.

Tom nodded. 'Which leads to question number three: what's the normal smuggling route?'

'Coasters, then small boats. Keep changing ports, boats, mules.'

'How do they hide cocaine on a boat?'

'Yachts, they don't. If we target them, they know we'll find it—just get it ashore quick as they can. Might pitch it overboard with a pot-buoy. Come in at night, so we can't pin them down. If we don't locate the buoy, some punk clam boat collects... Down in the Florida Keys, Tom, they even get to use buoys equipped with radar transponders.'

'How does the organisation handle the mules?' Tom asked, rubbing his hands. The wind was rising. 'Would the organisation provide suitcases with false bottoms, and so on?'

'Mule gets the package complete,' said Sam. 'Not told what's inside.'

Tom nodded. 'Question number four.'

'You're a very numbering guy, Tom.'

Tom smiled a little wryly. 'Keeps me focussed... West's murderer. How do you see him? Someone in the cocaine organisation?'

'I figure your murderer started out as West's target,' said Sam, 'and managed to turn the tables. Might be involved. But could be just some unlucky guy saw something he shouldn't.'

'And West himself, was he a distribution organiser?'

'Maybe: we'll know soon.' Sam applied himself to his binoculars again. He scrawled slow notes into a well-thumbed book.

Tom shivered. The sun broke through the clouds, and a patch of grass beside him shone suddenly emerald. Hopefully, he moved onto it, but the wind still battled his trouser-legs. He stood up and banged his arms around his body several times. Sam looked up and grinned.

'You think West was gunning for someone?' Tom asked. 'Pat thought the rifle might point to a smuggler.'

'Down in Florida, maybe,' said Sam. 'Up here, no. But yes, West could have been gunning for some guy, figured on meeting him at sea.'

'Right.'

Sam seemed lost in thought. Then, 'Uh, huh!' he said suddenly, and shook his head. 'Something for you.' He opened his briefcase, extracted a large envelope and waved it at Tom.

'The satellite pics?'

'Yup.'

Tom bundled the envelope into his own briefcase. 'Good… I'm sorry Sam,' he added. 'Too cold, need to go in.'

'Is OK,' said Sam, grinning.

'But did you say you might know more soon?'

'Ah,' said Sam. He wrote again in his notebook, and thought for a moment. 'Best keep this shtum… We got a big bust coming.'

'When?'

'Flying up to the Windy City this evening.'

98

'Chicago? Can't be windier than this.'

Sam laughed. 'You'd be surprised… Should bring us some juicy new intelligence, Tom. Pat'll tell you.'

*

Tom ran back to his room, dragged on a heavy pull-over, and walked slowly downstairs to the library, his legs and arms warming up gradually. Once settled at his desk, he resisted the temptation to light another of his stale Embassies and tilted back his library chair.

Sam and Pat seemed certain West was involved in US cocaine smuggling, and if they were right that certainly changed his case. It must surely connect with his disappearance: he'd probably taken that rifle along to eliminate someone else in the racket. The second rum bottle proved his intended victim must have been another of the competitors. Where better than mid-ocean, where the two of them would be isolated, and where, by listening to the reported positions, he'd know exactly where to find his victim? And then, perhaps, the victim managed to turn the tables? Stroking his chin, Tom considered this idea and found he rather liked it.

But who? Dr Todd? Chemists were useful in the manufacture of crack, even if Sam was right that most of the purification now happened in Colombia… Perhaps Todd got involved, and pushed his luck too far.

Eileen Meath? Her perfume business could be a cover for processing drugs, her outlets in London and Dublin distribution centres, her story of spitting in Plymouth a blind… But she still had her J's Jamaica.

Then he remembered the satellite photos and pulled them out of the envelope.

There were five large glossy prints. Each was labelled 1427 GMT / 25 June, and Tom guessed they were all made from the same image, at different enlargements. They had latitude and longitude markers along the edges.

Print 1 showed an area about fifty miles square, and someone had scrawled 'northern group' in marker pen at the top. Three positions had been ringed. The boats themselves were too small to be seen easily; Tom fished a hand-lens out of his work bag, and could then pick them out quite clearly. He read off the latitudes and longitudes and transferred the positions to his sketch chart.

He frowned. The new positions showed *Cas A*, *Flying Cloud*, and St *Louis Blues* disposed very much as they had reported on 24 June, but about 150 miles further west, as though the race had continued unaffected.

'But that shows,' said Tom to himself, 'he never turned away at all!'

Prints 2, 3 and 4 showed the three boats separately, at maximum magnification. The resolution was excellent; it was easy to see, for instance, *Cas A*'s two masts; Tom could even make out a blob standing at the wheel. There were scale markers inserted alongside the hull, and someone had written '44 feet' as the length. Tom had details of the various boats on file, and dug them out. *Cas A* was indeed 44 feet long. He turned to Prints 3 and 4: the measured lengths for *St Louis Blues* and *Flying Cloud* agreed too.

Tom reflected: 1427 GMT was about an hour before local noon—only four hours before West was due to report on 25 June. And Print 2 showed clearly that the ketch was still heading west with all sail set.

Well, thought Tom, this fitted Sam's idea that West

was using the race as cover for meeting a ship to pick up a drug consignment. For that he'd need to be further *west* than reported, to give himself time in hand for the rendezvous.

'But the photo means,' muttered Tom, 'it can *only* have been Dan or Dale.' Unless West chose not to report his position on the 25th, and it all happened later... But he'd never choose not to report when on his way to shoot someone—he needed his alibi. 'It's *got* to be Dan or Dale.'

Tom turned back to Print 1. Even with his hand lens he could find no other boats anywhere on it, and the experts would surely have marked for him anything that could be detected.

'So definitely *not* Dr Todd or Eileen,' he muttered, frustrated. He frowned. Dan ran a microwave company; he could build a radar responder.

'But he isn't the type, neither of them is.'

Perhaps Dan or Dale had been an innocent witness of something dodgy, and West had decided they couldn't safely be left alive? Well, possibly... But in that case, why did the intended victim, after he'd turned the tables on West, keep quiet about what had happened? You'd think he'd be anxious to tell the authorities as soon as possible, to make clear he'd acted in self-defence.

Print 5 showed an area of two hundred miles square, with the 'northern group' marked towards the top left-hand corner. Nothing was marked anywhere else, but the bottom right-hand corner of the print was covered in a blanket of cloud. Someone had written 'southern group concealed?' over it.

*

Frustrated and gloomy, Tom ran over to the steamy cafeteria for lunch. He ate quickly, then, wiping his mouth, carried his tray to the clearing racks. Dan and Dale needed re-interviews.

He walked over to Della's office. When she heard what he wanted, she stopped typing and peered at him over the top of her half-moon spectacles and shook her head slowly.

'Race winner's announced this afternoon—you know that?' she said. 'Three-thirty... But you got a problem, Mr Tallis. Dan didn't wait, took the train for Annapolis.'

'Damn!'

'All making plans. Dale van Twente, he's off to Boston. Long weekend, visiting his cousin, back Tuesday... Dr Todd leaves Monday, for England. Miss Meath and Miss Allison are still in the marina. Jane Allison's looking for someone to sail back with her.'

'I know she is,' said Tom.

He could at least re-interview Dr Todd. But then it occurred to him that he had no new evidence to press, and Dr Todd was not a man to be bounced easily into an incriminating admission. Better wait till he had more leverage.

Della was waiting, her mouth open.

'Forget it,' he said, and strode off to the library. Dan and Dale being unavailable, he decided to carry his folders down to Mike's boat to think. He could at least grab the opportunity to look closely at the yachts while they were still in the marina, and on the way talk to Ed. He made sure of pullover and windproof, and collected Mike's keys from the marina office.

Ed was still stitching serenely at the red sail. He had nothing new for Tom. He couldn't recall anything on

Flying Cloud that looked at all like a radar transponder.

By the pontoons, the rain had stopped, the wind had eased, and shadows of clouds were chasing one another down the river. Tom took a look at the dan buoy frame on *St Louis Blues*. The new buoy with its whip pole and flag fitted snugly into the frame. It was made to be removed in a hurry, and not lashed in; but as Ed had said, to get the sinker out of the rack you had to lift the float, already four feet above the water, another thirty inches or so: a wave big enough to do that would surely swamp or sink the boat at the same time—but there were no signs of damage. The buoy was tied by a short line to a horseshoe lifebuoy, bright yellow in the sunshine, which also fitted into a rack with no lashing.

Ugly Duckling was some distance away, and Tom could see no one on board. She looked tidy, but the trash can alongside was overflowing with bottles. An aromatic whiff floated up to his nose, and he sniffed around for its origin. Dr Todd had been renewing the teak oil on his grab handles and cockpit drainage grid. Wondering whether there might have been stains to disguise, Tom took a careful look at both, but found nothing.

As he pondered these details, he found he was staring blindly at *Ariel,* moored to the next pontoon. She was deserted, peaceful and solid. Raindrops hung from her mainsheet and green sail cover, and her deck was beginning to steam gently in the sun. He remembered Jane's unexpected offer. *Ariel* wasn't exactly a graceful boat. But her lines were good, the sort of boat solid enough to look after you out at sea.

At last, he picked his way onto Mike's boat, let himself in, and made tea. The cabin smelled musty. He sat for a while, thinking of Mike fighting for his company, wondering how long it would be before he got his boat home. Then he settled to review his files. No fresh ideas sprang to his rescue, and he felt discouraged.

Misses not much

At four, Tom wandered back to the administration building, and was taken aback to find the navy and white cruise car waiting outside. Through the glass of Della's office he saw Kidd standing beside her, his peaked cap pushed back over brown curls. They both looked up, and the patrolman shouldered his way out through the door. 'Move it!' he urged with a wave, and ran off towards the car.

Tom opened his mouth and shut it again. If Pat wanted him, all he would need was in the bulging brief case under his arm. He sprinted after Kidd. Two doors slammed, and tyres spewed gravel as they roared away.

*

Pat's office was stickily hot again, but crammed this time with uniformed men most of them overweight, and a couple of muscled women. The big ceiling fan spun silently. Pat himself was rolling up his shirt sleeves, and bawling hoarsely.

'You guys?' Fierce grin round the whole room. 'Read your goddam schedules? No mother-fuckin' foul ups, not this bright and beautiful day—not a one... *Ninety minutes*! You got that? *Six o'clock's* your fuckin' deadline, home and tidy and lickin' dirt.' He jammed his hands onto his hips, and swung his shoulders slowly around to look his men in the eye, one by one.

'Professional, OK? *All* them lousy punks, *all* of 'em. No cell calls! … *No* hits on attorneys… Forget them grievin' families, not one lousy buzz… Guy reaches for his candybar, shoot it out his hand.' Another big grin all around, wan smiles in return. 'I mean it! … Questions?'

Silence; but he held their gaze.

'Now out!'

The crowd filed away, checking holsters, slapping bullet-proof vests, talking quietly, and Tom found himself left standing by the door alongside the uniformed administrator.

Pat turned to them. 'No interruptions, Melissa.'

'Coffee, Sir?'

'Sure, sure.'

She disappeared, and Pat waved Tom to a chrome and leather seat. 'Big bust,' he observed.

'Sam told me.'

'He did?'

'Only he would need to fly to Chicago.'

'We been sweating on this since '97, Tom. Today's the big one… You want a heads-up?'

Tom nodded.

Pat leant back in his springy steel chair. 'Leonardo Donatello,' he began and wiped sweating hands up over his dark hair. 'Lucky Bambino. Chicago hood, big boss. This goddam bogeyman's been running cocaine into New England a darn long time. Along with a heap of other crap.' Pat slowly removed his watch, clawed a tissue from a box on the desk, and carefully wiped both wrists. He scrunched the tissue into a ball and pitched it accurately into a trash can six feet away. He glanced sharply at Tom.

'Right.'

'Ties up with a middleman. Name of Estoril, Huge

Colombian guy…' Pat pressed both palms down onto his desk and leant forward. 'And your Mr Charles West, Tom…'

'What about him?'

'We just discovered he was in deep with *both*.'

'Really? You're sure?'

'Crafted himself a real efficient supply chain.'

'Where's he selling?'

'Mostly Boston. University neighbourhoods, Ivy League kids… An' we're making to corral this whole sweet herd, right now, wipe out the lot, fast and clean… But we got this problem. Your five suspects. Any of 'em in with this outfit, d'you reckon?'

Tom thought. 'Hard to say.'

'Come *on*, Tom, come on! If they're in, we gotta *take* them. With the rest. Straight up… How's that evidence shaping?'

'Well,' said Tom. 'Sam gave me a set of satellite photos this morning—and they seem to show the only two left in the frame for the shooting are Dan Soberski & Dale van Twente.' He dug out the photos and explained.

Pat listened intently, frowning. '*Those* guys? … Holy shit! We ain't got nothing on them… Figure they're in?'

Melissa sashayed in, a tray carrying cafetière and mugs perched airily on one hand. She lowered it unsteadily onto Pat's desk and disappeared again. Pat poured himself a mug.

Tom poured his own. 'Can't tell, can I?' he said. 'Dan runs an electronics company, so he might be providing radar transponders. Dale's technically competent too. But I think it's far more likely one of them was unlucky enough to be a witness of something incriminating, and West set out to eliminate him, to be on the safe side.'

'So West intercepts him at sea? And your guy gets to grab the rifle?'

'That's my picture.'

'And shoots West, in self-defence? … But if he's so goddam innocent, why don't he dose out his story to the cops, Tom? Or to you?'

Tom shrugged.

Pat looked sharply at him. 'Where's these two guys now?'

Tom hesitated. 'Dan's off to Annapolis by train,' he said at last. 'Dale's visiting friends in Boston, Della knows where.'

'Hell! … OK, Tom. We go get 'em.'

'Arrest them anyway?'

'Sure, 'fore they hit on their pals.'

'They may be innocent.'

'We'll get to figure *that* out, soon enough. No harm done… Stop here.' Pat leapt up, and the door snapped to behind him.

Tom raised his eyebrows, visualising two comfortable families tumbled by arrests into confusion and anguish. He poured himself another coffee.

Pat was back within ten minutes. 'Dog's a-runnin'!' he said. 'And here's *another* turn-up… Feds picked up Stacey.'

'West's companion? He's in the gang too?'

'Sure is. Bigger'n West, they say. Skewered him, yesterday. And did they hit pay dirt!'

'Good stuff?'

'Stacey plea-bargained!'

'So soon? Why?'

'Ain't even sure of that yet,' said Pat, with a satisfied grin. 'But he done it, real peachy… Rollin' up the big names every which way, Englewood, Washington

Park, you name it... Feds can spare him for a day or two, Sam's going to fly him up tomorrow. Care to drop by?'

'Of course!'

'Eleven a.m. Oh, and Sam faxed you.' Pat jumped up and snatched a folder off a filing cabinet. He handed over a flimsy sheet of scribbled notes:

FOR TOM

Stacey says he met West 1987. W. was peddling drugs to students at MIT, low-level, and S. set him up in a more profitable line.

Says W. was gunning for someone during the race. W. wouldn't tell him who, or why.

Tom looked up. But Pat was working through a pile of files. 'Got that?' he mumbled, without raising his eyes. He turned to his laptop and began rattling away.

'Thanks,' said Tom. He poured himself a third mugful, and settled thoughtfully to drink. After a while, Melissa marched in to remove the coffee pot. She looked at Pat and jerked her blond head towards the door. Tom followed her out.

'Best leave him,' she whispered, and awarded him a Colgate smile. 'Go home. He wants you here eleven tomorrow.'

'I know.'

She phoned through to patrolman Kidd and, still smiling to herself, escorted Tom down to the basement in the beat-up elevator. On this trip, Tom observed, its familiar tang of disinfectant was overlaid by the sharp smell of fresh urine, but it didn't seem to disturb her.

*

Back in the library, Tom found a note from Della, asking him to call Plymouth. He mentally added five hours to his watch time and called Iain's home number.

'Tom here Jeanie—I won't keep him up late, I promise.'

After a minute: 'Tom?'

'How's it going?'

'We picked up his trail in the UK.'

'Good! Where?'

'University of Cambridge.' Iain was stifling a yawn. 'Calling himself Carl Easton.'

Tom wrote it down. 'Sure it was him?'

'Got a photo. Younger, of course, and his hair was blond. But it matched our pics very nicely, considering.'

'Right, good. Any history?'

'Yup... British father, German mother. German speaker, grew up in Bonn, high school there. University at Heidelberg.'

'*German.* Hm.'

'Then a Ph. D in computing.'

'Heidelberg too?'

'Aye. Moved to Cambridge in 1979 for research.'

'Still pretty young, I suppose?'

'Twenty-two.'

'And *was* there a link with radio astronomy?'

'Sort of. He was in the Computer Laboratory, but the Cambridge radio astronomers knew him—he wrote programs for them on commission. He wasn't liked. Too fond of pointing out others' mistakes.'

'When did he leave?'

'1985.'

'Hm... Six years.'

'In a hurry. The astronomers didn't know why. I

couldn't find out either at first, but it came out in the end... Big trouble.'

'What sort of trouble?'

'In this college. I got to interview their Senior Tutor.' Iain sniffed loudly.

Tom laughed. 'Classier than dear old Strathclyde?'

'Gardens, man. By the river.'

Tom essayed a doodle of two punts and a cloister.

'They made him what they call a Bye-Fellow.'

'What's that?'

'Half-way between student and staff.'

'So what was the big trouble?'

'That damn Tutor tried to choke me off, I had to knock into his thick head this was a murder enquiry. But in the end he told me... Sex, not drugs. Corrupting students.'

For a moment Tom began in imagination peopling his punts with muscular toy-boys in straw hats, but something made him stop.

'Some of the students went to pieces... Seems he knew how to draw them in deep—finished up thinking *they'd* seduced *him,* the poor buggers. So when they wanted out, they kept the guilty secrets to themselves, naturally. That bloody Tutor *assured* me he knew nothing of it till too late. But had a shrewd notion, dammit. Didn't want to put himself about... Eventually Easton went too far. Something he made one of the students let him do, with a knife.'

Tom remembered the decapitated kittens.

'It went wrong, the undergraduate got carved up. They couldn't get him into court—*said* he cowed the witnesses. But it appeared to me yon idiot's chief concern was avoiding the publicity. In the end all they did was bundle Easton out of his job. Shit sued them—but they had the guts to resist that.'

'OK, Iain,' said Tom. 'Nasty... It all fits.' He scrunched up his doodle and pitched the ball of paper quietly into the waste basket. 'Get the names?'

'Idiot won't release them.'

'Need them in the end,' said Tom.'

'Take a judge's order... That's *it* for me with ancient seats of learning!' Iain breathed heavily for a moment or two. 'Hell, man... Now, the rest... Stacey. Some fellows at the yacht club remembered a man of that name came down from London. That's all I found.'

'Right, Iain. I just heard the FBI have picked up Stacey in Chicago. Flying him up here tomorrow... Seems he knew West was gunning for someone in the race.'

'Was he, now?'

'Anything else?'

'Dale van Twente's landlady's a bit vague about the bottle. But on balance I'm thinking he never gave it her...'

'That's important, Iain. Can't you pin her down? Sort of woman who *would* remember?'

'No man: seventy, floats around her damn parlour in purple chiffon, vague about everything.'

'Hell!'

'That's about it, Tom.'

'Thanks, Iain.' said Tom. 'The more we hear about this victim the more worth shooting he seems.'

'Too right.'

Nasty, thought Tom as he settled the phone onto its cradle, and it does sort the background... But gives me no help whatever with who fired the rifle... Apart from the rum—that puts young Dale back in the frame.

He set off in reflective mood to find himself some supper.

Bootless inquisition

Next morning, Tom was ready with his briefcase when the cruise car drew up outside the old house. The sun was hotting up, and Patrolman Kidd's eyes were obscured behind shades.

'Nice day,' Tom said as they rolled smoothly into town, making a less hurried trip of it than the afternoon before.

'Yessir! Us guys is mighty happy.'

'You are?'

'Pay and a half.' Kidd grinned.

'Because of the bust?'

'Huge, Sir… Cells overflowing. Prisoners' breakfasts late.'

'Ah.'

At police headquarters the odour of the elevator had reverted to disinfectant. Pat, in shirtsleeves, fetched Tom iced water from the office machine.

'OK, OK,' he said, settling back into his low-slung easy chair. 'Stacey ain't here yet. But we can check out Soberski and van Twente.'

'You managed to run them down?'

'Feds took Dan off his train, so he won't be wise to the bust. But Dale they pick up at his cousin's home— so most likely he did hear… Dan, he hired himself an attorney. Dale ain't bothered.'

'Have you questioned them yet?'

'Julius will do that.'

'Julius?'

'Julius Koch, Customs Attorney, old partner of mine. You and me, we sit and listen.'

'You've briefed this Julius, then?'

'Pretty much.'

Tom nodded. He was uneasy that Dan and Dale had been swept up so uncompromisingly in Sam's enormous dragnet. But they were US citizens, it was out of his hands. The tower was noisy this morning with echoing corridors, slamming doors, and occasional raised voices or distant complaints. He sipped his iced water and waited.

After a few minutes, there was a discreet knock on the door. Pat looked up but didn't trouble to shout permission, and the door slowly opened. Framed in the opening was an impressively jowled man with a shiny bald head. His pale grey suit was double-breasted, his tie silvery, his glasses rimless, and his feet oddly small in glossy black shoes. Under one arm he clutched a large and well-worn brief case.

'Hi Pat,' he intoned resonantly, and strode forward. 'A *vurry* good morning to you... And Chief Inspector Tom Tallis? Good morning, Tom, to *you*, yes indeed.' The smile was fixed. The proffered right hand yielded in Tom's, as though there were no bones inside.

'Files OK, Julius?'

'Sure Pat, sure. Very clear, I thank you... Do you have a little iced water?'

Pat filled another plastic cup and watched as Julius sipped. Then he punched a number into his desk phone.

'Arrived, Eddy? ... We'll be right down.'

Pat jumped up. Julius downed his remaining water in two gulps, rose himself, and stepped firmly ahead of Pat. Tom followed.

The elevator dropped, slid rapidly past the basement car park and dived deep into the earth. When it finally clanked to a halt, its doors remained closed until Pat inserted a well-worn key into the control panel. A police guard in brown uniform was revealed, waiting silently beneath an unshaded wall light, in a long corridor of dark grey walls. A thin steel chain led in a shining curve down from his belt and up again to his side pocket.

'Number four, Eddy?'

'Yessir.' Eddy led the way. The floor squeaked under his feet and smelled of rubber.

He stopped beside a heavy steel door, flicked aside a view panel and peered through, then extracted a bunch of keys from his pocket, worked the lock, and stepped in first. Having checked the situation inside he stood back deferentially.

Dan was sitting at a steel table, untidy and unshaven, his attorney beside him. Her charcoal suit almost disappeared against the walls, but glossy lipstick in a russet shade and a lime-green silk scarf shone in the meagre light. Three empty chairs faced them across the table.

Julius marched in, and Pat and Tom followed. Dan made as if to rise, but a manicured hand restrained him. Eddy left the room and re-locked the door from outside.

Julius boomed: 'Mrs Greenbaum, Lippner & Casey?' He bowed.

'Anna Greenbaum.' She smiled engagingly in response but did not rise. 'Julius Koch?'

Julius nodded, and settled with an imperious creak onto the larger central chair facing Dan and Anna; Pat and Tom made relatively minor creaks to his right and left. Pat leant over and started an old-style tape recorder on a low table to his right. Its enormous reels jerked into silent rotation. He tapped at the desk microphone, and muttered into it: 'Suite four, July twenty-two…'

Julius opened his brief case, extracted five fat and dog-eared folders, and disposed them impressively on the table. 'You Mirandised?' he asked Dan sharply.

'Wouldn't sign,' grunted Pat.

Julius nodded and coughed. 'Tape running?' he queried in a rumbling undertone, and turned back to Dan. 'I'm gonna ask you a few easy questions,' he said in a fatherly, confiding voice. He nodded elaborately and boomed: '*You have the right, Dan, to remain silent. Anything you say can and will be used against you in a court of law … I see you hired yourself an attorney… You have the right to have your attorney present during any questioning. If, later on, you can no longer afford your attorney, one will be provided for you at government expense…* You understand all that?'

Dan nodded.

'Out loud, Dan, if you please.'

'I understand.'

Julius opened his brief case and found a form, pushed it towards Anna.

Anna checked the form. 'Sign there,' she said laconically to Dan, pointing. Dan took the form, studied it closely, and signed. He looked up.

Julius looked up, too. 'Now Dan,' he said. 'You got a fine family?'

Dan raised his eyebrows.

'You got a family?'

'Yes,' said Dan at last. 'Married, two kids.'

'And a business to care for?'

'Electronics enterprise.'

'OK. Well, Dan, you and I, we wanna handle this

right, don't we? Don't want to hurt your wife, nor your kids, nor your business. Not if we can help it. Cause they weren't involved, were they? With all those drugs? With that fucking heap of cocaine?'

Dan's head jerked back, and Anna sighed loudly. 'Mr Koch,' she said. 'My client here got himself arrested yesterday. Right off the train in Annapolis. On suspicion of *murder*. No mention of anything else. So what's with this spiel of drugs and cocaine?'

'On suspicion of murdering Charles West, a known drug dealer,' said Julius smoothly. 'You see, Dan, what we don't understand is whether you got yourself onto that boat *Cas A*, or whether West got himself onto your *Flying Cloud*? That's what we haven't got clear. Maybe he try to shoot you? Maybe you shoot him in self-defence? … How you get that hunting rifle into your hands?'

Anna looked sharply at Dan.

Dan was pale, but had himself in hand, Tom thought. 'I don't know what you're talking about, Sir,' he said. 'Like I said to Mr Tallis here, Charles West was never on my boat, and I was never on his. Yes, I heard Mr West was shot. But not by me… As I told Mr Tallis, I saw West's boat *Cas A* at sea on the nineteenth of June, when she passed between me and Dale van Twente, and I could still see her from time to time on the twentieth. I never saw her again after that— barring a distant sail that might have been her on the twenty-third.' He turned his head in mute appeal to Tom, who gave a small nod. Anna noticed it. A small hard smile flitted over her face.

'Dan,' said Julius in a tone of fatherly reproof. 'You just ain't understanding your position. We got three pieces of evidence against you.' He pulled an even fatter file from his brief case, and splayed out its contents. 'Hard evidence... Got them here. One: we know for sure some competitor other than West was on West's boat *Cas A.*' Julius looked up impressively, and Tom was careful not to nod again. 'Two: we got a satellite photo shows for certain sure you're the only competitor in a position to intercept *Cas A.*'

Tom blinked and turned to Dan.

'That can't be right,' said Dan promptly, frowning. 'I know the positions. If you think I could have intercepted West, then Dale van Twente could too, surely. Not that I think... ' Anna laid a restraining finger on his arm, and he stopped.

Julius went on as if he hadn't heard. 'Three: this Donatello mob you got yourself mixed up in. Down in Florida those guys been using radar transponders, and—you know what, Dan?—your corporation *manufactures* radar transponders. So: you make 'em to special order? Custom built?'

Anna looked questioningly at Dan.

'We *don't* manufacture transponders,' said Dan. 'We *could* make them, we're a microwave outfit, but we don't.'

'We can check you out there, Dan.'

'Feel free,' said Dan calmly. '... Though what you say, Mr Koch,' he added suddenly, 'reminds me of something Dale told me... ' He tailed off into silence.

'Dale told you?' said Julius incredulously. 'You *know* Dale van Twente? Talk to him? You two in *conspiracy*?'

'I got to know him after the race,' said Dan. For the first time he raised his voice. 'It was natural. We had sister boats, we'd sailed similar courses.'

'Indeed you did, Dan. Remarkably similar.'

'But I didn't know him at all before the race!'

Anna coughed and cleared her throat. '... Mr Koch!'

she said loudly. 'Seems like you're accusing my client here of a fair bit more than murder. Drugs, for instance, *and* conspiracy. And if that is so, it leads me to offer him certain advice. I advise him *now* to answer no more of your questions, your *leading* questions. For the time being... Until I hear from you *exactly* what my client's accused of—I'm pulling him, Mr Koch. And until I have a copy of that satellite photo right there on my desk, and until I've seen your written argument why it incriminates just my client and no one else—likewise, no more interrogation. Do I make myself clear?'

Julius' lips had clamped together.

'And now,' added Anna, 'can we discuss bail?'

'C'mon!' Julius growled. 'This is a murder rap, for chrissake.' Pat nodded. Dan had looked up hopefully when Anna intervened, but now one shoulder slumped, and he looked reproachfully at Tom.

Julius cleared his throat and rose. He offered no further comment. Pat intoned again into the microphone, stopped the tape-recorder and removed the tape. He pressed a button fixed under the table. After a pause Tom heard Eddy unlocking the door, and the three of them filed out. The door clanged shut behind them, leaving Anna incarcerated with her client.

This sad knot

The elevator whisked them back into the daylight and up to Pat's office. Three fresh beakerfuls of iced water were dribbled from the machine.

'Dan was quite right about the satellite evidence,' said Tom, sipping.

Pat looked at him, and grinned.

Julius paid no attention. 'So, Pat,' he said, ponderously. 'Anna does the clam-shell act, fast. But not before we learn something... This gang of two discussed transponders... Conspiracy! You agree, Tom?'

Tom felt it was time to defend certain standards. 'No,' he said.

Julius examined him severely. 'They sail very similar courses. Why?'

'Is a good question,' said Pat.

'Certainly,' said Tom. 'But you don't know the answer. It could be accidental, their boats were identical.'

Julius frowned dismissively. He opened his brief case and dug out a new folder. 'This Dale ready, Pat?'

'Sure.' Pat grinned again. 'Since midnight.'

'And *he* don't have no sassy attorney... Let's go.'

*

They found Dale in a smaller interview room, alone, and a good deal more unkempt than Dan. He jumped up angrily.

'What the *hell* is going on here, Mr Tallis?' he shouted.

Pat made a keep calm gesture, but Dale jammed his hands down on the steel table. 'A *murder* rap?' he demanded. 'How the hell d'you make *that* out?'

'Hey, hey, Dale' interrupted Julius. 'Let's have some procedure here!' His eyes still on Tom, Dale subsided unwillingly onto his chair. 'Tape running, Pat? Now Dale... You Mirandised?'

'He signed already,' said Pat.

'So he did,' said Julius. He extracted from his brief case his trademark fat files, located another folder, and whisked out a buff form, examined it. He nodded. 'You understand your statutory rights?'

'Could you *please*,' shouted Dale, 'explain to me who the hell you are and what the fuck's going on?'

Julius eyed him sternly. 'Best cool it,' he said. 'Julius Koch... US Customs Attorney. And this...'

'*Customs* attorney? Since when did customs investigate homicide?'

'Dale, Dale,' said Julius soothingly. '... This here is Pat Slieve, Chief of City Police, Newport, Rhode Island. And this is Chief Inspector Tom Tallis from Plymouth, England.'

Dale gave Tom a dirty look. 'We met,' he said. 'And Mr Tallis had his ears shut, it seems.'

'Now Dale, now,' said Julius reprovingly. 'You understand your rights?'

'Sure.'

'You got a fine family?'

'*Family?*' said Dale. His face was pink, now. 'Wife, one son... What the hell have they got to do with this?'

'And you're employed?'

'So what?'

'You employed?'

'Yes.'

'Who by?'

'IBM,' said Dale, reluctantly.

'Facility?'

'Yorktown Heights... Research engineer.'

'Engineer, hey! Well, Dale, you and I, we want to handle this right, don't we? Don't want no damage to your wife, nor to your boy, nor your employment. Not if we can help it. Cause they weren't involved, were they, Dale? With all those drugs, with that heap of coke?'

There was a long pause, and Tom sensed that Dale was at last understanding the depth of his predicament.

'Just what is all this, Mr Koch?'

'Your Charles West, riding high in a drugs outfit, weren't he, Dale? And you with him. We got evidence. Against *you*.' Julius picked a file off the table and flicked through it. 'One: we know for sure another of the competitors was on board *Cas A*.'

'Not me,' said Dale.

'Two: we got a satellite photo shows for *certain* you're the only competitor in a position to intercept *Cas A*.'

Dale swallowed.

'Three: this drugs gang, you know what? Down in Florida they're making use of radar transponders. And *you* been discussing transponders with Dan Soberski: that so, Dale?'

'So what?'

'You admit you did? You two working together?' asked Julius in his most mournful, understanding tone.

Dale stopped and considered. 'Look,' he said, breathing deeply. 'Dan's a radar engineer. Runs his own enterprise. I just told him something would interest him.'

'Like what?'

'Like drug smugglers using homemade radars and transponders at illegal frequencies.'

'Ah! How you know that?'

'Does it matter? From a work colleague.'

'That's a peculiar sort of gossip, to be picking over at work.'

'It's an engineering research lab, for God's sake.'

'Who's this colleague?'

'Guy works on signal processing.'

'Name?'

'Schneider, Gary Schneider... But Gary got it from another colleague, works on narrow channel receivers. And *he* got it from a guy in Verizon.'

'Cell phone Verizon?'

'Yeah. The Verizon guy said smugglers were interfering with the X band in Florida.'

'And Dan was interested?'

Dale stopped again. He ran both hands up through his hair and left them behind his head as he frowned at Julius.

'You better answer my question, Dale.'

Dale let his hands fall and looked down at the floor, his chest rising and falling. 'No,' he said, at last. 'No! Some godawful idiot gets me arrested on suspicion of murder. Seems it's *not* some crazy mistake, like I thought... And now you're interrogating me. You say you have evidence I shot West. You're asking me about some drugs outfit I never heard of, you're trying to make me implicate Dan in a conspiracy... *I need an attorney.*'

'An attorney, Dale? … You want to see your wife tonight?'

'Hell, Mr Koch! I need an attorney *now*, I've got a right to an attorney… How do I get to use a phone?'

Julius looked down at his hands. Pat said: 'I find you a phone, Dale… In a few hours, maybe.'

'*Hours*? Holy shit! Why?'

Pat and Julius exchanged a look. No one replied.

Julius slowly re-packed his brief case and stood up. Pat shut down the recorder and pressed the button under the table. Eddie came to escort Dale back to his cell. Tom caught Dale's eye as he was marched off, and collected from him a further very ugly look.

*

Back in Pat's office, Julius said at once: 'This sure *is* conspiracy, Pat. This gang of two, they shoot that guy. Won't be easy to prove, however.'

Tom said: 'But if Dan was interested in what Dale had to say about transponders, that shows it was all new to him.'

Julius seemed not to hear.

Pat said: 'More in that conversation than meets the eye, Tom.'

The desk phone rang. Pat answered the call, spoke quietly, returned the phone slowly to its cradle. 'Hell,' he remarked, shrugging. 'Seems Stacey won't be here till tomorrow… Say eleven, here in my office?'

'Right,' said Tom.

'And better review Dan and Dale after we question Stacey,' said Pat.

Julius nodded ponderously.

So Tom had once again to return frustrated to the yacht club. He travelled down in the whiffy elevator

124

with Julius, but didn't find much to say to him.

*

Back in the library, Tom tipped back his chair to think. According to Julius, Dan and Dale were in some sort of conspiracy. Tom had to admit it was a little odd they'd sailed such similar courses and discussed the gang's interest in radar transponders. But they *couldn't* have been in a conspiracy to intercept and shoot West, because they didn't have the boat speed to overtake him. On the contrary, Sam's FAX about Stacey had confirmed that West had been gunning for one of the competitors. Perhaps Dan and Dale had *jointly* feared an attack from West, and kept company for mutual protection. Perhaps West had turned back to attack one of them, but working together they had managed to defeat him?

But now, at all events, whether in conspiracy or not, the two of them were caught up in this drugs bust. It meant, in effect, that Tom's investigation was out of his hands. He'd probably have to abandon it—his flight home was supposed to be in three day's time, after all. And to make matters worse, the West case would now inevitably take a low priority in Newport.

Wearily, he turned to more petty matters. He called again the travel agent in Newport, where a husky-voiced woman explained languidly that his money had still not arrived from the UK, and told him to have a nice day. With sinking heart he fought his way, via sundry call centres at international rates, to a Barclays Personal Banker in Plymouth, who in a twittery voice assured him that his hard-earned money was already safely deposited with Citizen's Bank in Newport; she gave Tom the transaction code. Citizen's Bank proved easier to reach. A silky-voiced young man there wrote down the code, and left Tom with a heavy metal combo playing in his left ear. After five minutes he returned. He could find no trace of the transaction, and advised Tom to contact Barclays' head office in London.

Ridiculous, thought Tom. Everything was in a mess, he needed somewhere quiet to unwind. He walked down to the marina and collected the key to Mike's boat. But as he passed Della's office, she caught his eye through the glass and beckoned. He stopped, and she jumped up to open the door.

'Join me for some coffee, Mr Tallis?' she asked, conspiratorially, gently taking Tom's left forearm and elbow and drawing him in. She opened and held out a tin of sticky goodies. It carried a battered label representing a lady in an empire line dress driving a pony and gig, adorned with the logo *O'Leary, Parnell Square* in handsome italics. 'Eileen's,' said Della, 'gingerbread.' A little reluctantly, Tom took one and perched on the edge of her desk.

She spooned ground coffee into a cafetière with a clatter, filled it with boiling water, hunted in a cupboard. 'You making progress, Mr Tallis?'

Tom hesitated. 'Not much,' he admitted.

'But is it murder?' She was laughing at herself.

'You're as bad as my daughter! ... What do *you* think, Della?'

She became serious and shook her head.

'Why not?' he asked.

'Not capable of it. Not your five suspects.'

'Even if I can prove one of them was on *Cas A*?'

'Even then. Must have been some terrible accident.' She filled Tom's mug, filled her own, and settled comfortably on her office chair, facing him, knees

together but plump feet in high heels splayed sideways. 'You disappointed, Mr Tallis?'

Tom gave her a quizzical look. 'About what?'

'You got a long face, when I see you passing.'

'Let's say, I wanted to have made more progress.'

'But you *do* think it was murder?'

Tom laughed. 'Don't give up, do you?'

She shook her head. '*And* you're disappointed about
your trip home.'

Tom took a swig of coffee and frowned at the floor.
'Are you mothering me, Della?' he enquired.

She grinned broadly, leant forward and tapped his
knee. 'Why not, Mr Tallis? I'm house-mom here…
Mike Guerdon, he's a real good friend?'

'You've been talking to Jane Allison.'

'I like her…   Guess you *had* to turn her down?
Rules?'

'You know about that too?'

Della laughed. 'Was my idea,' she said. '*You* were
disappointed, and *she* was one truly exhausted
woman.' She looked shrewdly at Tom. 'Trying not to
show it, of course… Maybe you didn't realise?' Della
refilled Tom's mug and handed him another
gingerbread as though he were a hungry teenager who
needed comforting. 'Get your flight fixed?'

'No,' said Tom. 'The money hasn't come through.'

Della tutted, stood up, and perched next to Tom.
She draped an arm around his shoulder, and nodded
sympathetically.

*

By eleven next morning Tom was again sipping iced
water in one of Pat's tubular arm chairs. As a plea-
bargainer Stacey was not to be questioned under-

ground.

'No Julius today,' announced Pat. 'Got a suspect in Boston won't break. Figured they could use his grandpop technique.'

'Grandpop wasn't very successful yesterday,' said Tom.

'And that's fair comment,' agreed Pat equably. 'One of your suspects hired himself a sharp lawyer, and the other was smart enough to see the storm clouds a-rolling.'

'Think they're guilty?'

'Some of your evidence says so.'

There was a knock at the door. Sam entered, wearing a soft felt hat, and carrying a laptop and a rain-spattered nylon raincoat. He dumped all three onto Pat's cluttered side table. 'Hi there,' he said cheerfully to Tom.

'Where is the louse?' asked Pat.

'Pissing.'

Sam sat down, and few moments later a small man appeared in the doorway, face deadpan, mouth turned down at the corners, head on one side, grey hair and grey trousers both a little too long. He reminded Tom momentarily of Charlie Chaplin—but without those sad unfathomable pools for eyes: these were pale, alert and shrewd.

'Alfred Stacey?' asked Pat.

'Sure,' said Sam. 'Come in Alfie and sit down.'

Stacey scowled and looked carefully round the room. He settled into one of the tubular chairs, upright, knees together, hands clasped over them. Pat's face was stoney, but he rose and fetched iced water. Stacey took it silently, and sipped. 'Who's these gentlemen?' he asked Sam.

'Pat here's our Newport Police Chief.'

Stacey inspected him.

'And this is Tom Tallis from the British police.'

Stacey's eyebrows shot up. '*Commander* Talleys?' he enquired. 'Operation Tango?'

'No,' said Tom acidly.

The eyebrows dropped back.

'Let's get on with it,' said Pat, frowning.

Sam seemed relaxed about the situation. 'Now, Alfie' he said firmly. 'You know what the scenario is? You've agreed to come down to Newport and help us over one particular matter. And we've agreed it could be of some advantage to you. *Provided* you don't mess with us... On the same page, are we?'

Stacey nodded very slightly.

'OK. We went over some of this yesterday, but best if we take it again... When did you first meet Charles West?'

'1987,' said Stacey promptly.

'Where?'

'Sitting on a bench on Harvard Green. Wiv' a chic co-ed, who was part stoned, and out of 'er depth.'

'But he wasn't calling himself West then?'

'Carl Easton, 'e was.'

'And dealing in cheap resin?'

'On the MIT campus. Found it turned 'im a penny.'

Stacey's cockney style was irritating and to Tom didn't seem entirely natural. 'What was West doing at Harvard?' he asked. 'Was he employed?'

The pale eyes swung round. 'Yep.'

'Who by?'

'The Department of Physics.'

'Doing what?'

'Computing.'

Tom nodded.

'And you slotted him in with Lucky Bambino?'

prompted Sam.

'*After* a lot of argy-bargy.'

'Now Alfie: were you West's only link with the Donatello mob?'

'Yep.' Stacey's mouth turned down a little more at the edges. 'Lucky reckoned he was useful. Could mix import with yacht racing... So Lucky helped him buy a boat.'

'When was that?' asked Tom.

'1998... But that weren't the ketch.'

'Not *Cas A*?'

'That first was smaller... Called it *Wotan*.'

'*Wotan*?' asked Tom.

Stacey tipped his head back, and looked down his nose at Tom. 'Wagner, mate.'

Tom was thinking hard. 'What made him change boats?' he asked.

'Told me he needed something faster.'

'And he bought this *Cas A* from a guy in Florida?' asked Pat.

'Yep. Wiv' his own money, this time.'

'Money he made from dealing?' asked Tom.

'Must have been. He wasn't earning much.'

'And that was in 1999?' asked Tom.

'Summer '99.'

'Didn't he have a job back in England by then?'

'Yep... In a chemistry lab.'

'Why did he want a faster boat, Alfie?'

'Keen racer, wasn't 'e? ... But later, maybe he had another reason...'

'Go on,' said Tom.

'And 'e starts buying things... New desktop computer. But who wants a desktop on a boat?'

'Chart work?'

'Nah,' said Stacey. 'Had a chart display already.

The only app he had on this new machine was a desk-top publisher.'

'QuarkXPress?' asked Tom, remembering.

'That's the one… And next, he gets himself a bloody rifle. And he wants Lucky not to know about it… Psychopath, wasn't 'e? Thought I'd better keep an eye.'

'*You* reckoned him a psychopath?'

Stacey gave Tom a long cool look. 'Had my reasons.'

'But,' said Tom, 'he bought the rifle before that.'

'He did?' said Sam.

'He joined the Salisbury rifle club in 1997, and bought it soon after.'

'He was planning this for three years?'

'Looks like it,' said Tom.

'That's a very slow-burn plan,' said Sam.

'He have any slow-burn grudges?' Pat asked Stacey.

Stacey grinned. 'Plenty of grudges in the mob,' he said. 'But not Carl, and not from three years earlier.'

Tom hesitated. 'Did you discover any more about his plans?' he asked at last.

'Sort of.' Stacey again looked speculatively at Tom.

'And?'

'He'd entered in this race—told Lucky it'd be an opportunity. But then I found he had another reason… Got himself an enemy.'

Tom's head jerked up. 'He *told* you that?'

'Near enough, yes.'

'An enemy in the race?'

'Yep'

'Did he say who?'

'Kept that quiet.'

'Try him with the names, Tom,' said Pat, suddenly.

'Yes,' said Tom. 'Let's see if any of these mean anything, Alfie…'

131

'Mean anything?'

'Members of the gang? Enemies for West?'

Stacey blinked. 'OK.'

'Dan Soberski? … Dale van Twente? … Dr Todd? …'

'Southampton,' said Alfie immediately. 'Employer.'

'You sure?' asked Pat.

'Course I'm sure. Dr P. N. Todd. But Todd had nothing to do with the mob.'

'Certain?' asked Tom.

'Yep.'

'What about the others? Eileen Meath? Jane Allison? Laurel Delon?'

'None of those.'

'Not in the gang?'

'Nope.'

'Sure about the two Americans?' persisted Sam. 'Soberski and van Twente?'

'Certain sure.'

'Maybe West knew someone in the mob you're not acquainted with?' enquired Pat.

'No, mate. I had to know *all* his contacts, them's the rules.'

'Maybe he was cheating you?' asked Tom.

'He wouldn't.'

'How can you be sure?' asked Tom.

Stacey raised his eyebrows eloquently. 'He knew,' he said.

'Knew what?'

'How Mr Donatello liked things to be…'

'What d'you mean?' Tom received a pitying look, but no reply. 'What d'you mean?' he repeated.

Stacey sighed. 'Had to watch, didn't he?' he said at last. 'Like the rest of us.'

'Watch *what*?'

Stacey stared at Tom. 'Fingers,' he said, and shrugged. Seeing that Tom remained puzzled he added, 'Fucking salami slicer, squealers' fingers.' He nodded several times. 'Not aesthetic.' He smiled beatifically.

Tom swallowed and looked down.

After a moment Sam said, 'Did you know *all* the mules, Alfie?'

Stacey looked up. 'Yep,' he said. 'Recruiting mules was my job. Carl, he didn't know 'em.'

'So who d'you think this enemy was?'

'Dunno,' said Alfred. 'But he gave me a little hint, one day.'

'Which was?'

'I tell him to get that rifle off of his boat or I'll have to inform Lucky about it. And he says, "Won't be there long, Alfie." So I say: "What is all this, mate? Planning on shooting some geezer in the middle of Cowes Week?" And he says, "Not in the Solent, Alfie. Nor in the Channel, nor the North Sea, nor the Irish Sea. Out in the deep ocean, Alfie," he says, "that's 'ow it's planned." And he taps 'is nose.'

Tom considered this remark. 'He meant that, though his target might sail in those other places, it wasn't safe to shoot him there?' he asked.

Alfie considered. 'That's right,' he said. 'What I took him to mean.'

Pat demanded suddenly: 'That goddam sail race go through those areas?'

Sam's head jerked up. 'Not the North Sea or the Irish Sea,' he said.

Pat looked at Tom, who nodded.

'So who *is* this guy, Tom?' said Pat. 'Which of your suspects sails his boat in the North Sea and the Irish Sea?'

Tom thought for a moment. 'That argument rules out Dan and Dale,' he said, 'they only came over for the race. But the other four probably did cruise those waters.'

'You got a point there, mate,' said Stacey.

'Sure you remembered that conversation right?' Pat asked him. 'Rock-solid?'

'Sure as hell.'

Pat turned and looked gloomily at Sam. 'Shit,' he said, 'we arrested Dan and Dale.'

'You did? … Get anything?'

'Julius convinced himself they're in some god-almighty conspiracy. But we got no solid evidence, just they sailed close together and discussed transponders.'

'Transponders?' asked Stacey.

'Radar transponders used by drug smugglers.'

'I knows transponders,' said Stacey. 'And I know where Lucky gets 'em.'

'You do? Where?'

'Outfit in Long Beach.'

'California?' groaned Pat. 'Holy crap! Those two are East Coast guys… If I can't charge them, I gotta release them.'

'Best let them go,' said Sam.

Tom nodded. He felt relieved.

'Ask 'em first whether they ever cruise in British waters,' said Stacey firmly.

Tom looked at him.

'Out!' shouted Pat suddenly. 'Give the louse lunch Sam, stuff him a tuna malt. Then back here. We need to talk.' Their visitor was grinning, all sunshine suddenly, but Pat stared him out. 'See you again, two, three hours,' he growled.

Sam jerked his head, and the little man jumped to

his feet and ambled to the door, feet slightly splayed.

*

At first Tom thought Pat was going to produce his whiskey bottle, but it didn't reappear. Instead he asked Melissa to fix them all black coffee. Then he put his hands behind his head and waited, thinking, till at last Sam reappeared.

'Well, Tom,' he said then. 'Your case... Back to square one, ain't it?'

'It's all contradictions,' said Tom. 'The satellite picture shows only Dan and Dale had opportunity... '

Sam nodded dourly

'...but West's conversation with Stacey rules them out completely and rules the Europeans in... So I'm left with no solution at all.'

The other two looked at him.

'There is one further thing we can check.'

Pat looked up with a frown.

'West couldn't have been sure that he needed a faster boat, or had that conversation with Stacey about his plans, until he knew definitely his intended victim would be sailing in the race.'

Sam raised his eyebrows and nodded. He scrambled slowly to his feet and fetched his laptop. Keys rattled. '... He bought *Cas A* in July '99. And we can ask Stacey the date of his conversation with West.'

'No problem finding when the competitors entered the race,' said Tom, 'I'll let you know.'

'You're leaving in three days, Tom?' said Pat.

'That's true,' said Tom.

'And your goddam case is dead in the water?'

'I'm afraid it is,' said Tom.

'What we going to do then?'

'Not much we can do... If Laurel Delon, the French woman, turns up after I've gone, you said you could interview her?'

'Yeah, Tom,' said Pat. 'We can do that.'

'And if any evidence accumulates against Dan or Dale, you'll be ready to take action at this end?'

'Sure.'

'So far as the Europeans are concerned, I'll have to see what I can do from Plymouth... Unless anything turns up before I leave.'

*

It was still very hot as Patrolman Kidd drove Tom back to the club, but clouds were piling up in the east, and the humidity was rising.

Since it was Sunday, Tom took a more leisurely lunch than usual in the almost empty club cafeteria. Then, deciding he needed a rest from his case, he borrowed a map from Della, and during the afternoon took a walk inland from the clubhouse. He found himself following a trail over a promontory clothed in long-needled pines, resin-scented in the overbearing sun.

As he walked, he thought of Mike. How was he going to fetch his boat home once his troubles had blown over? For a moment Tom excited himself with the prospect that it might all be settled in a day or two, that Mike would jet back to Newport, and their little adventure could be revived. As he strode between the pines, hearing the occasional chatter of a chipmunk, trying to catch sight of bushy tail and watchful eyes, he found himself rehearsing what he'd learnt in his Yachtmaster Ocean classes, and tried to remember what it had been like taking sextant observations using the rooflines of the Crownhill housing estate as next best thing to a sea horizon… But it was all a dream: Consolidated Amory weren't going to relent, Mike must still be in there, fighting… Tomorrow he must settle his flight home, and tackle a final review of his case, however dead in the water Pat might consider it.

By six he was back at the clubhouse. Just before supper, Sam rang through with the information that Stacey's conversation with West had taken place in September 1999, during their earlier crossing of the Atlantic.

As Tom became drowsy in his huge bed he felt at first thankful that Dan and Dale were to be released. But then the humidity rose and, with the sheets sticking ever more tightly to his legs, he found himself increasingly irritated: mad with Consolidated Amory for having scuppered his cruise, exasperated with the banks for their dance of the veils over the money for his air ticket, hurt by Pat and Sam's fading interest in his case—and furious above all with himself, for having made so little progress.

This music crept

Tom lay angry in his huge bed. The night was very dark and he'd been woken by a nightmare that hovered just beyond recall. It had emerged, he could just about remember, by shape-shift out some particularly delightful earlier dream. Time's up, he thought furiously, investigation in tatters... Mike's bombshell, the loss of his cruise—that ripe apple snatched out of his very hand... And then Miss Allison's suggestion, that juicy replacement offered by a kindly bystander... Rain spattered relentlessly at the window

Suddenly, the vanished nightmare re-erupted fully armed, his chronic real-life flashback—Beth sprawled dead on the wet Dartmoor moss, himself devastated by unbanishable guilt as he finally gave up trying to revive her. To force it away he tried desperately to summon back the earlier dreamland delight, but it wouldn't reappear.

Thunder exploded overhead, and the rain-spatter changed abruptly to machine-gun hail. Doubly infuriated, Tom yanked both pillows over his head with a muffled yell.

*

The cafeteria at breakfast was almost deserted. By the time he had stacked his dirty plates, he was calmer, steeling himself to leave his investigation in some sort of shape. He sloshed his way to the library. The desk there was, he felt, developing a CID patina, carrying too much of his own detritus.

Citizen Bank first.

'Sure,' said the cashier sweetly, 'your draft is through, Sir.'

He arranged to draw the money in person the following morning.

'You're welcome, Sir. Have a good day.'

American Express. His flight was still available.

Less than two days, then. Progress or no progress, he had a report to write. He stood up and paced about the library, returned to the desk and found himself a clean sheet of ruled paper. Rain was still beating on the windows.

Three new issues, he thought, and wrote with a heavy underline:

Boat purchase timings

He looked at his watch: lunch should be over in Plymouth. He picked up the phone, and caught the secretary at the race office before she settled down to her afternoon's work.

Yes, she said, entries for the OSTAR Millenium had closed in May 1999 and been listed on the race web site. Proving cruises were to be complete by the end of July and all his six suspects had met this condition. West himself had been given special permission in July to change boats, and complete a further proving cruise during August.

'Thank you,' said Tom. 'That's very helpful.'

So West had indeed bought his new boat in the knowledge that his intended victim had entered the race, but unsure whether he or she would qualify by completing their proving cruise. A reasonable gamble.

Satellite pic interpretation

The satellite photographs unequivocally made *St Louis Blues* and *Flying Cloud* the only boats near enough to *Cas A* for any interception or rendezvous, provided it all happened before West's reporting time on the 25th.

But what if West had chosen not to report on the 25th and it all happened later? What reason could he have had for not reporting? If his target had been anyone other than Dale or Dan, he'd have needed to turn away from his reported course. And since he'd need an alibi, and wouldn't want to alert his victim, he would have had *every* reason to continue reporting plausible positions, if he'd been still alive to do so. Perhaps he'd been seen and identified by some vessel of which Tom was unaware, and so couldn't safely report a false position? Or perhaps he knew about Eileen's radio direction finder, and was afraid she might notice if he transmitted from an unexpected direction?

Tom frowned again, uneasily. He was much inclined to dismiss these speculations, and assume as before that it had all been over by the 25th. But in that case it *must* have been Dan or Dale.

He sighed, wrote down his conclusions neatly, and inserted a third heading:

Stacey's conversation with West

If West's target had been Dan or Dale, Stacey's conversation with him had to be discounted. Stacey was very clear that it had occurred, and had been sufficiently interested in it to make sure he hadn't misheard. But perhaps when West had mentioned the North Sea and the Irish Sea he'd been less specific than Stacey had assumed: maybe he'd just quoted them as typical places where a shooting would be too dangerous, where the radar coverage was too good. Perhaps he had in mind only that he *himself* often sailed in such places, not that his victim did.

Yes, Tom thought. Dan and Dale are *not* excluded by what West told Stacey, by no means.

*

He'd been cooped up in this damn library for too long—time to get his problem into the fresh air. Sheets of wet were still bucketing down, so he borrowed an umbrella from Della, set off for the low cliff-top in front of the big house, and marched vigorously up and down the waterlogged turf.

He'd been resisting his final conclusion—why? West's conversation with Stacey was *not* conclusive, there *was* no reason for West not to report, the satellite picture *did* tie it all down: *it just had to be Dan or Dale!* It wasn't that his argument was dodgy, just that Dan and Dale seemed too innocent. But, as Sam had remarked, they didn't have to be drug-runners. West might have set out to eliminate one of them simply because they'd been an innocent witness of something incriminating; and somehow, in self-defence, the intended victim had managed to turn the tables. *If that was what happened, there was still a good chance of forcing an admission.*

As he'd hoped, the fresh air and exercise had cleared his head. He still had to consider the mystery of how Dale managed to lose his buoy. Why had he never got round to asking him when he was available? Tom squelched determinedly off to the marina, Della's striped umbrella swaying sharply over his head. The buoy, however, told him no more than it had on his previous visit—and once again, as he was forcing his mind around the buoy-question, his gaze drifted idly across to *Ariel*, moored twenty feet away.

As he did so, the earlier of his two dreams during the night—the delightful one—imperceptibly reinserted itself into his consciousness... Yes, that was it—he'd been sailing on the Atlantic—somewhere in the Gulf Stream, porpoises playing about the boat—he'd been trying to take a sun sight... And with him, laughing at him, her grey eyes alight with amusement, had been... Jane Allison.

Bestow your luggage

Tom stood stock-still for more than a minute. Then he took two deep breaths, turned directly away from the pontoons and hurried back to the cliff top, umbrella bobbing. The rain was easing at last, and there were distant signs of light on the sound, to the south. He paced up and down.

Jane was no longer in the frame.

Eileen's radio bearing supported her reported position. West was in completely the wrong position for intercepting her. The drift evidence ruled her out. She still had her rum bottle... He'd argued it all to Sam and Pat, who'd agreed... And now the satellite picture had confirmed it: there was no conceivable way in which West and Jane could have coincided in the time available. At 240 miles behind, she was no more a suspect than Mike, 300 miles ahead. *If it had been OK to sail home with Mike, it was equally OK now to sail with Jane. His position had changed...* Or had it?

He hurried between the raindrops back to his room and stretched out on the enormous bed, hands behind his head.

The police code? Social contact with a suspect? ... He could imagine only too well what the Super would have said; it *ought* to have made him sweat. But it didn't. She *wasn't* a suspect, not now, any more than Mike had been. She was a friend of his friend. He'd be on leave.

Too compromising a situation? She was a doctor, a professional. This felt particularly encouraging: doctors, after all, handled potentially compromising situations every time they examined a patient, as a routine... Her invitation had felt like a genuine kindness, but in no way had it been any sort of invitation to dalliance. And it wouldn't be hard to keep it that way: the exhaustion, continual motion, and seasickness would be effective prophylactics against that particular disease. In fact there'd been something sharp and businesslike about her offer. It was perfectly possible to take it up in a spirit of friendly partnership.

But then he swung himself upright, sat on the side of his bed, head in both hands, and forced himself to think. No one's logic was perfect. What if his deductions were wrong? Yes, he felt reasonably confident, but Jane couldn't properly be ruled out as a suspect, could she, until the case was finally solved? Throughout his career he'd prided himself on his professionalism. If he were *wrong*, and it came out that he'd chosen to sail with her... And it certainly would come out, sooner or later...

His mind in turmoil, he found his way to the cafeteria for lunch.

Jane wasn't there.

After lunch he thought some more. There was another aspect to be considered. How might he behave if a thirty-three year old woman were shrieking orders at him in the teeth of a gale whose wisdom he doubted? From what he'd seen so far, he thought she had the confidence and capacity, and they both had enough common sense, to work this out safely. But, he reminded himself, he scarcely knew her, things might seem different under stress... *Ariel*, in the marina, had looked a sturdy and solid boat; he imagined himself heaving at the winches, coping with the heavy chain and anchor as they slid triumphantly in towards Plymouth…

He wasn't going to rush this decision.

The rain had stopped. He found Della's map and decided to repeat his walk of Sunday afternoon in the opposite direction. As he strode along, he set himself yet again to consider his professional position. But he discovered almost at once, partly with dismay, but partly also with considerable boyish excitement, that a switch seemed to have been reset in his head— professional propriety had intervened too late and fate had taken a grip. His deductions *were* solid, damn it, of course they were! He was *not*, if he could help it, going to miss this tantalising new chance of an Atlantic trip. Whatever the Super might think! Why not? It *was* perfectly possible to carry it off properly and carefully, and ensure that no harm came of it!

Yes.

Taken aback by his own decisiveness, he felt oddly light-headed. But he wouldn't rush to find her; that should be approached circumspectly.

It was still only 4.30 when he returned from the walk. To kill time he called Iain at home again, and went over with him his latest conclusions.

'No point in staying… The suspects are leaving, I can't stop them… I'll fax the Super a report, though he won't be too pleased with my progress… Yes, leave starts today, but my travel plans are still muddled… Tell you when I know… See you, Iain.'

He explored the library shelves, found a popular book on astronomy, took it upstairs to his room, and started absorbing what he could of radio telescopes. By supper time, as the light drained from the sky and the clouds blushed, he was still engrossed.

He came to with a start, tidied himself, and hurried down to eat. Once again Jane wasn't in the cafeteria, and over coffee he considered what he should say to her. Then, as she'd still not appeared, he walked slowly down to the marina. There was a light in *Ariel's* cabin. He walked up to the boat, clenched both fists for a moment, and called down:

'Anybody at home?'

Ariel swayed, and Jane peered up the companionway. 'Oh, it's you,' she said, rather solemnly. 'Hi! Come in.'

Tom clambered into the cockpit and backwards down the steps into the cabin.

'Why don't you sit there,' she said, pointing to the seat behind the chart table, and examined his face. 'You're going to be *serious* about something!'

'Not very serious,' he said, smiling. 'It's just, the situation's changed. I can take up your proposal.'

She looked at him.

'Your kind offer of a passage home... Instead of with Mike... If you'll still have me, that is.' He didn't try to explain, just sat upright, hands on knees.

For half a second her face was blank. She looked thoughtful, took one very long deep breath, and smiled at him. 'I haven't found anyone else,' she said.

'Is it OK?' asked Tom, a little worried.

'Yes—of course!' She grinned.

She's *pleased* thought Tom.

'Let's drink to it,' she said. 'What've I got?' She peered first into her fridge, then a drinks locker. 'There's some Budweiser, or, let's see, a liqueur?'

'Is that Cointreau?' asked Tom. 'I rather like that.'

'I'll join you then,' she said, 'But I don't have proper glasses.' She poured carefully judged doses into tumblers and found some water biscuits.

146

'Cheers!' said Tom.

Jane nodded and smiled without replying. Tom sipped and sipped again, then put the glass down and stretched out his legs. She waited, one arm along the top of the bunk cushion, glass in hand.

Tom was frowning.

'Maybe you've got something you want to say?' she asked.

'Well, yes,' said Tom. 'First, it's your boat and you're the boss.'

'When we're sailing. Of course.'

'Second, expenses. I'd like to pay for my keep.'

'All right,' said Jane after a pause.

'The other thing's about my investigation,' said Tom. 'I'll have to work on it when I have time: I've got a report to write. Obviously, I won't be able to discuss it with you. It may make me rather an absent companion.'

'That's all right,' she said. 'I won't be inquisitive. In fact I'd very much rather keep it that way... And you may find me an absent companion too. I'm like most single-handers, fond of my own company.'

'That was all.'

'OK.' A little nod. 'Now, when I have men on *Ariel*, there are a couple of things I like to be clear about. Just to avoid muddles. One: we share the cooking.' She looked up.

'Yes.'

'Two. A bit crude, I'm afraid, but I've learnt from experience: no peeing over the side to save going below, not when I'm about. I'm old fashioned about that.' She gave a little smile: 'OK?'

Tom found he was smiling too. 'Yes,' he said.

That seemed to end the heavyweight exchanges, and she sipped her Cointreau. Tom asked about the boat.

147

Most of the money for it had come when her father died.

'He was a doctor, too,' she said, 'but I told you that before... I suppose we ought to think about when to start. My original plan was Wednesday—but that only leaves two days. Would that give you time?'

'Yes,' said Tom. 'Two days more than I'd originally planned.' He went on to ask about personal kit and equipment, and Jane explained what preparations she still had to make.

'And the berths,' said Jane. 'Will you be OK in the fore-cabin? I can clear the lockers.'

And so it was settled. Before Tom left, she made mugs of hot chocolate as a night-cap, deftly and seriously. Tom thanked her again for her invitation, clambered a little awkwardly out of the cockpit and carefully picked his way off the pontoon in the dark.

*

When he got back to his room, he took a deep breath, and laid his plans. Tomorrow he must cancel his air ticket and sort out the money. Then wind up his investigation. He would rather have solved the whole thing himself, and shown Sam and Pat what the Devon and Cornwall was capable of. But it now seemed that either Dan or Dale must have shot West, and they were US citizens. He was in no position to pursue them—time to hand over to Pat or the FBI anyway. He just needed to write his report. He shrugged. Never mind. He wasn't going to let professional disappointment spoil his voyage home.

He planned the rest of his time. His preliminary report would take two or three hours. Then he needed to see both Sam and Pat for a last conference. A final phone call to Iain. That wouldn't leave much of Tuesday for personal preparations. He'd check over with Jane tomorrow that the equipment list was complete. Then he must get into Newport and buy some gifts and souvenirs, and perhaps one or two surprise items of food, to show willing on the cooking front. Drink, too, and spare batteries for his camera. It would take an hour or two to get his gear stowed in *Ariel*. And he must call Miranda to explain what he was up to, and leave a message for Jack. He really ought to ring Mike as well. It was going to be a busy last day.

His plan settled, he lay on the bed pondering his exchanges with Jane. Knows how she wants things, he thought. Quite right, too. And quite pleased to have me, I think.

He got himself organised for sleep.

'It'll do!' he found himself saying aloud, with considerable satisfaction. 'It'll take us a little while to work things out, but it'll do. Well Miranda, I don't know what you'll think of what your old dad's getting up to, but it's going to happen anyway, whatever *you* think about it.'

And in due course, sleep came easily to him.

Without grudge or grumblings

Tom was steering. It was 11 o'clock on 26th July. Fifteen miles south of Newport, *Ariel* was close-hauled, setting genoa and full main, driving south-east against a gentle southerly and nodding to herself as she rode easily over the swells rolling down from Martha's Vineyard. The city skyline was already out of sight. To the west, he could still make out Point Judith through the haze, astern and unimportant. What mattered next was the corner of the Vineyard, low, but increasingly hard against the eastern sky, a safe ten degrees under the port bow.

Jane, seated on the cabin top, was watching him. Her gaze wasn't critical or intrusive. She seemed calmed by contact with boat and sea. Although he knew so little of her, Tom felt peaceful too. If she'd been in a more communicative mood, he'd have given her a very cheerful grin.

He'd been a little anxious when asked to take *Ariel* out of the marina; he hadn't conned so large a boat before, and wasn't used to wheel steering. But it proved easy enough, like a quiet day trip from Plymouth. She'd controlled the engine, and gone quietly around hoisting the sails, working the winches as they beat out of the sound, tossing her brown curls, he noticed, in the fresh sea air. She had the single-hander's habit of always clipping on her safety harness, even in this gentle breeze. She managed it without fuss: apart from the noise of the sliding shackle on the span wire, he scarcely noticed it as she moved around in her orange waterproofs. The mooring lines and fenders were stowed, the engine shut down. The courtesy ensign had come fluttering down to her raised brown hand, sail covers had disappeared, hatches and ventilators had all been checked. To count off the buoys in the channel, she'd brought up her big binoculars. Now, they hung black and weighty from her neck.

At last she shook herself, nodded, and said: 'Guess we'd better sort out watches.'

'Right.'

'In busy waters, one of us needs to stay awake. But with self-steering the crew on watch doesn't have to be on deck all the time. How about six-hour watches, one of us eight-till-two, the other two-till-eight?'

'I should think so.' He'd no experience of long passages.

'For the night watches, the off-duty crew sleeps, duty crew makes a night-cap or gets breakfast. During the day, off-duty gets the meal: lunch or early supper. OK?'

'Sounds good.'

'Which d'you want, eight-till-two, or two-till-eight?'

Tom laughed. 'Hold on,' he said, 'Let me get it straight... Suppose I do eight-till-two? Which means I get the night-caps? And the suppers, during your daytime two-till-eight?'

'That's it,' said Jane. 'That leaves me with breakfast and lunch... Good! And you're on watch now, so maybe I'll dig out some elevenses.' She gave him a quick grin and wriggled down the companion.

Five minutes later she stuck her head up again, pushed two steaming mugs of cocoa at him with a few pieces of English fudge, and climbed back into the cockpit. He hadn't been asked what he wanted, but savoured the soft cubes contentedly. She sipped her cocoa and watched the sea.

When they'd finished, she said, 'In a bit, we'll get James going... My coachman,' she added, responding to Tom's puzzled look, and pointed to the self-steering gear behind the stern. 'Home, James! I tell him... Used one of these before?'

'No,' said Tom.

'Helps to get the sails balanced first. Close-hauled like this, I usually reduce the mainsail a bit. Makes life easier if the wind strengthens... Slab reefing. Know the routine?'

'I think so.'

Responding to her nod as in a half-familiar dream, Tom eased the mainsheet to reduce the wind pressure on the sail. In a few brisk movements, she had the boom supported and the mainsail lowered a few feet; loosened, it slatted to and fro above their heads in the light wind. *Ariel* stumbled and slowed as she lost drive.

Tom watched as she grabbed the churning sail by the mast, and forced the reef cringle down onto its hook. Working together, they tightened halyard and clew line to re-stretch the upper part of the sail. Then Jane, kneeling on the cabin top, worked backwards along the boom, bullying the lowest slab of canvas into a neat sausage, strapping it down as she went, panting a little. When she'd finished Tom eased the topping lift, bowsed down the sheet, and steered a little away from the wind: the mainsail quivered, quietened and began to draw, the tackle creaked, and *Ariel* leaned to the breeze as she recovered speed. From the drag on the wheel, Tom could feel that the sails were now pulling her up to windward only very gently.

'On second thoughts, let's leave James till later,' said Jane, 'I ought to do a bit of navigating.' But she didn't start anything immediately and sat watching the sea. After a while she said: 'I suppose it was the race committee got you into this investigation?'

'No,' said Tom, wondering how much he should say. 'It was the Navy... A frigate found *Cas A* adrift at sea.'

She took a while to absorb this information. 'And something made them suspicious?'

'Yes.'

'They brought her into Plymouth?'

'Yes.'

'Which was how you got assigned to the case?'

Tom nodded.

She thought for a while. 'I got to know the place a bit before the race. Where do you live? In the city centre?'

'No. Crownhill.'

'Where's that?'

'Three miles north—the A38 runs through it... We moved there nine years ago.'

She hesitated, then smiled. 'And who is *we*?'

He felt himself frown and looked down. After a while he raised his head again. 'Jack was ten and Miranda twelve.'

She looked at him, then clasped her hands together beneath her chin, head a little on one side. After a while she said, 'They'll be at college by now?'

'Yes,' said Tom. He told her what Jack and Miranda did.

She nodded. 'I'd better get on,' she said. She found a hand-bearing compass, took and jotted down a few bearings. 'OK on deck for a bit?'

'Yes.'

She handed him the binoculars and disappeared to plot her results on the chart. Tom focussed the glasses and took a good look round to check on nearby shipping. There were just two yachts, posing no problems, one ahead and one behind, following much the same course as *Ariel* at about the same speed. The wind had freed a little, so he was able to ease the sheets and keep steady on the course Jane had set to pass a little south of the tip of Martha's Vineyard.

*

After a couple more miles Jane reappeared. 'Now for James,' she said, climbing onto the stern deck. 'His job is to keep *Ariel* pointing at a set angle to the wind.'

Tom was keen to take it all in. He'd been aware of the big red self-steering vane since first seeing *Ariel*— you couldn't miss it, mounted high up just behind the stern, like a huge weathercock swinging freely on a vertical hinge. Looking at it again now, he could see, mounted on the same hinge, a blade like a long thin rudder, which stuck down several feet into the water. He peered at it, understanding nothing.

'The push of the water on that blade does the steering,' said Jane. 'Watch.' Leaning over the back of the boat, she angled the blade, using both hands. The water flowing past pushed it sideways, and the whole vane-blade system suddenly rocked. 'Look under the stern deck.' She climbed forward, and pointed into the locker behind Tom's feet.

Still very puzzled, he stuck his head down, and saw in the gloom a stout fore-and-aft shaft, which stuck through the stern of the boat. Fixed to this shaft was a stainless steel quadrant. 'The blade makes the quadrant rock on that shaft?'

Jane nodded. 'You've got it.' The quadrant was touching a wire rope, to which it could be clamped.

She was pointing. 'That's the steering cable...' She crouched down and clamped the cable to the quadrant. 'Now, can you unfix the cable from the wheel, please?' She showed Tom how to do this, and leant again over the stern. 'Now watch—I can steer just by turning the blade.'

Intrigued, Tom released the now useless spokes of the wheel. As Jane angled the blade, the flow of water pushed it sideways, the blade turned the shaft and quadrant, the quadrant pulled the steering cable, and the cable turned the rudder. She angled the blade the other way, and the rudder movement was reversed.

'Right,' said Tom.

She was watching his face, to be sure he was following. 'OK? Now, the final step is to make the wind control the blade.'

She leant again over the back. Tom saw that the wind vane and the blade could be clamped together, so that they swung on the hinge as a unit. Jane tightened the clamp, and straightened up. 'That's it,' she said. 'All done!'

Tom watched. Gradually *Ariel* drifted a little off course. Immediately, the wind started to blow on one side of the wind-vane. This angled the blade on the vertical hinge—which turned the rudder and brought *Ariel* smartly back on course. 'Magic!' he said.

'Think you've got it?'

'I think so... How reliable is it?' He was determined to grasp the finer points.

'Good on most points of sailing,' said Jane. 'But James doesn't like a quartering wind and sea.'

'Why not?'

'You know what happens when you're on a broad

reach, if a swell swings you round to windward?'

'Yeah—the mainsail yanks like hell, and you broach!'

'It can take a terrific heave to get back on course, can't it? Well, James can't produce that heave.'

'Right,' said Tom. '… And what happens if the wind strengthens?'

'That's OK, as long as the boat keeps moving. The settings don't change.'

'And your course is linked to the wind direction? If the wind swings round while you're asleep, your course changes?'

'Yes, of course. But you can anticipate. And if a cold front comes through, you're not going to sleep through the squalls, anyway.'

Tom nodded. It was a lot to take in.

*

Jane disappeared to get lunch, and Tom, relieved by James of steering duty, settled into his cockpit seat in the sun and let his mind run on their passage plan. To Martha's Vinyard and round the corner to Nantucket, shallow water. From Nantucket Light, a deeper two hundred and fifty miles across the Gulf of Maine to Cape Sable in Nova Scotia; then along the coast and across Cabot Strait and the shallows of the Grand Banks, another five hundred miles to the corner of Newfoundland, Cape Race; and Cape Race would be springboard for their leap over deep ocean, eighteen hundred miles into the English Channel.

At one o'clock, the lunch appeared: tinned soup, a lot of rye biscuits, coleslaw from plastic pots, pastrami from a pack, fresh peaches, and very thick Turkish coffee cooked in a little copper pot, with sugar—a standard of catering Tom could live with, though he wouldn't have chosen the Turkish coffee himself. They ate in the cockpit, watching James make his small adjustments to *Ariel*'s course. The wake wasn't as straight as Tom would have expected from a good human helmsman, but averaged over five minutes there was no doubt it was reasonably consistent. They were now half way to the corner of Martha's Vineyard, the mouth of Buzzard's Bay wide open to their left.

He was finding the discipline of sailing very satisfying and as they downed the last of their coffee he said: 'Mostly in life, I'm rather cautious… But this transatlantic crossing really got to me—I wanted the adventure like a naïve schoolboy.'

'I know you did.' She was smiling again.

'But adventure involves risk. How do you feel about *danger*, Jane? In sailing, I mean.'

She laughed.

'Your single-handing's much dodgier than this, isn't it? Why do you do it?'

Her look became more cautious. 'I'd several reasons for going in for it,' she said at last. 'Mostly, maybe, I liked relying on myself. It needs decisiveness, and I like that too…'

'But the dangers?'

She laughed again. 'If you mean, do I have an adventurous streak, yes, I do. But I don't take unnecessary risks.'

'The diagnosis has to be properly assessed?'

'Exactly.'

*

Once off-watch below, Tom stretched out on his bunk, knowing that the day had already burnt up a

157

good deal of nervous energy. Typical professional, he thought, girls' boarding school probably... But ready to open up a bit. He shut his eyes and dozed for a while.

He woke an hour later, the skin over his temples taut. *Ariel* was rolling, and although his head was at rest in the bunk, it felt as if clamped to a helter-skelter, whose swerves across the cabin were synchronised with a periodic tightening over his stomach. Oh well, he thought. He wasn't usually physically sick; in fact, he coped better than most of his sailing friends.

He slowly dug out his case notes, and struggled again with the satellite photos and that northerly group of three boats. But his stomach was in no state for detailed analysis, and he flopped down on his bunk, jarring his tender head.

Jane came into the main cabin to make a chart plot, and peered forward at him.

'Oh!' she said. She laughed. 'You'll do better on deck.'

Tom clambered past her into the fresh air, gulped. Sight of the horizon quietened his stomach almost at once.

She stuck her head up to see how he was doing. 'Could you cope with some tea?' she asked. 'If I make it weak?' The motion obviously had no effect on her.

The tea, laced with plenty of sugar, and sipped very slowly, more or less settled the matter. Could have been worse, thought Tom. 'Try a dry biscuit,' she said, and went to find one. She returned, and settled near him on the cockpit seat.

'Funny about your having kids,' she said.

'*Funny?*'

'It hadn't crossed my mind you were a family man... Silly—I should've asked.'

For a while Tom didn't reply, and she hesitated. 'My wife died nine years ago,' he said at last.

She gave a tiny nod, then waited, mouth half open, as though ready to apologise for having persisted.

Tom frowned.

'That was before you moved to Crownhill?' She seemed anxious to get it straight in her mind.

He nodded.

'What was her name?'

'Beth,' said Tom and regretted at once having given it. He lowered his gaze.

When he looked up he realised her eyes were closed. He waited, puzzled.

Suddenly she said: 'Tom! '

'What?'

'What I said to you earlier about danger wasn't honest… It's not true that I never take foolish risks.'

He looked at her.

'I *do…*'

'You do?'

'Well, I just did, didn't I?'

'Pressing me about my family?'

'Yes… And sometimes over really big things…'

'Not with boats?'

She gave a little laugh. 'No… With people.'

'People?'

'Men, people I know… Or so someone once told me.'

'And they were right?'

'Yes, they were… This person said, sometimes you think you can walk on fucking water…'

'You haven't seemed at all like that to me.'

'No,' she said, and frowned. 'Just as well!' She smiled at him, then looked down towards the galley. 'Better tidy up. Before I come on watch.'

*

To keep his nausea at bay, Tom brought his note-books into the cockpit where he could see the horizon, while Jane went below to work at the chart. He found himself wondering again whether Dan or Dale might be less innocent than they seemed. Dale had been the more prickly, but his story about the kittens had sounded like a man encountering West's sadistic streak for first time, not an accomplice. Dan, though apparently equally nice, had been more cool and reticent. His VHF conversations with Dale had sounded relaxed. But since they were out of sight of each other and the conversations had been quite short, that really meant nothing.

He climbed below and settled at the cabin table to write up his conclusions, frowning; Jane glanced over thoughtfully, and after a few minutes went up on deck. Nausea crept over Tom again. He checked his arguments, and slowly got them down on paper. He wasn't very satisfied. Never mind, repeated thinking around the problem usually got you there, in the end.

Seven o'clock took him by surprise. He tidied away his files and stretched cautiously. Swallowing with determination as he bent down, he dug out from the back of the refrigerator the escalopes of veal and blueberry fool he'd hidden in preparation for his first meal as ship's cook.

Noontide sun

It was ten o'clock of a crisp morning, the wind still gentle and southerly, and *Ariel* was heading north-east on a very broad reach with no land in sight. Against the palest of backdrops, Tom could see a few yachts, and ten miles to the luminous south-east was a line of coasters in tiny silhouette, on passage to Nova Scotia. Beyond them he could catch occasional dim glimpses of larger vessels bound for the English Channel. With the swell surging slow and oily, *Ariel* was rolling heavily. But James could cope—and so, to his pleasure and relief, could Tom.

When he'd come on deck the night before, Martha's Vineyard had been already behind them, and the low line of Nantucket Island lay stretched to their left, the sun sinking behind it. Soon after ten, as the western dayglow died, they'd passed Nantucket Light, and set out towards the star-spattered eastern horizon. Jane had gone down to sleep, and as Tom's watch continued, the faint western brightness dimmed, while the flashes of the lighthouse seemed at first to strengthen as his eyes adjusted to the gathering darkness, and then to weaken as the miles slipped quietly away. The water gliding beneath *Ariel's* keel gave an occasional drawn-out chuckle, and gentle wind thrummed in the rigging. Not long before Jane's alarm clock shattered the peace, the sails had become visible again as the moon rose ahead. By the time she had appeared sweater-muffled in the cockpit, it was standing three fingers above a fragmented mall of light glittering on the sea. Tom had dropped into his bunk more exhausted than he knew. He had fallen directly into a dreamless sleep, unbroken till Jane shook his shoulder to offer him coffee and a hot bacon sandwich, with sunlight streaming through the portholes.

Now, with Jane asleep again and James in control, Tom was free to let his mind wander. Had his supper been too ambitious? She'd been appreciative—but more enthusiastic, he'd thought at the time, than seemed quite natural, and the bottle of Bailey's bought to round off the meal had stayed hidden in his bunk.

With its beady eye on Tom, a solitary tern was swaying on the slipstream from the mainsail, slender wings barely fluttering. He watched as it banked and skated away down wind.

Doubt about his supper wasn't the only thing leaving Tom uneasy. He was enjoying the sailing, but his case was in the doldrums. Pick over his scenario for flaws? Well, there were plenty:

One: neither Dan nor Dale made a convincing drug smuggler; nor even Dr Todd.

Two: if West had wanted to eliminate a drugs rival or an innocent witness, he'd surely have wanted to do it quickly. But it had taken years of planning to get them both into the same single-handed race: as Sam had said, an extremely slow-burn plan. Tom pulled distractedly at his hair—he should have grappled more with this aspect of the problem.

Three: the intended victim would have realised his danger, never allowed West on board.

Four: even if the intended victim hadn't realised his danger, how could West have got close enough? He could have planned to fire his rifle from a distance.

But that didn't wash—he'd still need to dispose of the body, and for that he must get onto his victim's boat, leaving himself the insuperable problem of managing two boats at once, both under way. No, West would have to get both boats stopped and in contact before attacking, perhaps by feigning illness, or pretending he needed to borrow equipment. His need to get at close quarters might explain how the intended victim got the better of him.

At this point in Tom's deliberations, Jane came up barefoot to enjoy the sun, wearing under her safety harness a sky-blue T-shirt, and what looked like a pair of men's tennis shorts. She was carrying a small dark blue book and Tom recognised *Persuasion*.

After she had read a page or two, Tom asked: 'Can you sort me out on something?'

She looked up.

'I need to know whether it's possible for two single handers to get alongside each other and make fast in mid-Atlantic.'

She didn't answer at once. 'It can be done,' she said at last, and then inspected her bare toes for some time. But when she finally turned back to Tom, her grey eyes had narrowed and the corners of her mouth were turned down. 'Look!' she said. 'I thought we'd agreed we weren't going to discuss your case.' She stretched one hand firmly over the sheet winch beside her.

He saw the tension in her forearm muscles and looked back at her face.

'I thought we were going to be just a crew,' she added.

Tom said nothing.

'I'd like an answer, actually.'

'You're right,' said Tom quickly. 'I was out of order.' He looked down, and gripped the cockpit seat.

Eventually, he raised his head to face her—but to his surprise, and then relief mixed with irritation, she was head down again in her book. Her determined objection seemed to have dissolved as quickly as it had flared. After a while, she turned a page, but caught Tom's eye as she did so.

She peered speculatively at him, and laughed. 'Forget it,' she said, and read on.

*

After another few pages, she seemed to finish a chapter and looked at her watch. 'Getting near noon. Want to try a sight?'

'Yes,' said Tom. 'Good idea.' He'd practised using a sextant on land, and had learnt that if he could read the elevation of the sun above the horizon to an accuracy of one minute of arc, then he could work out a position line for *Ariel* accurate to one sea mile. But precision of that sort wasn't going to be easy from the rolling deck of a small boat.

Jane first consulted the almanac to work out the time of local noon, when the sun would be highest. There was about half an hour to go and she went below to dig out the equipment.

'I've got one decent sextant,' she said, on reappearing, 'and one of those cheap plastic ones. You take the good one, I'll take the plastic, and see how we compare. If we start by just taking the noon elevation we shan't need to fuss about the exact time.' She handed him a varnished wooden case and a small notebook.

Tom opened the case, and lifted out the beautiful brass instrument, gripping it with his right hand. Standing in the cockpit, he braced his legs and put his right eye to the small telescope, trying to remember from his evening class how it worked. His view passed through the sloping horizon glass in front of the telescope, and through its unsilvered left side he could see the horizon. He screwed the eyepiece in and out to get it in focus.

'Got it?' asked Jane. 'Try setting the scale to zero.'

He was enjoying himself, but her voice still had a slight edge, he thought. In the silvered right side of the horizon glass a cloud was mirrored, and he remembered that this part of his view was reflected twice, once in the horizon glass itself, and once in the index glass, a second mirror mounted on a moveable arm, which swung around a hinge at the top of the sextant. The angle of swing could be read off a brass scale, and Tom now set this scale to zero.

'Two horizons?'

'Yes,' said Tom. Sure enough, he could now see the horizon on both sides of the horizon glass.

'Do they agree?'

'The right horizon's a fraction higher.'

'Twiddle the screw, then.'

Tom found with his left hand the screw used for making small adjustments to the angle of the index arm, and turned it until the two horizons were level.

'OK. Read the scale and write down the index error.'

'Plus three minutes of arc,' said Tom.

'That's the easy bit!' said Jane. 'Now fold down all three shades.'

Tom pulled down three pieces of dark glass to cover the right hand field of view, to protect his eyes. To find the sun's image he had to adjust both his direction of view, by swinging his hips, and, with his left hand, the angle of the index arm. He'd tried this on land, and found it hard. It sometimes took a long 'square search', going patiently round and round in expanding rectangles, before the Sun's neat, round shape popped up in the horizon glass. He found he had to prop his legs very firmly but leave his upper half free to counteract *Ariel's* rolling and swinging around her proper course. While hunting for the Sun's image through the telescope it was helpful to keep his free eye half open, to remind himself where the Sun was.

'Got it!' Once he'd found the image it was easier to hold it in view while he twiddled the screw to bring it roughly into line with the horizon in his split field of view.

'It's still rising,' said Jane. 'See if you can get the elevation.'

Tom now had to adjust the screw so that the lower edge of the Sun on the right was exactly kissing the horizon on the left. He noticed how the double mirror arrangement had the effect of locking together the images of the Sun and the horizon: if he or *Ariel* jiggled about, the two images jiggled as one in the telescope, and it was quite easy to follow them with his eye, to see whether the Sun was touching the horizon or not. But the problem was that, as *Ariel* rose and fell on the swell and waves a few hundred yards away raised their crests, the horizon itself seemed to change: it was surprisingly hard to be sure exactly where it was.

He went on practising for a while. But the angles he read off to Jane were nothing like consistent enough— they were varying over about thirty minutes of arc.

'Don't worry,' she said. 'That's pretty good for a first try.'

Tom took a short rest.

'We're getting near,' said Jane, who was watching the sun through the plastic sextant.

Tom tried again and lost the sun's image, but recaptured it after a struggle. The image was still creeping up compared to the horizon. He gently twisted the screw to bring it down again. The sun crept up very slowly. He brought it very gently down again. The sun stood still. Then, after what seemed a long time, he could tell that it had begun to sink. He was on the point of adjusting the screw again when he remembered that he mustn't do that: he had to measure the *greatest* height, the noon height. He rubbed his knee to get the circulation going again. He carefully wrote down the reading on the index scale, and checked it. Then he remembered he had to subtract the index error.

'68° 6′,' he announced.

'And I got 67° 50′,' said Jane. 'You work out the latitudes.'

Tom put the sextant safely away in its box, and then made the standard corrections for refraction of the atmosphere and semi-diameter of the Sun in his notebook.

'What about height of eye above the sea?' he asked, looking down at the water. 'Would two metres be about right?'

'Yes,' said Jane, 'subtract 2.5 minutes.'

Having worked out the corrected altitude for the centre of the Sun, Tom looked up in the almanac the Sun's declination (its angle north of the equator) for the time of observation. Then 90° minus corrected altitude plus north declination gave north latitude: easy! He plotted the two latitudes on the chart, and was irritated to find that Jane's was much nearer than his to *Ariel*'s estimated position.

'That's a lot better than my first ever try,' said Jane. 'My altitude was smaller than yours, wasn't it? Did you remember to check that the sextant was vertical, by swinging it to get the Sun as low on the horizon as possible? It's easy to be a few minutes too big if you don't.'

Tom kicked himself mentally: they'd taught him that.

'Right! Now we must wait till about six,' said Jane, 'to get a position line that'll tell us how far east we are. For that we need to record the exact time. I'll read the watch for you.'

*

Jane got the lunch, while Tom enjoyed the warmth of the sun. After the drinking chocolate, Tom produced his Bailey's.

'Oh, good!' said Jane. 'I like that stuff even better than Cointreau.' She seemed to have forgotten about her earlier protest. But Tom had not forgotten, and he'd remembered what she'd been reading. At home, Miranda had been pushing him to try Jane Austen, and he too had recently read *Persuasion,* and admired its sensitive but self-controlled heroine. Perhaps Anne Elliot, who kept her strong feelings to herself and knew the Navy List so well, had something in common with Jane Allison.

Off watch, he spent most of the afternoon reminding himself how the astronavigation tables were laid out in Jane's copy of Macmillan's Almanac. It was easy to see what her preferred navigational methods were: the Moon and star columns were unblemished, but the altitude correction table for the Sun and the Sun's positions for most of the summer months were thumbed grey, and the page giving the Sun's positions in June had come loose and been neatly stuck back with invisible sellotape. With this revision behind him, he made a considerable success of getting the evening position line, in spite of being forced to use the top edge of the Sun's image, because the lower edge was hidden by a thin streak of high cloud.

That high cloud heralded a change in the weather. By 2 a.m. the wind had veered south-west and risen to Force 5, and Tom, not trusting James to avoid a gybe, was doing the steering himself. When they changed watch, the glass was falling. After listening to the coastguard weather report, they set a smaller jib, took in two reefs, gybed deliberately in anticipation of a westerly, and rigged a preventer on the boom. Once below, Tom tied up the canvas lee-cloth at the side of his bunk, to hold himself safely in if *Ariel* started jumping around. As he dropped off to sleep, the rushing of the water on the other side of the planking was insistent.

The westerly came, and they rushed north-east all night and half the next day in very murky weather. The cold front came through about mid-day, squalling up to Force 7, and leaving them with a raw north-westerly. *Ariel* rushed onwards, and Tom distinguished himself by producing a basic but tasty stew in very bumpy conditions without getting near to throwing up. In the evening they saw the light on Cape Sable and started their tourist-hop along the Nova Scotia coast in discouraging circumstances. Next day they managed to see a good deal of the coast, but it remained cold, with the wind in the north, the land giving them shelter. The wind didn't ease till late the following day, when they'd left Cape Breton Island behind and were setting out across Cabot Strait to Cape Race on the corner of Newfoundland. Then, perversely, it backed round to south-west and dropped away to almost nothing, leaving *Ariel* rolling on the big swell still sweeping down the strait from the north.

Tom had by now settled pretty well into the routine, and his sea-sickness had gone. He was physically tired most of the time, busy being a sailor, and had spent no more time on his case at all. But then, late on 31st July, while he was waiting for the weather forecast, he picked up a news bulletin:

> *The final competitor in the OSTAR Millenium singlehanded race arrived St John's Newfoundland late yesterday. Frenchwoman Laurel Delon's* Bon Appetit *dismasted l0th July. With her radio broken and unable to call for help, Laurel was spotted by a Russian factory ship 18th July and towed in. Collapsed on coming ashore, she is now in hospital.*

Tom's flickering interest in his case burst back into flame. He told Jane.

'*Collapsed*?' she said. 'Did they say what happened?'

'Dismasted.' Tom gave her the details.

'That's all they said?'

'Yes.'

'Say it again.'

Tom obliged.

'Eight days, trying to cope. Then that ship… She's going to need help… We'd better call in there, Tom, it's not far.' She looked concernedly at him. 'Might be stuck for a while. But I owe her, she's been a real friend to me.'

'Fair enough.' said Tom. 'It's OK by me.'

Melted into thin air

It took them two days to get into St John's. Rounding Cape Race they met the cold Labrador current, bringing fog and a dying wind. Jane became silent, and then, on the second day, anxious about strategy: she kept studying the fickle wind-shifts and tidal streams, coaxing *Ariel* on her way. When they eventually motored in through the narrows, the Douglas firs on the steep south shore stood motionless, each above its unruffled reflection. Ahead and to their right, the city's buildings clung to the opposite slope, perched above cranes and unhurried quays.

It was mid-morning. Their quarantine flag brought a sleek customs launch ranging alongside, its commander intent on confiscating US handguns. But he knew about Laurel and the Russians. Jane fetched the local chart. 'Where's her boat now?' she asked, urgent.

'Navy Dock.' He showed her.

'Can we moor there?'

'No. You want the yacht anchorage.'

'Isn't there a marina?'

'Conception Bay.' He pointed again.

'But that's miles!'

'Afraid so.'

So they had to leave *Ariel* on a buoy near the narrows. Tom pumped up the dinghy and they puttered noisily towards the town.

They found *Bon Appetit* moored forlornly, both

aluminium masts folded a few feet above deck, a tangle of twisted rigging still to be cleared. Jane's mouth tightened. A port official had the keys, but wouldn't let them on board. Laurel was still in St Clare's Mercy, he said.

It was a brisk climb, Jane pushing on impatiently. Tom lagged a little, noticing the stores. St John's felt more provincial than Newport—and more like home, perhaps because the ubiquitous stars and stripes had disappeared.

From the door of the ward, Jane picked out Laurel's bed and hurried forward, almost running, then knelt beside her. Following cautiously, Tom looked down at a wide and weatherbeaten face, eyes closed, unmoving on a cream institutional pillow. The nurse found a junior doctor, who told them Laurel was heavily sedated; he suggested returning at seven.

They found a hamburger bar for a late lunch, and laid plans. 'That hospital seems OK,' Jane said. 'We've got to get her some funds, and contact her family. Maybe we can organise a boat yard.'

They found a phone booth and fixed *Ariel* a temporary berth with the Royal Newfoundland Yacht Club on Conception Bay, then Jane went off to restock fresh food. It didn't seem to have occurred to her, Tom noted, that he might be interested in Laurel as a suspect.

While she was gone he took the opportunity of calling Newport and Plymouth. Sam Greenbaum's checks on Dan and Dale had thrown up nothing. Iain Gemmill confirmed that the money for *Cas A* had come from Columbia. The forensic chemists were still puzzled by the stain on West's clothing. It wasn't algae; there was uncertain talk about pigments. Tom then considered his own objectives. He couldn't question Laurel in her present state, but if he and Jane could get on board *Bon Appetit* Laurel's log and chart would tell him most of what he needed to know.

When Jane returned, they found their way up the hill to the south of the harbour and took a long but rather silent walk through firs in bark-scented mist. Afterwards, they found a waterside restaurant got up to resemble the Prospect of Whitby: the lobsters were good, the beer watery.

At seven, they were back at the hospital, Jane in command of herself, but, Tom thought, still in a state of suppressed anxiety. Laurel was awake. Jane went straight up to the bed, kissed her, and held her hand. After a moment's dazed uncertainty, Laurel's mouth creased into a slow grin, and she sank back into her pillows, tears welling in her large brown eyes. The nurse asked her whether she could cope with visitors. The English of her reply was halting and thick.

It took time before she was ready to say much; but as Jane smiled, murmured and began to rattle away in French, Laurel blinked her tears away, muttered a little, and then, gradually, and with pauses to gather strength, poured out her story. Tom struggled to follow. Perched on a huge wave, *Bon Appetit* had swung right away from the wind in a vicious squall, and broached. A shroud and the triatic stay had parted, both masts had collapsed, and for many hours her boat had been out of control, dragged sideways in the howling gale by wreckage in the water that Laurel wasn't able to clear. With her radio dead, there'd been eight days of mind-numbing continuous labour with no help in sight, before the *Novy Mir* had appeared through a rainsquall and responded to her red flares.

As she described this ordeal her voice strengthened. Tom was impressed. Listening, he realised that Laurel wasn't the Parisian sophisticate he'd somehow expected, but a Breton farmer's daughter. She and Jane had common friends, some in Laurel's village, others who sailed on the south Brittany coast. The chatter swung between the practical matter of Laurel's disaster and idle gossip. There were pauses, but easy chatter was what it was. As time went on, there were gestures and animation from Jane, and gentle smiles from Laurel. Tom was struck, not for the first time, by the difference between women talking to women and women talking to men. He thought he'd been getting on quite well with Jane—but not like this. He'd been aware of her femaleness, yet her manner to him, he felt, had been camaraderie, an entente cordiale between states whose boundaries were sharply drawn. Well—he didn't know her very well yet.

Jane asked whether they could look over *Bon Appetit* to see what needed to be done. Laurel scrawled a note of permission for the port official, then sank back and screwed her wrinkled eyes tight shut. Jane, smiled, kissed Laurel's damp forehead and hustled Tom out of the ward.

*

They spent the next morning sailing *Ariel* round to Conception Bay, and confirmed that the marina there had facilities to re-rig *Bon Appetit*. Jane, now obviously much happier, grabbed the chance to stock up on cable clamps and shackles from the chandlery.

After lunch they took a taxi downtown, Tom with case papers tucked inconspicuously into the back of his rucksack. They were now able to get aboard *Bon Appetit*. Below decks she was a little tidier, but very wet: water was showing above the cabin floor, whether from leaks or waves slopping aboard during the tow they couldn't tell, and their first job was to pump her dry. However, the batteries were flat—which meant they couldn't start the diesel engine, and had no artificial light. They couldn't start the diesel by hand either, but did manage to light the paraffin heater, and a reek of wet bedding and hot plastic threatened them as condensation streamed off the cabin windows.

Jane sorted through the ship's papers and Laurel's bank records, and threw out rotting food. Then she set off for the hospital again.

Tom decided that, permission or not, now was his chance. He couldn't find Laurel's J's Jamaica, in her drinks cabinet or anywhere. Her log, observation book and nautical almanac were safe in the chart drawer, and merely damp, but her North Atlantic chart had been floating on the floor. He hung it on a string above the heater grill, and settled down to study the log and observations.

*

Laurel's regular navigation had been by GPS, but she seemed to have taken sun sights every few days as a check. He first transcribed her sextant readings for the important few days onto dry paper and recalculated them using her own almanac. No problems there, the positions agreed with those recorded in her log. So he began to plot them onto his own sketch chart.

As he did so he felt his eyebrows crawl up and gave a whistle of surprise: it was quickly apparent that during the whole of the important period, from 21st to 24th June, Laurel had been extremely close to Charles West, or so it seemed. On the 21st she had been some twenty-five miles northeast of *Cas A*. She'd slowly closed with and overhauled her: on the 22nd she'd passed about ten miles to the north and on the all important 24th she was some five miles ahead to the west.

He double-checked, but there was no doubt. One would have thought that the two skippers would have been bound to see each other. She was, however, too far away to be seen by Dan or Dale.

Did that make Laurel the chief suspect? Tom extracted from his rucksack the satellite photos taken at 1427 GMT on 25th June. He knew what he'd find, but had to check. The sea near *Cas A* wasn't obscured by cloud, and, search as he would, he could find no sign of *Bon Appetit* on it, either ahead or astern. Moreover, neither West nor Laurel had recorded sighting the other.

According to Laurel her radio had been out of action, so neither she nor West would have known the other's position. Didn't that rule her out as a suspect? It did in the scenario in which West first deliberately approached his intended victim, for he couldn't have known where to find her. The other way round was less obvious. If Laurel had only pretended that her radio was damaged, she could have known where West was. But wouldn't she in that case have used the radio to save herself during the storm? Tom made a mental note to check it out. His schoolboy French could cope with Laurel's log. She had indeed recorded the radio's failure on 17th June, and after that her records of competitors' positions had ceased.

So why wasn't *Bon Appetit* visible on the satellite pictures? She was as large as *Cas A* and should be equally easy to see. At that point a rather obvious thought occurred to Tom. Both boats were large ketches. Perhaps the vessel on the satellite image was *Bon Appetit* and not *Cas A* at all? He returned to the photos: even on the most enlarged print there just wasn't enough detail to be sure. His list of boat lengths was back on *Ariel* and he had no measuring tape, but he clambered up onto the quay and paced out *Bon Appetit*'s length. Sure enough, she was forty-five feet, near enough the same as *Cas A*.

What did that imply? If the ketch on the photo was *Cas A* then, as he'd worked out earlier, the possible suspects were Dan and Dale, plus possibly Dr Todd and Eileen Meath, to whom must now be added Laurel—for on this scenario Laurel must have falsified her position, and be hidden under the cloud bank too.

But if, as seemed more likely, the ketch visible on the photo was *Bon Appetit*, then by the 24th West had deliberately moved away from the northern group, all of whom would be ruled out as suspects. Where could he have been, in that case?

Well, this was Scenario 4 again, and, since West had turned south, he must have been gunning either for Dr Todd or for Eileen Meath. He couldn't have been aiming for Jane because, as before, intercepting her would have left him too far to the east.

Was there another way of reading it? Suppose it was Laurel who'd been West's intended victim. He would have lost track of her when her radio broke down, but on, say, the 22nd, hey presto, they meet by chance at sea! He grabs his chance and attacks her; she gets the better of him, and sails on, sending *Cas A* south into the cloud bank. The strain of it all explains Laurel's collapse when she arrives at St John's. But it didn't *feel* right: in the hospital Laurel had poured out her emotions about the storm with such an obvious sense of release—she didn't sound like a woman under the continuing stress of a second trauma. And the idea didn't work for another reason: West had continued transmitting until the 24th.

Could Laurel have killed West earlier, and faked his last few transmissions? Scarcely possible, with her strong accent and woman's voice.

Tom suddenly felt a little guilty. He sighed, returned the log book to its drawer, packed his rucksack, and settled down once again to spring-cleaning.

*

About five o'clock, Jane returned very cheerful, and looked around the cabin. 'That's a bit tidier!'

'Could she talk?'

'She could. The doctor *said* we tired her too much last night, but I wasn't going to be browbeaten. I talked through her money. She's skint... I'm going to lend her some.'

'Is that a problem?'

'Oh no.'

'She's quite a toughie!'

Jane laughed. 'Breton sailor. And a lovely person, Tom. Mad keen on sailing, always pretty much on her beam ends financially.'

'How did she buy that big boat?' asked Tom.

'I don't know. Her dad got some farm subsidy money and gave all his children some capital, but I think most of hers had to go on training, and buying into her shop.'

'What shop's that?'

'She's a pharmacist. After that she won a bit on the French lottery, too, which got her enough to set up on her own. It was later she bought the boat, but I just don't know how that was managed. Must have been pretty difficult.'

'You met her in Brittany?'

178

'At Glénans.'

'Doing what?'

'Ocean navigation course.' She grinned at him. 'I thought she was *bound* to ask about you, but she never did... She's happy for me to negotiate with the boatyard... Wants me to bring some of her things, and we'll need to get that damaged radio repaired. It's rather specialised—not sure they can do it in St John's.'

'Like me to look into that?' said Tom.

'Good idea, thanks... Where's her log?'

'I dried it out,' said Tom, and extracted it from the chart drawer. Jane jammed it into a holdall with a lot of Laurel's clothes and other documents.

They found a taxi, rolled back to the yacht club contentedly and clambered aboard *Ariel*. Tom tidied his stuff away discreetly and got on with cooking supper.

*

Over a few days they sorted things out. Tom found an electronic engineer who could tell him what he wanted. He thought long and hard about talking to Laurel. But what was needed was either serious questioning or none at all, and the doctor surely wouldn't let him quiz her in her present state. Neither would Jane—and he didn't want to poison the atmosphere for the rest of their voyage home. So he contacted the Royal Canadian Mounted Police, briefed them and put them in touch with Pat. They agreed to question Laurel before she left St John's. It was unsatisfactory—and very tantalising—but couldn't be helped. He also rang Plymouth and spoke to Jack, now home for the vacation.

In the meantime Jane had organised the repairs on *Bon Appetit*. They paid Laurel a final visit—and at last

179

she asked who Tom was. Jane laughed.

'Ah!' she said, '*definitely* on the mend! ... He's a guy who got let down by someone for a spin across the pond. Well behaved on good days—and earning his passage home as cook!' She and Laurel parted very warmly and a little tearfully.

Later that afternoon Tom discovered from the engineer that Laurel's radio was indeed damaged, and in a way difficult to fake: a transistor in the power supply had blown, making it useless for both reception and transmission. Of course, there was no way of knowing when this had happened.

*

They took *Ariel* out to sea on the evening tide, having spent five days in St John's. The wind was gentle and westerly again.

'Be a while before we see land again,' he said.

'Yes,' she said absently.

*

To Tom's disappointment, by supper time Jane was deep in thought again and looking drawn. As he poured the coffee she looked up and said:

'I'm worrying, Tom.'

'About what? Laurel?'

'Yes.'

'Well you shouldn't,' he said. 'You've done a splendid job.'

'It's not that...'

'What, then?'

'I know we agreed not to talk about your investigation, Tom...'

He looked cautiously at her.

'But I can't help wondering... Her radio wasn't working...'

'True.'

'Which must mean you can't have eliminated her as a suspect?'

He frowned. 'Either we have a rule or we don't,' he said.

She screwed up her eyes. 'Look,' she appealed, 'it's just, I can't *bear* having you suspicious of her, Tom... She's a very dear friend.'

'But it's a good rule... I know I was tempted to break it earlier, but I was wrong.'

Jane shook her head with what might have been frustration, or rather more, and looked more upset than ever.

*

When he had breakfast ready next morning he found her sitting knees-to-chin on the damp and misty foredeck. 'Please, Tom,' she said, *'can't* you set my mind at rest?'

'How?'

'By telling me she isn't a suspect?'

'Look,' said Tom. '*Everyone* remains a suspect until they're completely ruled out by the evidence. That's how it works... Come and get your coffee.'

When she was well into the eggs and bacon, she asked, 'Well, with no radio reports from her, you'll have needed to know what was in her log. Obviously.'

Tom said nothing.

'So why didn't you look?'

Still Tom said nothing.

But she'd seen something in his face. '*Oh*!' she cried. 'You *did*! Before I took it away?'

He neither nodded nor shook his head.

'You *appalling* man!' She burst suddenly into tears, but screwed them quickly away from her eyes with both hands. 'And what the hell did it say? Where was she on the 24th?' Tom's mouth twitched, and her eyes narrowed. 'Shit!'

He shrugged.

'It's *bad*, isn't it?'

He shrugged again, more elaborately and looked hard at her. 'Ten miles ahead of *Cas A*,' he admitted eventually.

She compressed her mouth and glared. There was a very long pause. At last she said: 'Then why the *hell* didn't you question her?'

'In no state for it.'

'But she'll have to be questioned?'

'Of course.'

'When she gets home to Brittany?'

'I don't know. We'll see.'

*

Jane said no more until Tom came on deck for his stint at 2 a.m.—they'd swapped watches for a change.

'Tom!' she said. 'You avoided at breakfast saying she'd be questioned *in France*. Did you fix up for her to be questioned *in St John's after we left?*'

He hesitated. 'Yes,' he said at last. 'I did.'

'I should have guessed, I should have stayed to help her.' She went on, but more uncertainly. 'We must go back.'

'*No*,' said Tom. 'You can't change anything. It would've been tough for her if we'd stayed and I'd questioned her. It won't be any worse from the Canadians. They'll get a French speaker. Laurel isn't a tender flower. If she's innocent—and you obviously

182

think she is—she'll get over the questioning.'

'You're trusting the Mounties to get it right, aren't you? Sorry Tom, but *I* don't think you police are always so bloody wonderful. You're *dangerous.*'

'Why the hell d'you say that?'

'Because you're so capable of getting things wrong! Getting innocent people into the most awful trouble. And *I'll* be left not knowing what state she's in—and all the way home *you'll* be wondering what they dug out of her guts. What a delightful trip we're going to have!' Jane's voice has risen in pitch, but again she seemed uncertain. 'When will they do it?'

'From what the doctor said, not for several days, perhaps a week.'

'A *week*…' She was thinking again, perturbed. 'And questioning after that… We can't afford the time.'

Tom said nothing.

'*And* if we stayed I'd be sure to get so terrified I wouldn't know what to do with myself…'

'*Terrified?* Why?'

She looked sharply at him but made no attempt to answer. 'Maybe you're right,' she said at last, made a face and shrugged. 'Press on, try not to think about it?'

Again, Tom said nothing.

'What do you think?'

'That *is* what I think,' said Tom.

She frowned deeply. But she seemed to have retained some sense of fairness, too. 'I'm sorry, Tom,' she said after thinking for a while. 'I shouldn't have said you were an appalling man. Just, you had a mucky, dirty, appalling *job.*' She stumbled down the companion ladder and threw herself onto her bunk.

For Tom, who identified with his work, that was scarcely an improvement. And he wasn't going to be able to put the investigation out of his head, either: it was all in the melting pot again. He tried to concentrate on the simple problem of steering *Ariel* efficiently eastwards in search of the gulf stream, but with little success.

Most auspicious star

There followed several days during which, as if by consent, they concentrated on the sailing. *Ariel* ran steadily eastwards with a settled following wind. Imperceptibly their soundings increased, the sightings of fishing trawlers became rarer, and the swells wound themselves higher. They met the main part of the cold Labrador current, and a pale green slop came shouldering towards them through luminous banks of fog. They crossed the Flemish Cap, where the echo sounder found the bottom again, and then, almost without realising it, they were past the edge of the continental shelf, the ocean bottom dropping away thousands of feet beneath them. Gradually, they found themselves surrounded by North Atlantic swells, majestic and deliberate. Each huge grey mountain range rolled *Ariel* up, up from behind, like a great cupped hand bowling her downhill, forcing her through and round and over the waves of her own size that ran across the immense forward slope; then caught her up, and held her poised aloft, so that for a moment they could view an open terrain of distant equally unstoppable and equally unhurried ridges—and finally hustled past with a great hiss and a wrench at the wheel, leaving *Ariel* struggling up a watery gradient, through white streaks spread backwards from the ridge's retreating crest like thin combed hair. The ocean's insistent rhythm moulded them to itself. *Ariel* had become a lonely and wind-borne sojourner whose voice was the whine of the wind in her steel rigging, as solo and lacking in love as the cries of the sea birds. Her two crew, when they thought and felt at all, did so more and more in isolation.

Yet they hadn't forgotten the feelings with which they'd left St John's. Jane remained tense and Tom suspected that in some obscure respect she felt guilty. One morning, as she was marking up the chart, he saw tears on her cheek.

Catching his enquiring glance she angrily grabbed a tissue.

'Laurel?' he asked.

'Of course! Should've stayed.'

'Why?'

'Stupid police.' Her damp eyes caught his.

Now he felt angry.

Her head dropped. 'Should have turned back...'

'We agreed not to,' said Tom.

'She's not well!'

'They'll wait till she's better.'

He saw her lips tighten.

What he suspected—and it hurt—was that Jane, forced to confront the coarseness of police work, was disgusted by his professional scepticism. Perhaps she could forgive Tom for being suspicious of herself, but wanted him to melt in the glow of Laurel's integrity. Which was a little hard, for Tom *had* warmed to Laurel.

*

In the following days Jane left the Laurel question well alone, and Tom at last got the feeling that she was trying to find friendlier topics. Perhaps she had understood his affection for his profession, because one day at teatime she suddenly asked: 'What took you into policing?'

He wondered how much to say. 'Pure accident,' he said at last.

'How?'

'I did electronic engineering at college. But my final-year project was on computer recognition of finger-prints, so I tried for forensic science. The interview chairman was a retired AC. He seemed to think I'd make a detective, and set about persuading me, then and there.'

'Go on,' said Jane, peering into the biscuit box. She handed him another.

'I was flattered, I suppose. Anyway, I decided to apply for that too, and—surprise, surprise—they offered me the police, but not the forensics.'

'Did you find it very tough?'

'My parents thought I wouldn't cope. But I did.'

'And found it attractive?'

'It's the contact with people. Often foul, sometimes just gritty, always *human*. And the retired AC was right: I am a good detective.'

Jane didn't comment. But after a while she nodded, gently.

'And what,' Tom enquired, after a while, 'made you choose to be a doctor? Following father's footsteps?'

She looked up sharply. '*No!*' she said with a toss of her head. 'That was what *he* expected of me. The very last thing *I* wanted… What fucking era was he living in? … I could *never* have started out accepting the reins from him like that.'

'Wanted to do your own thing?'

'Of *course*! What d'you *think*, Tom? She squeezed her eyes shut for a moment, then forced her lips tightly together and shook her head. 'Big gap in age,' she added. 'Mother was forty-two when she had me. I was an only. She died before I qualified. Massive stroke, hit Father very hard. Then *he* died… I didn't join the Maldon practice till much later.'

'So something made you change your mind?'

'Yes… Yes, it did… I was doing biology at university. And…' her voice trailed off. She looked blindly out at the sea, then, equally unfocussed, at Tom. '*Then* I got seriously ill… Forced me to rethink… The woman treating me got me onto an even keel. I owe everything to her. She made a huge impression.'

*

Two days later they were sitting in the cockpit, and Tom was amusing himself making an eye-splice on a spare length of rope, when Jane began to talk about the characters at the Point Judith Yacht Club. She'd liked Della.

'She noticed everything.'

'Could say that again!'

'Well, yes. But it's not every woman who'll lend her best clothes to a stranger, someone she's known only two hours.'

'You?'

'Mine were damp… Complete smart outfit—black dress, hideous floppy throat bow, even shoes.'

Tom looked up. He remembered Jane as they'd first met in the restaurant, and his irritation at the court heels clicking beside him as they walked. 'Why did you need them?'

'To visit someone… You didn't like them, did you?'

'Didn't I?'

'No! And *she* knew that throat bow wasn't me…'

188

For whom would it have been so important to look smart, but unimportant to look good?

'… *and* she laughed outright seeing her stuff on me, looking all wrong, told me not to worry! Takes something.'

*

Some days later as she was preparing supper, Jane asked: 'What was your Beth like?' She was busy opening tins, and didn't look up.

He hesitated. 'I can't describe her,' he said. He splayed his elbows behind him on the bunk cushion.

'Was she clever?'

'She wasn't at all intellectual…' Tom's eyes were focussed somewhere far beyond the cabin ceiling, and he paused. '… She had a sort of knack of eternal youth.'

Now Jane did raise her eyes. 'There was an age gap?'

'No, no. Not in years… And she levelled with me— she was good at levelling.'

Jane filled a saucepan, lit the gas, and set about grating cheese. 'How did you meet?'

'It was winter.' Tom smiled. 'I was a young sergeant in a police car. Found her out of petrol in the snow. Curly hair, blue eyes. I took one look at her, she laughed, and that was it.'

'Where were you? … I'm trying to imagine.'

'Five miles out of Widdecombe.'

'What was she doing out on Dartmoor?'

'She was a farmer's daughter, lived near Tiverton… She always loved the moor…' Tom paused, uncertainly.

Jane went on grating, but Tom remained silent. 'The moor?'

'Yes,' said Tom, eventually. 'We used to walk up there, rain or shine...'

Jane stopped her work, and looked at him.

'And it was where she died,' he added.

She placed the grater gently on the worktop.

'We were walking, the four of us. And she collapsed. By the clapper bridge above Avon Dam reservoir.'

'Heart attack?'

'That's what they told me.'

'How awful...'

'She gripped at my shirt, took two strong breaths, and sank down, dragged me down. I tried mouth-to-mouth. I sent the kids running different ways to get help: Miranda along the path to Lud Gate, and Jack to the reservoir building which is nearer, but there's no path... Then I was on my own with her. I kept it up for a whole hour, but it was useless—her pulse had gone. It was very hot. Both covered in sweat, her dead and me alive.'

Jane's hands on the worktop had moved an inch towards him and stopped.

'It was another half hour before they came. I covered her up to keep the sun off, and went and sat on a rock ten yards away, and tried to get a grip on myself— she'd gone, no more point in anything, I thought... I should have used cardiac massage.' He made two tight fists. 'Didn't know how, hadn't done the course. They told me I could quite likely have saved her, if I'd been quick... And then I had to cope with the kids, and they had to cope with me.'

He looked up. His view of Jane was blurred, but he could tell her mouth was a little open, her eyes shining—like Beth's when moved. Damn, he thought to himself. Impulsively, he moved towards the companion ladder, eased his way past, and took his memory on deck. He made some sheet adjustments and stayed to watch the Atlantic. After quite a while Jane passed him up his hot soup with the usual toast. She'd added a little sherry to the soup.

*

After another two days they met the gulf stream, and felt warmer. There were occasional porpoises now, and as time went on, the animals began to play around *Ariel's* bow. Tom watched them for hours, and tried to photograph them. They were graceful and extremely strong, like racehorses. An arm of the high-pressure belt that attaches itself to the Azores stretched out towards *Ariel*, bringing blue skies with almost no cloud and a gentler south-westerly. The water changed from grey to ultramarine. At night the wind eased and the sky was clear. Tom started taking star sights just after dusk when there was still enough light to give a clear horizon. He found it hard at first to be sure he had the right star in the sextant telescope, but the calculations were easier than with the Sun. He was by now getting positions that agreed with Jane's to within three or four miles, and she was willing to let him do most of the navigation.

In fact she was leaving him to his own devices a good deal. She seemed to have deferred *Persuasion* in favour of *Medical Taxonomy*, but didn't discuss either of them with Tom, and spent a lot of time on deck watching the sea, or checking the rigging, or, for a change, taking over the steering from James.

She was not always so distant, however. Four days later, Tom was in the saloon, working intently through the parts of the Yachtsman's Handbook that referred to heavy weather sailing. To his right, Jane was sitting on the settee berth, her head cradled in her arms on the table, lost in a reverie. In turning the large page, he accidentally brushed the back of her hand.

She pulled it back sharply, then frowned.

'Sorry,' he said absently. 'What's your theory about man-overboard drill?'

She sat up slowly, gazed at his errant brown hand, and laughed. 'Mister serious policeman!'

'What?'

'Working up for your Yachtmaster?'

'Why not?

'Man overboard, what do they say?' she asked, and grabbed the book. 'I think the beam-reach method is good.'

'That's what they taught me.'

'I reckon there are two things more important than the manoeuvre itself.' She leant back. 'The first is: always stay clipped on, so you don't go OB in the first place. For single-handers that's the *only* consideration. The other is realising the problem is not so much getting back to the guy in the water, but getting him *out* of the water.'

'Ever done it for real?'

'Once. Lovely big man, a builder.' She was smiling again. 'Got knocked out by the boom as it went over. Luckily the water was warm. He was completely inert, sodden. Even with three of us lifting, we just couldn't begin to haul him over the side by hand. Then we saw he wasn't breathing. Someone got into the water and started mouth-to-mouth.'

'How did you get him on board?'

'Lowered the mainsail, set up the topping lift, and used the boom as a derrick.'

'How?'

'Undid the mainsheet tackle from the traveller and shackled it to his harness. We hoisted him up like a sack, swung the boom in, and dumped him in the cockpit.'

'And he was OK?'

'Yes, in the end. He had a feeble pulse, and we had to keep up the artificial respiration for nearly half an hour before he was breathing reliably. But he's OK now and still building houses!'

*

After dusk that evening, Tom was taking star sights as usual. He took three, on widely spaced bearings, to get three intersecting position lines. The sky was very clear and the horizon good, making the whole exercise a pleasure. First Antares, α-Scorpio, very low on the south-south-east horizon. First magnitude and easy. Then, a bit higher in the west, Regulus, the handle of the Sickle, also bright. Finally, he would usually have taken Polaris. But, tiring of the pole star, and seeing Cassiopeia and thinking of *Cas A*, he took instead the star at the middle of the W, thinking he could look it up later. When he did so, he found he'd been lucky to see it so easily. γ-Cas was an irregular variable, not always easy to observe. When he plotted the three position lines on the chart, they crossed *exactly* on top of his estimated position. Tom smiled to himself. No navigator could ask for more things to go right on one occasion. It was a good omen. Perhaps it even meant he'd be able to discover *Cas A's* fate after all.

Ancient and fish-like smell

Encouraged by his successful star sights, Tom in his watches below returned to his investigation with vigour. He didn't quite know why the omen had encouraged him, for Laurel's records left the possibilities much more open than before.

If the ketch visible on the satellite photo of 25th June was *Cas A*, then Dan, Dale, Dr Todd and possibly Eileen Meath and Laurel were the suspects—and where on earth was Laurel? On the other hand, if it was *Bon Appetit* on the photo, then West must have secretly turned south some time between 20th and 22nd June, leaving Dr Todd and Eileen Meath as suspects but excluding the northern group—unless one of them had eliminated West earlier, sent *Cas A* south on her own, and faked the last few transmissions.

So navigational calculation left everything open. This drove him to reconsider the characters of his suspects and their behaviour under questioning. But this was old ground. None of them had ever struck him as a likely villain. Dr Todd and Eileen Meath remained slightly more suspect than the others, but no firm evidence linked either of them with *Cas A*. Yet these discouraging reflections left Tom's renewed enthusiasm undimmed. For some reason he felt confident that the answer was available and that he'd find it soon.

The second day after the star sights, on tuning in the evening weather bulletin, he heard for the first time of hurricane Nathan. After tearaway youth in the Caribbean, Nathan was now enjoying robust maturity off the coast of Carolina and careering northwards. Tom pulled out the North Atlantic Pilot from beside the new pack of hand flares in the rack above the chart table, and studied thoughtfully what it had to say about hurricanes: they usually died out on the eastern seaboard of the US.

He returned to his two prime suspects. In spite of the discouraging lack of incentive, he decided to check all the fixes made by Dr Todd and Eileen Meath from the 22nd June onwards. Why he chose to do this wasn't clear: he'd done it all before. He started with Eileen Meath. To his considerable surprise, her position on the 22nd came out a hundred miles further east than expected. Tom checked his calculation once without finding any error, and then it was time to go on watch.

He was extremely puzzled: he'd been doing astro-navigation for two weeks without making serious mistakes. Why had he suddenly made a gross error and been unable to detect it? This troubled him throughout his watch, but he stuck to his duty and concentrated on sailing *Ariel*. There was plenty of time to sort out errors later. At 2 a.m. he went straight to his bunk and slept.

Jane woke him at 7.30 and they listened to the new forecast. Nathan was still moving rapidly, and turning eastwards.

'Mm. I wonder!' said Jane, 'It's nearly a thousand miles away, but they do sometimes feed up into the

Atlantic—not as hurricanes, just unpleasantly deep depressions.'

When Tom came off watch after lunch the weather was still much as before. At last he could get back to his calculations. But still he could find no mistake. Starting from as early as 15th June, Eileen Meath's positions as calculated from her sights lagged increasingly behind her reported fixes. On the 24th she was nearly a hundred and fifty miles further east than reported. At last, substantial evidence! But was it? Tom had done all these calculations before, and his sums had then *agreed* with Eileen's reported positions. If she'd deceived him in Newport, how had she managed it? As a check that he had indeed been tricked and not made a mistake he recalculated *Ariel's* positions for the same dates, using the same values for the Sun's positions taken from the almanac. *Ariel's* positions all came out exactly as Jane had reported them. Tom said nothing to Jane about all this, but went on watch in a fever of perplexity. Throughout that watch he was relentlessly driving himself to grasp how it was that Eileen had tricked him. And what was he to make now of her reported radio bearings?

Next morning it was clear from the bulletin that the remains of hurricane Nathan would be passing close to the north of them in about twenty-four hours' time. The barometer had already started to fall slowly. For the moment the weather remained clear and sunny with the wind southerly and only Force 3. Jane and Tom went carefully over the boat checking the rigging and hatch covers. Tom made preparations for doing quick hot stews and soups and washed out all the thermos flasks.

When he came off watch, he had another go at positions and dates, this time with Dr Todd. To his consternation, he found that *Ugly Duckling's* positions behaved exactly like *Shamrock's:* from 15th June the fixes calculated from Dr Todd's raw sights started to lag behind what he'd reported, and finished up nearly 150 miles further east on 24th June. Tom felt his head would burst: what the hell was going on? Were Dr Todd and Eileen Meath acting in concert, and, if so, what was the point of being further behind than they were reporting, when West was well *ahead,* even of their reported positions?

By the time he went on watch, the coming gale was beginning to make itself apparent. The sunset sky was streaked with scars of mare's tails from west to east, and the barometer falling sharply. The wind had veered to south-west, but was still only Force 4. The sea was confused, but in spite of the relatively light wind a sullen swell was growing, from the same direction. As a precaution, they took in two reefs in the mainsail and set the number two jib before Jane went below.

Very thick clouds quickly covered the stars, and the night became inky black, leaving Tom with only the orange glow from the compass and the shaded chart table light to keep him company: outside *Ariel* nothing was to be seen but the occasional foam as a wave crest tumbled alongside. James seemed able to manage without attention. By the 2 a.m. change of watch the wind had risen to the middle of Force 6.

'You should have called me earlier,' said Jane.

They switched on the deck lights and Tom brought *Ariel* up to the wind, which howled and snatched at them in the dark. They replaced the number two with the storm jib, Jane almost invisible as she worked on the foredeck. That done, and guessing what was coming, she took the mainsail off completely. They lashed down the boom and hoisted a reefed trysail.

'Getting near Force 7,' she said, 'but we can run on for a bit.'

At first it seemed absurdly quiet after she turned *Ariel* away from the wind again. Tom got himself into his bunk. But an hour later he was still awake, and could tell that the wind had risen further. Then came a change of motion and sound as Jane turned *Ariel* back into the wind: she must be heaving to. At once the urgent swaying and rush changed to an easier but jerky, buoyant motion, and the wind howl in the rigging rose higher. He heard her close the companionway hatch and come below. Later there came a belting roar as the rain of the warm front poured onto them. He heard her go up on deck to look round and come down again, wet oilskins squeaking.

*

When he took over at eight, it was a wild morning. They were now in the warm sector, and low dark clouds were roaring overhead from the west. The wind had risen to Force 8, and the swell was building up steadily. *Ariel* was still hove-to on starboard tack, pointing south-west to face the waves diagonally, and riding like a cork as though picking her way between the smaller crests. The motion, though quite manageable, was very jerky, and the waves themselves awe inspiring: the crests towered over *Ariel's* bow as they swept down towards them, roaring and tumbling. Jane had switched on the radar detector, but they appeared to be alone.

'I could have carried on with just the jib,' shouted Jane, 'but James won't steer safely downwind in a high sea and it takes a lot of concentration to do it by hand.

Better to heave to and save our energy for later if we're in for a really big blow. I'll get some sleep while I can,' she went on, wiping salt water and hair out of her eyes. 'Should be all right like this for a while. But this is a proper gale, and it's still strengthening. If the average wind or the gusts get much worse, or if she starts staggering around or lying over, or if the wave crests start breaking much more, you call me. Keep the washboards in and for God's sake stay clipped on while you're outside!'

She was gone, and Tom was in charge.

He decided he'd better start by getting a clear idea of what the conditions were like now, so that if it got worse, he would recognise the change. He had been in gusts up to Force 8 before and Jane's confidence was infectious; he felt more elated than scared. The masthead anemometer was showing the wind speed. It rose and fell rhythmically with the waves, down to 30 knots or less in the troughs and up to about 36 knots on the crests, and very steady in direction. But at deck level the variation was much greater. There were moments in the troughs when the wind seemed to drop right down to nothing behind the cabin top, and Tom could even hear himself humming the *1812 Overture.* But on the crests there was no hiding place: the wind felt as though it was driving directly through Tom's oilskins and into all three layers of woollens beneath them. Jane had lashed the wheel down and adjusted the sails so that *Ariel* needed no attention: she lay about 60° off the wind with her starboard bow to the waves, making little headway and leaving a big swirling eddy to windward. Her handkerchief-sized sails stayed drum tight with no sign of flogging and little vibration. As each great wave crest passed, her bow was thrown upward and further off the wind and the wheel snatched at its lashings, but with a quick swoop she lay over and swung stiffly to the wind as the crest passed beneath her.

Tom watched the waves carefully. They were much taller than any he'd seen before, but well spaced and not impossibly steep. Very long plumes of spray were being driven off the main crests, and were dashed into his face just before *Ariel* surmounted each ridge. On the smaller scale, the sea surface was scarred by white horses, but the main swell was quite regular, and there was only the occasional tumbling of a sharper than usual crest.

He could see a reasonable distance only when *Ariel* was on top of a wave, and the spray and lowering light made it hard to see very much even then, especially to windward, even though that was down-light. Tom contrived to keep some sort of watch by sweeping the horizon as best he could through the older pair of binoculars every ten minutes, but it wasn't very satisfactory. He felt glad of the radar detector.

After half an hour he began to realise how much the noise and buffetting and wind-chill were taking out of him. No need to stay on deck all the time. He wriggled down the companion, closing the washboards behind him, and got himself some hot soup from the thermos. Jane was an inert shape in her sleeping bag wedged into the quarter berth, and he didn't wake her. With *Ariel* jumping about like a rubber duck in a Jacuzzi it was extremely difficult to keep the soup still enough to drink: he jammed his feet against the opposite bunk and didn't risk filling his mug more than a third full. The barometer was still falling, and he wondered whether he'd escape being sick: no signs so far, though the inescapable jerking motion did make him dizzy. He stuffed a roll down after the soup.

There was no prospect of doing any useful navigating. He struggled through to the front cabin to fetch a towel, and found the motion there much more violent—in the main cabin he was more or less at the centre of the boat where there was violent pitching and rolling, but not too much jumping up and down, just the swoop... swoop... as the waves passed. But in the fore cabin he found he could barely lie on his bunk, because every time *Ariel's* bow jumped over a wave crest he was first flung violently upwards and then left almost in mid-air as the bow fell away—he had to cling to the mattress to feel secure.

As he returned to the main cabin, the radar alarm went off, and Jane sat up, questioningly. Tom struggled on deck as fast as he could, peered around, and seeing nothing, tried with the binoculars. The alarm continued to bleep once a minute, but nothing appeared through the murk. In the cabin, Jane began donning her oilskins.

Tom was panicking: hove-to, they couldn't manoeuvre quickly, they might need steerage way... He jumped to cast off the bar-tight jib sheet, but before he could, suddenly, there was a darker shape to his right, something he couldn't see clearly, the spray was bad. Then all at once he saw clearly the high steel wall of a ship, only a hundred yards away, neat rows of containers like Lego bricks on her deck. She was rolling slightly and slicing eastward at some enormous speed through those steaming waves as though the gale weren't happening, and apparently completely oblivious of *Ariel*. Fortunately, she would pass well behind them. She faded rapidly into the murk, but Tom could still hear—or feel—the powerful throbbing of her engines penetrating oddly through shrieks of the wind. For the first time he felt frightened. *Ariel* had her radar reflector hoisted, but it was obvious that the container ship's deck officers had been unaware of her. He carefully cleated the jib sheet again, as Jane climbed on deck.

'Too bloody close,' was all she said. 'I could hear his engines down there. One of those things you can't do much about.' She climbed back down to her bunk.

*

After that, Tom didn't feel easy staying below decks, and he crouched in the cockpit in the lee of the cabin roof, uncertainty developing at the pit of his stomach. It was hard not to imagine the steel prow of that ship crunching in a split second through *Ariel's* two inches of fibreglass, and the maelstrom of icy water that would follow. The wind had risen a little more. On the tops of the waves the anemometer was now showing 38 knots or more quite often—getting near to Force 9. The driving spray was becoming more continuous, making it harder and harder to see, and the wave tops were boiling up more often. For some time now *Ariel* had been burying her nose with a crash as she slid down the backs of the waves, and great showers of water spurted out to each side. Now solid lumps were coming aboard amidships sometimes as the wave crests swept past. They shot down the side-decks. A larger one than usual came pouring into the cockpit as Tom jumped out of its way. It filled the floor to a depth of a foot or so. That was alarming, to be paddling in the cockpit. The water gurgled out of the self-draining holes, but slowly. Four waves later a great gust flung *Ariel* onto her side as the crest passed, and swinging sideways-on she was rolled violently from side to side.

Tom opened the hatch a crack. 'I think it's getting too much for her,' he shouted down.

Jane was already into her oilskins again. 'I thought it was,' she said as she struggled into the cockpit and clipped herself on. She looked around. 'Time to go down wind,' she shouted. 'Have the sails off. You unlash the wheel and keep us very close up.'

She sheeted in the lee jib sheet and eased the weather one, letting the storm jib come gradually amidships. *Ariel* started to move ahead, and Tom kept her feathering up to the wind. Jane went forward, clipped herself on very securely, and sat down on the plunging foredeck. As Tom cautiously eased off the halyard, she got herself directly under the storm jib, so that by wrapping her arms around it she could keep the lower part under firm control. The sail snatched violently at her and water poured over her body, but eventually she had it almost lowered and lashed to the pulpit so that just the top foot or two of canvas caught the wind. Tom made fast the halyard. He'd admired Jane's management of the sail and was glad to see her working her way aft and then safely back into the cockpit.

'I'll take the wheel now. You do the trysail,' she said.

Tom transferred his safety strap to the span wire and inched his way forward over the bouncing deck clutching a long lashing, until he could stand nervously beside the mast. When he was ready Jane, choosing a moment as *Ariel* was sliding down into the relative quietness of a wave trough, let the trysail halyard run quickly, and Tom dragged the sail down and put one turn of the lashing around it. Jane was already swinging *Ariel* round, and there was a violent roll, Tom hanging on to the sail and his lashing as best he could. By the time the next crest came, *Ariel* was safe, already heading down wind, the tiny scrap of storm jib helping to pull her round. The wind was now driving into the loose folds of trysail, and Jane smiled as Tom struggled to smother it and lash it into some sort of parcel by the mast. He inched his way back to the cockpit, his fingers raw, but fingernails intact.

Ariel was no longer at rest in the water, but travelling with the gale at a considerable speed. Jane was steering carefully, putting the stern exactly to every wave as it passed. There was some wild rolling, but the jerky motion of being hove-to was gone, and because *Ariel* was now travelling with them, the waves passed under her more slowly, giving an easier swing to the switchback.

'Try it,' said Jane, and gave him the wheel.

Tom quickly realised why steering downwind in a big sea is considered the trickiest part of the helmsman's art: the danger was the waves, bearing down from behind, but he couldn't be always facing backwards to watch them—it made him disoriented. But it was necessary, by some sort of sixth sense, to know when the wave was about to do something unusual, and, particularly if the crest showed signs of breaking, to present the stern of the boat to it *exactly* square. He also realised that the helmsman was much more exposed to the wind in this position—and to the water, if the wave broke over the stern.

'What do I do if we get pooped?' he yelled.

'Hang on to the wheel like grim death! Just remember, if the washboards are closed, very little water can get inside, and it'll drain out of the cockpit if you wait, even it's up to your middle! I think we should take shorter spells, not more than an hour,' she shouted.

She watched for quite a while to see how he did, and then went below to get warm and dry before her turn.

Tom thought he was steering OK, and the heavy work on the wheel did something to keep him warm. But now he was scared—a lot more scared than Jane seemed to be. Well, it was a question of experience and knowing what the ship could take. And the crew.

What frightened him was those huge crests bearing down from behind. There was a long moment of suspense while *Ariel* ski'ed down the front slope of the wave, as though trying to avoid the pursuit, but each time the slope ahead of him grew longer and steeper as the wave caught *Ariel* up, and the wall of water behind seemed to grow more overhanging and more menacing. Then each time, quite calmly, *Ariel* found herself caught by the wave crest and subsided backwards; and it swept past embracing the waist of the ship, with a sighing, falling hiss, as though *Ariel* were a Sabine resigning herself to the grip of an amorous galloping Neptune.

To keep himself cheerful he sang something simpler than the *1812 Overture – Ilkley Moor*. He could give it a good, brisk rhythm. After exhausting all the traditional verses he could remember, he found himself concocting maritime ones:

'*Where* did she put the working jib? On Ilkley Moor b'hat 'at! Where did she put the working jib? Where did she put the working jib? ... '

This went on for some time, and he got neither warmer nor colder. No water came into the cockpit, and he slowly gained in confidence.

'Why can't I find the bloody sun?' sang Tom, thinking of his sextant. Not too hard to understand, he laughed to himself, peering at the dark vortices of wispy cloud roaring past above his head.

At this point Tom realised that the wind was beginning to turn to the north west. Then, very gradually, he began to detect signs that there were *two* swells crossing each other: a long low rounded one from roughly south-west, and the much higher, wind-driven one which now proceeded to follow the wind round to the north-west. The trouble was that this made the main wave crests much less regular: where one of the new swells crossed the old, the crest was flung much higher and threatened to arch forward like a wave arriving on a beach. In a few places in the murky distance he could see great torrents of falling water. He imagined uneasily what it would be like if one of them fell tumbling into his cockpit.

'*Whose* almanac was it I used,' sang Tom very loudly, 'on Ilkley Moor b'hat 'at? Whose almanac was it I used? Whose almanac was it I used? On Ilkley Moor b'hat 'at? On Ilkley Moor b'hat 'at! … '

He stopped. What the hell made me sing *that,* asked Tom. He thought for a while.

'That's *it*, of course,' he said out loud after some time, the skin on the back of his hands tingling… This won't do, he thought, you've got to concentrate on those horrible waves. And one part of his head did just that, but another part remained busy assembling the whole solution to his problem, quite effortlessly and quickly. He knew now why there was invisible sellotape in Jane's copy of Macmillan's. He remembered how Ed had referred to Jane having used a Very pistol near the start of the race, and had a shrewd idea why it had vanished and been replaced by a bundle of hand-held flares. He even understood why Eileen's radio bearings hadn't alerted him to what West had achieved.

He knew why West had been careful to wear shades

in Plymouth before the race, and was pretty certain, too, what had made Jane seriously ill as a student. He could even *half* understand, though it seemed absolutely extraordinary, why she had invited him to join her for the voyage home. The only thing that *didn't* fit was the J's Jamaica. Well, he could invent ways of explaining that too.

He felt humiliated and manipulated. He found himself contemplating why his subconscious had been able to explain all this evidence so readily while his conscious mind had been blocked. He concentrated on his steering very hard for what seemed a long time. He also found that he was now very scared indeed, though he might have been hard pressed to say exactly why.

Almost, he wanted her to come late on watch; but Jane relieved him promptly on the hour, looked at the threatening wave crests and pulled a face. Tom watched as she clipped her safety harness on and stood up to the wheel. She caught his eye, turned her head and, puzzled by his expression, turned her whole body and looked much harder. Tom tried to avert his gaze, but found it fixed on hers as if by bonds. It was Jane who looked down, and then, slowly, up again. The elastic tightness on her face had been displaced by slack-jawed disintegration. Making what seemed to Tom a huge effort, she filled her lungs and yelled into the screaming wind: 'You *know*, don't you? ... You've *worked it out!*'

'Yes,' bellowed Tom. 'Yes... I know!'

She nodded, and suddenly staggered. Spray streaked her, wet curls were blowing from under her oilskin hood.

Tom thought her ready to collapse. 'But we've got to get ourselves through this bloody storm first!' he yelled in a panic.

She stared intensely at him and narrowed her eyes. Then she gripped the spokes of the wheel, filled her lungs again deeply, turned to face the towering waves, and waved him dismissively to get below.

Pour down stinking pitch

Tom staggered down the companion steps, jammed the washboards shut behind him, and wedged himself behind the chart table without removing his oilskins, shivering uncontrollably. Salt water dribbled over the chart. This won't do, he thought. But his shivering worsened. Ashamed, he worked his way into the fore cabin and flung himself onto his bunk. To control the trembles in his shoulders he screwed himself into a ball, face into the wet oilskin, and burst into a stream of explosive swearing. After a while this exhausted itself, and his shivering eased a little.

Waves were passing steadily, and though some were throwing *Ariel's* tail higher into the air than others, the motion felt under control, and had a rhythm to it. He wriggled back to the companion steps and watched her through the cracks between the washboards. Her small hands were firm on the wheel, her eyes, focussed on the horizon, strained but steady: it hasn't affected her steering, he thought. Tom's fear wasn't gone, but it became more rational; and though his shivering didn't stop either, he thought now of soup. He found and gulped down a third of a mugful from the thermos, and then another third. He found himself a tot of rum.

The barometer was starting to creep up—perhaps conditions would start to improve soon. He'd be steering again in less than forty minutes—needed all the warmth and rest he could get. He mopped his oilskins with a towel, covered himself with all the bedding he could find, and dozed.

The next thing he knew was a great hammering on the washboards, and seawater pouring down the companionway into the cabin. He scrambled out of his bunk and hauled himself up the steps: a wave had filled the cockpit and flung Jane against the boards, but she was already back at the wheel. Tom could see that *Ariel's* stern lay dangerously low in the wave trough.

'Don't come up,' shrieked Jane. 'Stay where you are and pump!'

Tom did as he was told, frantically. It took more than five hundred strokes to pump *Ariel* dry. He returned to the crack. The cockpit had drained, and Jane was steering steadily again, but her hands on the wheel looked raw and blue. He found her some rubber gloves and passed them out; she gave him a distracted smile. He dried himself again, and went back to his bunk. This time he didn't doze, but watched the clock creeping round until his time should be due.

Suddenly he knew something was wrong: *Ariel* was starting to stand on her nose so steeply that he felt sure she must turn head over heels. As everything started to slide down the cabin, he was overwhelmed by a new noise—a rushing, hideous roar. Then daylight was blotted out and water cascaded all about him. He had the impression that *Ariel* was nose-diving hundreds of feet below the surface, as a great rumbling of trapped air bubbles churned around her hull. He closed his eyes as he tumbled down into the bow of the boat.

Slowly, things sorted themselves out a little. Some of the light returned. *Ariel* shook herself like a dog appearing out of surf, rolling uncontrollably through three or four swings. Tom struggled to his feet. The main cabin floor was deep in water. He flung himself at the pump. After thirty strokes, he was shouting at himself to calm down and pump steadily, but his breath was coming in retching gasps before he had the water below floor level.

He felt a little safer. But, hell, what was happening on deck? He dashed at the ladder, banging his shins uselessly on the steps. The washboards had all survived and the water had drained away, but Jane wasn't at the wheel. He threw the boards aside and staggered into the cockpit. The webbing holding the liferaft was broken. The raft itself was still there, wedged under the wheel at the back of the cockpit. It had smashed one of the floor gratings into little pieces. Both lifebuoys and the Dan buoy had gone, and some of the port side stanchions and guard wire had been swept away. The wind vane of the self-steering gear had disappeared completely. He looked forward, unbelieving: the mast was standing, that little piece of jib still pulling.

But Jane was gone.

Tom grabbed the wheel and swung *Ariel* around stern to the waves. She must be somewhere in the water behind him, up wind. His set his jaw. He tried to start the engine. Miraculously, on the third attempt, the Volvo fired. He set half revs, and swung *Ariel* round to starboard in the next trough. The gale caught that remaining scrap of jib, and stopped him turning more than sixty degrees. Full revs! Not more than half-way round. A huge wave loomed to his right and rolled *Ariel* over onto her left side, pouring right over the boat. Tom saw it coming, and managed to clip himself on in time. Water churned around him. The diesel kept running, and he swung *Ariel* away down wind again. Things settled down, leaving him panting and shivering.

God, how far back was she now? She must be near the Dan buoy, with its flag—he ought to be able to find that. Anyway, the first thing was to get that bit of jib down so that it couldn't stop him making the turn. He managed to lash the wheel central, clipped himself onto the safety wire and staggered forward down the port side.

As he did so, something caught his eye. There was a safety clip attached to the port lower shroud, and its strap led down into the water. He peered over. She was there, on the end of the strap. No sign of life, churned around face-down by the water, a bundle of oilskin and floating hair. Tom clenched his teeth again and then took a great gulp of air. She must have seen the wave coming and run forward to clip herself on by the mast, hoping to be safer there. Holding the shroud with one hand he hauled on her safety strap with the other. Her body turned over. Blood was oozing from her scalp. He managed to lift her an inch or two out of the water, but no more.

'God save us!' he mouthed. But at least he knew where she was.

There was another great crash, and heavy water poured over him again, powerful water that tried to undermine his footing and sweep him off the deck: in spite of the lashed tiller, *Ariel* was not remaining stern-on to the waves. He hung on grimly as the water drained away. He remembered Jane had a sea anchor. He staggered back to the cockpit, and dragged it from its locker with a mooring warp, extended it, made fast the warp to anchor and stern cleat, tightened all his knots, switched off the engine, and threw the anchor over the stern. There was a violent jerk as the canvas of the anchor caught the water, and *Ariel* swung herself tail-to-wind again.

He staggered forward, unclipped the main halyard and lowered the end of it until he could shackle it to the inboard end of Jane's safety strap by the shroud. Then he worked his way back to the cockpit, jammed a winch handle into his oilskin pocket, and returned, dragging a spare jib sheet with him. Lying down and using both hands he was just able to tie the jib sheet onto Jane's harness as a back-up safety line. He made the other end fast, and could then safely release from the shroud the inboard end of the safety strap. He got the winch handle onto the winch, and racked the halyard in. The orange sack that was Jane rose very slowly out of the water, swaying as inertly as a body on a gibbet, bumping against the rubbing strake. He pulled her inboard and lowered her to the deck. Untying the back-up safety line, but leaving the halyard attached in case of accidents, he bundled her ahead of him along the side deck against the spray, panting as he pushed, tipped her over the coaming onto the cockpit seat. She slithered over the wet seat and crashed onto the cockpit floor. Panting and grunting, Tom unhitched the halyard and safety strap, yanked out the washboards, climbed half down the steps, and hauled Jane after him like a sack of vegetables, doing his best to brake her descent. She bumped down the companionway and thumped onto the cabin floor, water streaming off her.

The ship had to come next. Back into the cockpit to make sure *Ariel* was balancing herself between the wind acting on that bit of jib, the pull of the sea anchor and the lashed tiller. Not ideal, but promising. The wind howled on. He slammed the washboards back into position, and tumbled down again into the cabin.

Airways clear... He spread her on the floor and yanked her jaw down. Even the inside of her mouth seemed deathly cold to his probing fingers, and she didn't retch. No, not breathing. How long had she been face down in the water? Mouth-to-mouth... His warm teeth grated on her icy ones. Her chest rose: good, windpipe not blocked. Five good breaths. Any pulse? He couldn't get at her neck because of the oilskins, tried her wrist: nothing there. Unzip that oilskin, fingers on neck... Not a proper pulse, but deep under his fingers there was a faint fluttering, strange under that icy cold flesh. Five more good breaths... Again that fluttering. Her heart was doing some-thing—but was it enough? He ought to try cardiac massage... He pressed her down flat on her back, set himself with braced arms over her breastbone, threw his full weight down. Eighty a minute, it was, and use *thumping* pressure, don't stop even if the ribs break. He could hear water bubbling around in her lungs... Then two breaths every fifteen compressions...

After ten minutes, he thought he could feel a change. From somewhere deep inside her body, warmth was reaching the surface: her cheeks were kitchen meat instead of chilled meat. Her pulse showed a few, barely perceptible beats before breaking again into that strange fluttering. He thumped on. After another five minutes her pulse seemed fairly steady, and he switched to mouth-to-mouth and less heart massage. Another five minutes and he gave up the massage entirely. He watched for signs of spontaneous breath-ing, but there were none. His muscles were starting to crack up and the breathing into her made him dizzy and sick. But it was a further half hour of mouth-to mouth before she showed very faint signs of spontaneous breaths, so slight he could hardly be sure.

He should be doing more to warm her, but it didn't seem safe to give up the respiration. After another quarter of an hour he could definitely *hear* her breathing, and hear a very slight bubbling inside her chest. Safer to leave her on the floor, in case he had to do the massage again. So he put her in the recovery position, covered her, oilskins and all, with his own sleeping bag, there on the floor, before he realised that water was still slopping about in the cabin. Damn! Never mind, he still had her own bag in reserve. He pumped the hull dry, breaking off every fifty strokes to check; her thighs and arms now trembled occasionally.

He could tell from the motion that *Ariel* was still looking after herself: the next priority was to get Jane warm. He spread her dry sleeping bag on the main cabin bunk, and found a towel. Getting her wet clothes off was a thoroughly indelicate struggle. He hoisted her naked onto the bunk and zipped her in, spread blankets, checked that those shallow bubbling breaths hadn't stopped. Her clammy throat and breasts and nipples left him with a sense of awe, and undeserved appropriation. And there was something else, which he'd rather been expecting: on her flat belly, down from navel to black pubic hair, was a long wandering scar. A peculiar shape, not an operation scar.

Tom was now extremely tired, and starting to shiver again. Hypothermia—he must think about hypothermia. People resuscitated from drowning often relapsed, didn't they? Look it up... the *Yachtsman's Handbook*, first-aid section. He read it doggedly through—and found his mind entirely blank. He tried again. Yes, they did relapse—'take to hospital as soon as possible'. Hypothermia: 'It is probably unwise to use cardiac massage.' Well, it had worked! 'Remove wet clothing.' Done. 'Dry and wrap in blankets or sleeping bag, preferably with another person to generate heat.'

Tom frowned. He got the last of the soup from the thermos inside him. He stuck his head outside to check that *Ariel* was still lying reasonably steady, head down-wind. Then he struggled out of all his clothes, stacking trousers, pullover and oilskins ready for emergencies, and wriggled in with her. Her body was very, very cold, and his shivering became more violent. He turned her back towards him, and enfolded her with his arms and legs, trying with small movements to keep some circulation of his own going while putting as little pressure on her as he could. Those strange, slight, bubbling breaths at odd intervals went on, and so did Tom's continual shivering. The action was over. His eyes filled with tears. He'd done the best he could. It was up to providence now.

All this time the strong pitching as the waves passed under them had continued, without let-up. From inside her sleeping bag it felt like the determined rocking of a cradle. Twice before, while he'd been frantically breathing into her, Tom had heard waves slop into the cockpit, and eventually drain away. Now came a larger one. A little water came through the wash boards. It was obvious from the motion that the cockpit had filled, and *Ariel* was wallowing stern down in the trough. Tom started up in a panic. But *Ariel* survived the next wave… and the next. Through the wind noise he could hear the water gurgling out of the drain pipes. It was all right, going to be all right. Tom drowsed, shivered, drowsed again, and finally slept.

Ariel, unconcerned, picked her way down-wind through the storm as before.

Backward and abysm of time

An hour later, Tom woke, guilty for having slept. In his arms, Jane was still unconscious, but snoring loudly and irregularly; her hands and feet felt very cold, but the middle of her a good deal warmer, her pulse light but steady. He slipped out of the sleeping bag, hauled on some dry clothes, and climbed on deck. The wind had dropped to the high end of Force 6, though the swells were still very large. He adjusted the sea anchor line to stop it chafing.

It was already 5 pm. Hurrying back below, he dressed Jane as best he could, adding gloves and socks. He washed and bandaged the cut on her temple, topped her off with a woolly hat, found and filled a hot water bottle, and slipped it in beside her.

He slapped her hand, but there was no response, and he could hear bubbling in her lungs. Time to use the radio, make an urgency signal. To be ready for the operator he scribbled down a list of medical questions.

But seawater must have got inside the long-range set: the panel light came on, but he could receive nothing, not even static. He went on deck to check the aerial connections. He tried making a transmission anyway, in the hope that the transmit circuits might be working. He repeated it on the VHF set, but the chance of anyone being within VHF range was remote—*Ariel* was well south of the main shipping lane. He got no response.

If communication was out, what were the best

tactics? Carry on eastwards and rely on his own resources? No—he needed medical help. Turn back towards Newfoundland? Too long a beat. Head north towards the shipping lane? No question—the shipping lane was best. Not a good place for a single-hander at night, but the risk must be taken.

That made him think of the self-steering gear, and he remembered that the main wind vane had disappeared completely. Unsteady over the heavy sea, he perched on the transom to see if anything else remained. By some miracle the rest of the gear hadn't been wrenched off completely by the great wave, and he thought it might be possible to improvise a new vane using sailcloth. But the vertical shaft was bent through ten degrees and jammed in its bearings. His attempts to lever it straight *in situ* failed completely. So—nothing doing in the short term. He knew it was difficult to make a boat sail itself in a given direction simply by balancing the sails, and for the moment left *Ariel* as she was. He should be able to remove the vane shaft from the transom once the swell had died down a bit; it might then be possible to hammer it straight. But that would have to wait.

Depressed, and dizzy with the perpetual urgent swaying, he got himself a dose of hot stew with a wedge of bread, and tried to think. He very much wanted Jane to show some sign of consciousness. So when he next replaced her hot water bottle he again tried slapping her hand, very hard this time. To his surprise, her eyelids fluttered open for a second and closed again. He watched. Ten minutes later, he tried again. She opened her eyes, shut them at once, and muttered something incomprehensible. After a few minutes, the muttering started again, and then, suddenly, she was very sick, a lot of it simply

218

seawater.

The next few hours were miserable. She was repeatedly sick, she choked, and the deeper breaths that this involved seemed to give her intense pain: she screwed up her face, drew up her knees and clutched at her lungs. Then, when not choking, she started to cough, sometimes dry hacks, and sometimes coughing up dollops of water. Tom mopped it up and did his best to calm her, and there were spells when she again seemed comatose, and her breathing became very shallow. Then it would strengthen, and there'd be another fit of painful coughing. Her face was blotchy, and the mutterings remained unintelligible. Eventually, the activity died away, and she was left sweaty, inert, cold and with a very fast pulse. Tom had no idea what to do. He tried his urgency radio message again, and did his best to keep her warm.

For the next three hours she lay still, and very gradually recovered her temperature and steady pulse. Tom made himself tea, and watched. Nothing further happened, and eventually he found some biscuits and cheese for a very late supper. He needed rest, decided he must set and reset the alarm clock at two hour intervals during the night, climbed into his wet sleeping bag on the bunk opposite, and dropped almost at once into a strange sleep, studded with frantic dreams.

Three times in the night the alarm trilled, he checked Jane by torchlight, found no change, lay back and let those strange dreams multiply.

In the half-light next morning, he heard her moaning. He jumped up. She was lifting her head and peering at him. He grabbed her gloved hand and stroked it. The corner of her mouth creased a fraction, and her head sank back, relieved. Tom wept again: it was another stage.

*

After that, though it took many hours, things gradually improved. The wind continued to ease. Jane began taking sips of warm drink in her bunk, and for short periods seemed to be thinking clearly, though on that first day after the storm she said almost nothing. Towards evening Tom caught her looking at him with what seemed a very tender smile. He felt oddly disconcerted. The smile disappeared.

At breakfast next day she remarked, 'My safety strap must have held?'

Tom nodded.

'And you hauled me out of the water, the way we said?'

'With the main halyard.'

She closed her eyes.

At lunch, as Tom handed her a mug containing a mouthful or two of tepid soup, she suddenly looked anxious and asked, 'How much damage?'

'Nothing really serious. The mast survived. No big leaks. We're sailing again. But James is badly screwed up.'

Her eyes almost closed. 'That was some wave!'

'I could only feel it.'

'I saw it was going to break right over me, so I ran forward and clipped on... After that I can't remember.' She put her mug down, leant back, and closed her eyes.

At supper time, to Tom's immense relief, she sat up properly, and began to tell him a little of what her medical treatment required.

On the third day, suddenly, she seemed clear headed, though very tired. 'The bruising round my sternum's still something horrible,' she said. 'I guess that was heart massage.'

'Yes,' said Tom. 'I did what they taught me.'

'You must have done it right.'

'Hope so... Your pulse was fluttering. I was afraid I was going to lose you the way I lost Beth.'

'Oh Tom, yes... And mouth-to-mouth?'

'Yes.'

'How long was I not breathing, before you started?'

'Five minutes? Probably a lot more—I don't know.'

'*A lot more than five minutes!*'

'Yes.'

'I ought to be dead!'

Tom said nothing.

'Was I hypothermic?'

'You felt very cold. It was ages before I could feel any warmth at all.'

'Maybe that saved me.'

They checked her pulse and blood pressure. She found a stethoscope and got him to listen to her lungs. 'Just an occasional bubbling noise when you breathe out,' he reported.

'No crackles when I breathe in?'

He tried again. 'No... What would that mean?'

'Oedema—water in the capillaries... You said I coughed up a lot?'

'Yes.'

'Doesn't seem to have irritated my lung tissues too much,' she said. 'What we have to avoid now is pneumonia.' Under instruction, Tom gave her a precautionary injection of antibiotic.

*

On the fourth day, to Tom's considerable surprise, she told him firmly that the case for flagging down a

221

ship had passed, and seemed cheered by the dreadful din as Tom hammered straight James' vertical shaft. For the moment, he asked no questions.

The weather had settled to a warm and sunny westerly, and the swell was manageable again. Tom set proper sails, and found, with some advice, how to make *Ariel* sail herself in roughly the right direction without James' help. He also took some sights, and was surprised how much distance they'd made eastwards during the storm. Finally, after a long struggle, he persuaded James to work again, and could feel, from the seafaring point of view at least, that the passage was finally back under control.

Jane's lack of interest in flagging down a ship worried him: it felt as though, for the moment, and for some reason, she wanted to keep the two of them alone, cocooned together.

She seemed content to convalesce slowly, and there was a good deal of pain and sleeplessness. On the sixth day she climbed on deck for the first time, in dark glasses because the sunlight hurt her eyes. She still seemed weak, unready to face unfinished business.

*

On the eighth day, however, she felt strong enough to steer for a bit.

'You saved my life,' she remarked in a small voice after some time at the wheel.

'I suppose so,' said Tom, seriously, watching.

'Yes,' said Jane. She frowned, and thought for a while, scanning the horizon.

After half an hour, Tom made some coffee. 'Will you take over, now, please?' she asked. She settled down in a sheltered spot, sipped at her mug, and looked up at him. 'Time to talk, perhaps.'

Tom set James to handle the steering and sat down opposite.

'I don't know how much you worked out,' she said.

Tom looked seriously at her. 'We knew West meant to kill someone,' he said. 'And then I deduced it had to be you.'

She screwed up her eyes and nodded.

'But *he* was the one who finished up dead.' He hesitated. 'I don't understand yet how or why.'

'No,' she said.

'Do you want to tell me?'

She thought for a while, and then said, 'His real name was Carl Easton.' She pressed her lips together. 'He was half German.'

'We got that far.'

She nodded. 'I knew he had it in for me. But I'd no idea he was gunning for me in the race.'

'No idea at all?'

'I hadn't seen him for ten years. I knew there was a competitor named Charles West, but I'd no way of knowing he was Carl—I never met him. I set off... And very early one morning in mid-Atlantic I was asleep, leaving *Ariel* to sail herself. It was a gentle Force 2. And there was this loud bump...'

Her coffee mug had begun to shake. She put it down on the cockpit seat, and clenched her fingers together.

'I stuck my head up the companionway, and... there he was standing on my foredeck. Holding a fucking rifle.'

Tom held himself very still.

'I knew who it was all right, but my mind was racing because I'd no idea how he'd got there or what was happening. He'd got his boat up under my lee, using one of those big orange racing buoys as an enormous fender, and lashed her to *Ariel* bow and stern; both boats were ghosting along westwards still.'

She pressed her hands down fiercely onto the seat.

'He was wearing a pair of shades, though it was hardly light. I felt sick... Worse... He'd come to *get* me...'

'To kill you?'

'Yes.'

'How could you be sure?'

'I knew *Carl*, and he was carrying that rifle.'

'You felt certain?'

'*Yes*. Absolutely... Neither of us said a word. All I could think of was my flare pistol—I kept it loaded, and it was near my right hand in the companionway. I climbed on deck with it behind my back. He took two deliberate steps forward, started to swing the rifle round and up, with both hands, slowly. I took a step forward, whipped up my pistol and fired. There was a terrific whoosh. The flare hit him in the neck. He fell backwards and cracked his head on the deck-edge, then tumbled over the edge and finished up on the orange buoy between the boats. The flare was wedged behind his life jacket, orange smoke and flames roaring out.

'His rifle had fallen on the deck. I rushed forward and picked it up. He was lying down there on the buoy. His face and chest were all scorched.

'I pointed it at him and pulled the trigger. Nothing. Probably got a safety catch, I thought. I found something I thought might be the catch, and pushed it, and tried again. This time the rifle knocked me backwards onto the cabin top. When I could look at him again most of the top of his head was blown away.'

She was swallowing. The wind had risen a little,

and *Ariel* was creaking, moving faster through the water, making appreciative noises. 'Hunting ammunition,' said Tom, quietly.

'I was sick, terribly sick. Then I looked around. No boats in sight. I found my rum bottle, and had a big swig. I put it in my oilskin pocket, and tried to think… I'd *murdered* him.' She slowly raised her head.

Tom neither nodded nor shook his head.

She screwed up her eyes. '*I had!* Got to make it look like an accident. He must sink, as though he'd gone overboard, and not be found, but the rifle mustn't be missing—that would be suspicious. I got down onto the mooring buoy and got his life jacket off. I emptied his pockets and found his keys. I found his kedge anchor to weigh him down, and tied it to him with a mooring rope. It was horrible. I pushed him off the buoy. His long hair, what was left of it, spread out in the water, and he sank, face up. Good riddance. I cleaned up the rifle and locked it back in its rack. He had a chart, on which he'd plotted out his positions and mine.'

'Did you look at the fixes?' asked Tom quickly.

'Yes,' said Jane. 'And I realised he had me a hundred and fifty miles farther west than I'd reported. I couldn't understand why. Anyway, that chart was incriminating—nothing must suggest we'd been near each other—so I burnt it and pitched the ashes overboard. I washed the blood and hair off his boat's topsides. Bits of bone too. And brains… I looked very carefully to make sure it all looked natural.

'Then I set his sails for heaving to and pushed his boat off my shrouds. It hove to all right. I cut a hole in that orange buoy and sank it. He must have brought it with him specially, there was an inflator for it in one of his lockers.'

'What did you do with the life jacket?' asked Tom.

'I couldn't get the blood off it, so I couldn't leave it in *Cas A*. But there was nothing to identify it. I left it floating in the sea. I dropped his keys into the sea, and set my course again. The wind was light, and that horrible boat of his stayed in sight for hours, but luckily no one else appeared.

'I can't remember the three days after that. I must have managed somehow, and I know I made my regular radio reports. I couldn't eat anything, and drank a lot and started shaking. But in a funny way I felt I'd cleansed myself of him in a way I couldn't before. And that I'd a sort of right to do what I did.'

'*Cleansed*?' asked Tom. 'A *right* to do it?'

She looked at him as though he were deranged. '*Yes*,' she said.

'A right?'

'To stay alive… Not to die… I thought I did, at least!' She dropped her head into her hands.

'Was he conscious when you shot him?'

But she seemed to have ground to a halt and didn't answer.

He paused, and after a while poured her another mug of coffee.

'But why the hell didn't you *tell* anyone?' he asked at last. 'Use your radio? Inform the police in Newport? He'd come to attack you, and you'd shot him in self-defence. Far, far safer to tell the authorities at once… What you did doesn't make sense, Jane.'

She looked doubtful and tired. 'Well, *I* thought it did. I didn't radio because I wasn't sure whether anyone would believe it had really been self-defence… I wasn't sure *myself* it was self-defence.'

'And why on earth did you then go and offer me this passage, without saying a bloody thing about the situation? Did you think *at all* about the position you were putting me in?'

She turned to him and opened her eyes wide. 'Ah,' she said, and paused. 'That's another story.'

'But wasn't it crazy and absolutely extraordinary?'

She looked stricken. 'I don't know,' she said. 'I expect I'm about to find out.'

*

Each time Tom considered the astonishing position Jane had so insouciantly drawn him into, he got angry. And more and more uneasy. He would need to handle the situation *absolutely* by the book—except that in this case the book provided no useful precedent whatever.

He considered her story with some care. Obviously, she'd set out to deceive him. On the other hand, she'd now made no bones about giving him a straight description of what had happened. He didn't doubt its essential truth. But the coolness of the shooting shocked him. Justified? Perhaps, in terms of what he knew of West. But *she* knew much less. She hadn't seen him for ten years—how could she have been so sure of what he intended? He very much doubted whether, in her shoes, he could have brought himself to pull that trigger so promptly. Could she have had some strong motive in addition to self-defence? He himself might, for the time being, be prepared to accept the shooting as justified, but Carl had been defenceless when she did it: by any ordinary standard she was, *prima facie*, a murderer.

There was much more to be asked, but he decided to wait. However, at coffee after lunch Jane leant back against the bunk cushion and enquired quietly:

'How did he manage it?'

'You don't need to know the details, Jane.'

'I don't give a toss about how you worked it out. But I *would* damn well like to be told how he set me up.'

Tom paused. 'He doctored your almanac,' he said.

'My Macmillan's? *Doctored* it?'

'He got onto your boat in Plymouth, cut out the page for June and replaced it with one having altered figures for the sun's distance east. He pretended the sun was further east than it was for the days he wanted, and then made it catch up again.'

Her mouth had fallen open. 'And I never noticed?'

Tom fetched the heavy volume from the chart table shelf, and showed her the invisible sellotape. 'He had a desk-top publisher on his PC, so it wasn't difficult for him to print off a decent facsimile of the page.'

'And he knew enough astronomy to work out the changes needed!'

'Exactly. I think he was a remarkably clever man.'

Jane's mouth tightened.

'He must have known you had no GPS. And that you always navigated by sun sights—he didn't bother to adjust the star or the moon tables to correspond. How could he have been certain about all that?'

She thought for a while, then made a face. 'The RYA published a cruise log of mine once. In their magazine.'

'And it described your navigation methods?'

'Yes.'

'When was this?'

'Three years ago.'

'That figures. We know he'd been planning this for a long time.'

'How long?'

'Since 1997. Maybe longer

'*God.*'

'He must have burgled *Ariel* in Plymouth. Would that have been easy?'

'There was a security gate; I didn't always lock the boat.'

'Once out in the Atlantic, you'd start reporting positions further east than your true position. *He* would know your true position, but everyone else would think you were further east. He could then cut south at a narrow angle from his reported track, rendezvous with you in a spot well away from other competitors, sink *Ariel* after he'd done you in, and cut back northwards without having lost much distance. He would have seemed too far away to be suspected.'

'When I looked at his chart, I realised he must have been transmitting false positions for days.' Her face was becoming more and more tense.

'He'd bought himself a boat large enough to have a bit of speed in hand over you and sailed slowly in the first part of the race. By keeping careful track of everyone's reported positions he could be sure not to try the manoeuvre unless both you and he were isolated. If he'd had to abandon it, you'd have come back on track and no one would've noticed. You would just have thought you were sailing faster during the second half of the voyage—which is what happened. You told me.'

'Had me pretty effectively sewn up, hadn't he?'

'A remarkably clever slow-burn plot.'

'As you'd expect. Nothing wrong with his intellect.' Tom pursed his lips.

'Absolutely characteristic.' She pressed fingers hard into her eyes for a moment.

'Only one thing went wrong. He couldn't know Laurel's real positions were right on top of his false ones.'

'I know. I was terrified you'd think it was *her*.'

'Two things puzzled me. One I've sorted out already. Eileen Meath had some radio bearings that seemed to confirm your reported positions.'

'Yes, I heard that.'

'But then I remembered that radio bearings don't distinguish between forward and back bearings. Eileen's bearings were accurate, but you were west of her, not east... The other thing was the rum bottles.'

Jane made a face, and picked up her mug again. 'I realised I'd left mine on *Cas A*. It must've fallen out when I was hunting for his kedge.'

'But you *told* me it was in your medicine cabinet. And Ed found one there.'

'That, I'm afraid, was a substitute I scavenged from the marina garbage can.'

Tom raised his eyebrows.

'And I thought I'd better drop my flare pistol into the sea, too,' added Jane. 'I bought some hand-held flares in Newport.'

'So I saw. But you'd told Ed earlier that you had a Very pistol, and he told me,' said Tom.

Gather to a head

Next morning, as Jane was frying bacon for breakfast, Tom leant back against the bunk cushion and said firmly, 'There's quite a few more things I need to get straight.'

The low morning sun was shining through the forward portholes and lighting up her face. She put down the pan and looked at him, shading her eyes. 'I'm not trying to hide anything, Tom,' she said. 'Not any more.'

'Sure?'

She nodded. 'What don't you understand?'

'First of all, why you asked me to join you on *Ariel*.'

'Oh yes,' said Jane. She pushed uncombed hair out of her eyes, slithered bacon onto the plates and started making fried bread.

'You said it was another story.'

She looked up at him and seemed to be thinking. At last she said, 'Well, so it was.'

'Can you tell me?'

'Of course… It was because of Father Michael.'

'Who the hell's Father Michael?'

She gave a wry smile, then looked serious again. 'Someone who helped me.'

'A priest?'

'Yes.'

'Why?'

'I was a mess! I'd killed a man. I needed to talk it

through.'

'With someone who would keep it secret?'

'Yes… Della told me where to find one.'

'Ah!' said Tom.

'What?'

'That was when she lent you her clothes?'

Jane smiled a little. 'That's right… I was brought up Presbyterian, but I got myself into Newport and found the right church and went in to see when they heard confession. I walked round and round the Plaza and came back at the proper time. I got myself into the box and shut the curtain. I told the priest through the screen that I'd killed someone. He said it wasn't a sin if it was in self-defence, and told me to pray for my victim. That was all. I asked if that was it, and he said if I needed to talk more, to go to the clergy-house.'

She slid the fried bread onto the plates, dumped them on the table and sat down opposite Tom. He cut up his bacon, took a mouthful and looked up expectantly.

'So that's what I did.' She looked thoughtfully at him. 'An old servant man took me to see Father Michael, and brought us a pot of tea. Father Michael listened very carefully. I told him the awful things that happened when I was a student. That I was afraid it *wasn't* really just self-defence, that I'd been angry, I'd wanted Carl dead—so it was murder. I started crying and had to stop, but he just waited for me to recover. When I'd finished, he thought for a long time, and then told me he had four things to say.

'First, in spite of what I'd told him about being angry, he *didn't* think it was murder because I really had been in mortal peril—yes, he said, my anger for Carl had been a sin, and I needed forgiveness for it, but that didn't make me a murderess. Second that Carl

232

had been a wicked man—he said Carl's soul stood in need of my prayers. Third that I'd sinned against myself and against my parents, and I needed confession and forgiveness for that—I told him Mum and Dad were dead. Fourth was the police. He wanted me to go and tell them.'

Tom felt his eyebrow twitch.

'Well, any decent citizen would. But I was still so angry with Carl: after all he'd done to me, I said, why should he be allowed to force me through a police grilling before I was ready? I knew they'd found *Cas A*. I knew I'd probably have to confess to someone in the end—but not in Newport, I wanted to get home first. I thought there was a chance I wouldn't be suspected straight away, and then I'd have the voyage home to come to terms with what I'd done, and work out what to do.'

Tom shook his head.

Jane looked up. 'He was just like you. Said it'd be bound to cause trouble. But, I insisted, did I have a *moral* duty to confess at once?' She gave a little sigh and peered at the puffy western clouds visible up the companionway.

'He thought for quite a long time. In the end he said, *perhaps*, because it was in self-defence, strictly speaking I had no absolute moral duty to give myself up... '

'Stupid man,' said Tom, more loudly than he'd intended.

'... but only if I could ensure that no innocent person suffered on my account. He repeated that condition several times, and urged me again to go to the police or a lawyer. At last he put his hands on my head and gave me a blessing. He seemed sad—I think he wasn't sure he'd said the right things. Then he rang a little hand bell, and the old man came again and showed me out onto the pavement.

'Well, even if Father Michael wasn't feeling sure, *I* felt better. He seemed to think I *wasn't* a murderer, and when I thought about that, I cried some more, and tried to think about what I should do.' She looked up, unsure.

Tom nodded. His irritation was mounting.

'I was hurrying along, and I started thinking about legal jurisdictions. If I was going to be accused of murder, I *certainly* didn't want it to be in the USA, where they have the death penalty. And even if I got a prison sentence, I didn't want to be in danger of rotting for life in some appalling American jail. It felt like a pretty compelling reason for keeping quiet.'

'You and Carl were both on *Ariel* when you shot him, weren't you?' said Tom.

'Yes, and I *thought* that probably made it British jurisdiction, but of course I couldn't ask anyone. I couldn't just gamble on it.

'When I got back to the club, Della introduced us, and you interviewed me. It was the first thing that happened. I suppose I thought… well, if that's the policeman chasing me, I could be doing a lot worse. And he's British. I decided I didn't *have* to tell you my story, not straight away. But I wanted to be sure that if I *did* have to explain to someone, it could be you, and not some bullying American cop. Then, when you said you were based in Plymouth, I realised I knew who you were, and that Mike had said you were fair-minded. *Then*, when I heard you needed a passage home, it seemed a heaven-sent way of doing what Father Michael had said—being in a position to make sure no one else suffered on my behalf, without necessarily having to spill the beans.'

'That was absolutely crazy, Jane!'

'It *wasn't*! If things got sticky, you'd be there and I could confess,' she said hotly. 'But I had very good reasons for preferring not to, till I was safely back in England.'

'As cool as that!' said Tom. It hurt. At the time Jane's invitation had come to him as a generous suggestion, something from a simple world outside his investigation. She'd made a fool of him, manipulated him.

Jane was watching him closely, her mouth compressed. She made a little face. But she said no more.

*

The next day, Jane seemed upset, and Tom wasn't surprised when she took to her bunk again. Grudgingly he found himself seeing things a little more from her point of view. He still felt extremely perturbed at how promptly she had pulled the trigger. But what he knew of Carl's history forced him at last to concede that it was in reality justified: she would have stood essentially no chance if the two of them had been cooped up alone together for any length of time.

The next stage of his questioning was sure to be distressing, and he decided to leave it till she was more recovered. The weather remained easy. He found himself busy with all the sailing and navigating, and concocting nourishing meals. Jane seemed to spend a lot of time reading, and he noticed it was still *Medical Taxonomy*.

'What happened to *Persuasion*?' he asked. 'Did you abandon it?'

She didn't reply immediately. 'Didn't suit my mood,' she said at last.

*

Two days later, Jane was more herself, and Tom felt he could hazard the next step.

'We've still a lot more ground to cover, you know,' he said cautiously. They were seated together in the cockpit enjoying the sun and the westerly breeze.

'Like what?'

'Well, for instance, why Carl wanted to kill you.'

She looked mournfully at him.

'I'd been hoping it wouldn't be necessary to go into that just yet,' he went on uncertainly. 'But if, for instance, we're to think about your legal position, I need to know.'

She thought for a while. 'I'm not sure I can be objective about all that, Tom.'

'You don't have to,' he said. 'It's only the essential facts I need. And you needn't tell me *anything* if you don't want to,' he added. 'Not now. We could take all that once we're back in Plymouth.'

She looked steadily at him.

'What do you think?' said Tom.

She took a deep breath. 'I'd rather wait,' she said.

*

By tea time, however, she had changed her mind. 'I was wrong,' she said. 'I want to tell you *now*.' They were once again in the cockpit, and she had been watching him. She seemed to gain confidence from his face. 'Like I said, I don't *want* to be concealing things from you, Tom, not any more.'

'Are you sure?'

'Yes... I don't know how much you know.'

'About Cambridge? We discovered Carl got into

236

trouble there over a student. For some reason we thought it was a man.'

'Well, he was involved with men too... I'm sorry Tom—this is awful.'

Tom said nothing.

She glanced up, then set her eyes firmly on the cockpit floor. 'There's a whole heap of nasty, crude stuff...'

Tom nodded.

'I was a complete innocent. Wildly romantic, never had a boy friend. My parents cared about me, but they were too *old*, too staid, too upright, I couldn't stand it... So what did *I* want?' A frown, still at the cockpit floor. 'Everything! Success! A double first, to keep Mother happy. But I was frantic to get right outside their tiny world, to *live* life. I wasn't going to be afraid.'

'Was that bad?'

She nodded firmly. 'It was when it came to sex... I wanted something *huge*. But it was all just wild imagination inside my stupid head. There were boys in my year I liked; but too gawky, too shy... And then Carl appeared.'

Tom frowned.

'I was a virgin, terribly naïve. And suddenly *there* he was, fair and blue-eyed, mature, vigorous. With something *challenging*, just in the way he looked at me, and terribly, terribly attractive. My crazy romantic imagination took wings. I was in bed with him within three weeks... *Completely* blind to what he really was.'

'How did you meet?'

'He was *teaching* me... College supervisions. Authority figure, rôle model, even. He was a good teacher, and I liked that.' She looked up at last, her face an anguished appeal of a sort that Tom hadn't seen in her before.

He nodded.

'I thought at first it was the real thing, that I was sharing something huge with him.'

'But you weren't?'

'He knew, you see. How to make me think I'd swept him off his feet, that *he* was the vulnerable one.'

Her voice was low and she was watching him closely. She clasped her hands tightly together. 'He was laughing, right from the start. All that hellish time, he was using me. He knew *exactly* what I was like, how to turn me on, how to string me along... I thought I was in seventh heaven.

'It lasted six weeks... What happened then was weird. I came to realise I *didn't* actually like him. In fact, he was horrible. But in some lunatic way I'd come to *need* him... He'd become a sort of sex-status fix.'

Tom frowned again.

She angrily pushed the bases of both hands into her eyes and blinked. 'That *wasn't* the real me. But it happened... And it was still a long time before I even half understood. The first shock was finding about the others, men and women. But it was so bloody important to me that I could make the sex thing work with him: he was supposed to think *I* was his real inspiration, his muse, that these others counted for nothing, they weren't really in the picture.'

'But they *were* in the picture. He even got specialised prostitutes up from London... what degenerate, debauched sort of person would go that far? And he got me doing things I didn't want... And he knew how to make me feel these damned ideas had come from me when they *hadn't*, they really hadn't. It got worse. The things he wanted got nastier. In the end he wanted... I really don't know why, it was just horrible... he wanted to *have* me covered in my own blood.

Just that. In the end, he carved me up with a lino knife, so he could have what he wanted.' Her head jerked up.

Tom flinched.

'I suppose he thought he'd got me just where he needed, and I wouldn't squeal. I was drunk. He didn't mean to kill me, or anything: I found later he'd set the blade so only a quarter of an inch stuck out. We were on the floor, he'd hidden it under the rug.

'When the pain came and I realised what he'd done, it was as though some huge door at last clanged shut in my head—anger tore through me and the pain vanished. I *screamed,* more horribly than I thought I could. I got violent—kicked his balls and went for his throat. But he just punched me down and scarpered pretty smartly. My neighbours came and found me all bloody. They called an ambulance, the hospital stitched me up, and someone told the senior tutor.

'I was too hurt and ashamed of what I'd got into with Carl to take him to court, and he tried to brazen it out. In the end, though, the College sacked him.

'He found out where I was. Came and raged at me. Nobody held him back, or kept him away. He shrieked his ruin was all my fault, he hated my guts, he'd *get* me one day… And then he disappeared.

'I was in terrible trouble. I had a breakdown. Couldn't explain one little bit to my poor parents, could I? One anti-depressant after another for more than a year—and then Mum died. Father was frantic.

'In the end, though, I got this therapist. Who cared. And my crazy romantic streak didn't end there, I was soon convinced I was in love with *her.* She just laughed at me, got me switched from science, started again in medicine… I was two years in therapy.'

Tom was wondering whether to slow her down.

239

'No,' she said, watching him. 'I've started now. But we might be warmer down inside.'

He set James to work and made some coffee.

She rummaged in a tin and found a battered pack of cigarettes, lit one and offered him another. He took it, lit it from hers. Their fingers touched. Neither of them had smoked in the other's presence before. She coughed violently, and he wondered what it was doing to her lungs. He inhaled, and could feel the nicotine coursing round his veins.

'I never worried too much about where Carl had gone or what he might do. The trauma blew him right out of my life. If I thought of him as anywhere, it was in hell…

'My anger was grinding away all that time. With myself as well as him, with my crazy fantasy. But any sane adult could see that if he'd had any glimmer of goodness or morality about him, it would have finished up as something different.

'In the end, I got into some sort of equipoise. I was lucky. The clinical course is tough, and I survived that. I even learnt to make jokes about sex. But sex itself had become completely hopeless. Still is. I'd *destroyed* it for myself.'

Rushing me over the jumps, thought Tom, and felt a surge of annoyance. 'Or maybe Carl destroyed it for you,' he said diplomatically.

'No, I'm just as much to blame.'

'What goes wrong?' he asked without thinking—he was feeling deeply enraged about Carl in a way he hadn't before.

Her eyebrows shot up. 'Bloody hell, Tom!'

'Sorry,' he said. He gave her a wry smile.

Her eyes searched his. 'Physical revulsion,' she said at last. She started coughing again.

Tom looked down.

'It's not that I don't want men. I do. But the instant it gets physical, fucking bloody Carl just blots the other poor guy out. And then I go rigid, literally rigid. Or I'm physically sick. *That's* what goes wrong.'

Tom said nothing.

'I get afraid, terrified, of a man as a man… That's why I won't let men pee over the side. I don't want to know any more.'

She turned her head away from him, and hesitated for a long time. 'So,' she said at last, 'there you have it. You saved my life… But you didn't have a clue *what* you were saving, did you?'

'No,' said Tom.

'A stupid feckless teenage debauchee!'

Tom thought for a while. 'Better understanding than not understanding, don't you think?' he said.

She looked surprised, and shook her head doubtfully. Then she frowned as though gathering her thoughts, and took a breath to continue.

'Stop,' he said quickly. 'You need a break. I'll take your watch.'

For a moment, she looked grateful, then peered around the cabin as though searching for help, her mouth working. She scrambled into her sleeping bag, turned away from him, curled up and covered her head with the bedding.

Tom looked down at her. He gripped the cabin table for a few moments. Then he swallowed hard, donned his oilskins, and went on deck. The sky was darkening rapidly.

Spiriting gently

As he began his watch and set about adjusting James' settings, Tom found himself raging furiously, and then raging again, at the despoiling of the young Jane. Professionally, though, he needed to disengage from that reaction. What happened next, therefore, alarmed him considerably: he discovered that *something*, somewhere, was urging him to rush in and offer Jane... what? ... A gift, some life-hungry gift powerful enough—if he could find it in himself—to heal the trauma that Carl had inflicted.

*

He was appalled. Wherever had *that* come from?

One part at least of his reaction had been straight-forward. The self-contained and confident companion he'd set out with had vanished, he felt, like smoke curling in the wind: she stood revealed as a naive and thoughtless risk-taker. Or so his head was telling him.

But his heart was hearing a different story. Jane's launching herself so passionately to grab her destiny by the horns had resonated almost unbearably with something long asleep inside Tom. Her eighteen-year-old determination not to be afraid of life had shone out to him not as a fault but as a beacon.

And this in turn, he soon discovered, had made it impossible for him to treat her any longer as devious.

Considerably to his surprise, he found that he could no longer conceive of her as guilty of *anything*. Originally, when she had described the shooting, she'd seemed to him suspiciously cool, far too ready to pull the trigger. But now he was unable to countenance the notion of any sort of concealed motive. It now seemed appallingly obvious that the man she'd been forced to confront had been totally evil and totally ruthless: if she were to secure the *slightest* chance of survival there'd been absolutely nothing else she could have done—and he caught himself, in imagination, sharing her predicament, pulling the trigger with her.

*

For the next three days she seemed exhausted, and Tom stuck doggedly to his sailing duties, while the policeman in him enquired brutally why his head was being so vigorously overruled by his heart. Indeed, his policeman-self went on to enquire with emphasis, for how *long* precisely had his heart held the upper hand?

Hadn't he been aware in himself, if he was honest, almost from their very first meeting, of a certain unprofessional lack of guardedness? That invitation to join her: by day he'd been reassuring himself so very carefully of his sound judgement. But by night, hadn't she and *Ariel* been dancing in his dreams?

And if that had been the case, what had been the attraction? Partly, of course, the offer of adventure, and her own adventurousness. But, he soon recognised, intertwined with her alarming readiness to take risks he'd been aware of something else. However dangerous and maddening her plan might have been, she'd *trusted* in him to quite an extraordinary degree. She'd been convinced in their very first meeting that she'd be safer with him than with anyone else. And he remembered how, on that first day at sea, she'd felt driven to admit her fault—as though she owed him, in fact, a warning, perhaps even come near to confessing. And when it had finally come to telling her story, she'd held absolutely nothing back—on the contrary she'd seemed determined to reveal herself wholly to him, however terrible a light it might place her in.

And hadn't there been another attraction? Hadn't the wild streak now revealed in her been perplexingly twinned with its direct opposite, a stalwart steadiness? He knew how he'd enjoyed her instruction in the art of navigation, how he'd come to rely on her seamanship, her medical expertise. And hadn't she all along taken a caring interest in his career, in his family? Her fury at him after St John's was revealed as nothing but frantic fear that he might accuse Laurel in her place—it had arisen simply because she was a loyal friend. Perhaps it was that intriguing wedding of wildness with steadiness that had beguiled him the most.

During three night watches, as he gazed over the moonlit sea, Tom found himself puzzling time and again over *why* the effect of her story on him had been so unnerving, and felt more and more uneasy.

*

The heart of a man may proceed crabwise, but will usually exert an irresistible force in the end. It wasn't until the end of the third day that Tom at last admitted the scale of his problem. Like lightening out of a clear sky Jane's story had smashed his professional detachment to smithereens. His heart was engaged, and demanding commitment.

So he stood at the very edge of a precipice, more appalled than ever.

*

These new feelings did not abate—far from it—and on the fourth day, when off watch during the afternoon, he retreated to his bunk to struggle with them. *Ariel* was now within a week's sail of Ireland, and his heart was still clamouring at him: to shelter her, to be joined with her... But what middle-aged stupidity was this? If his career was to survive it was absolutely essential to crush it. She was his *suspect*—a suspect *murderer*, damn it. And even more to the point, her emotional lacerations were raw—her traumatised disgust with sex couldn't simply be wished away. If he let escape the *slightest* hint of his unruly new feelings, what inexcusable harm might he not do?

The rigging screws above creaked continuously as *Ariel* hustled onward... He'd saved her life... He found himself seared by the memory of holding her shivering body naked in his arms. He tried to extinguish the flames by conjuring loyal memories of Beth, but his dead wife's shade gave him no help: she seemed just to smile over his bewilderment...

He turned over on the bunk. Then he heard a creak. He swung himself up and cracked his head on a deck beam, listening... Steps sounded on the companion ladder... The water tumbling on the other side of the fibreglass was urgent... At last there came a familiar rustle from the pages of the log book... Then more steps; silence, prolonging itself... She must be back on deck.

No, he insisted, *never*, of *course* not... It could never work. He rubbed his head and dropped back onto the pillow. Once we're ashore, there'll be the investigation and the case—which I must be central to... And if she gets safely through all that, the chances are she'll recover from her trauma and fall for someone of her own age... Which will be what she really needs... How, oh *how*, could I ever have allowed myself to imagine otherwise?

*

That evening at supper he thought she looked a little sad. But she'd rustled him up a favourite: buttered egg and strips of smoked salmon on thick brown toast, black pepper and a pinch of herbs.

'That was good,' he said. It felt like a peace offering and, though he couldn't see why any such thing might be needed, he felt touched.

*

Six hours later he was waiting in the cabin for the 2 am change of watch when Jane, usually so secure in moving around the boat, slipped while climbing backwards down the companion ladder. Tom, waiting ready below, grabbed her flailing right hand. She gripped him firmly, let him take her weight, and jumped down. As she did so, her cheek brushed his, and she looked at him.

'Sorry,' he said quickly.

'My fault.'

He said no more, but hurried scorched on deck.

*

Over the next few days, gradually, Jane settled to the remaining work of the cruise. Whether she was allowing her thoughts to move beyond the release of con-

246

fessing, he couldn't tell. At times, she watched him with some intensity. At others she seemed playful. She made no further effort to discuss her situation, and neither did Tom, who was thinking of what had still to come.

*

The gentle westerlies continued. The ocean beneath them was growing shallower and at last, one warm and quiet morning, Tom said firmly, 'Plymouth in three days. Things to be faced.'

'Yes,' said Jane. The sea was still empty, and they were sitting on the foredeck for a change.

'You need to do some thinking… You've got a good case of self-defence.'

She said nothing.

'I mean it.'

'He was unconscious, Tom.'

'I've thought it through.'

She looked sceptical. 'And morally?' she said at last.

'Morally too.'

Her eyes closed, and she took a slow breath.

'But,' he added, 'you're going to have to convince a jury.'

'I knew it would come to that,' she said at last. 'And anyway, I need to be held to account, by someone.' She pushed one hand up through her curls. 'But not by you.'

Tom frowned. 'Why?'

She blinked quickly.

'Why?' he insisted.

'Not impartial enough.'

'Aren't I?' he asked.

Her eyes were on the horizon.

Tom sighed. 'You see,' he urged, 'you can't escape it.

My Super will want to play this one strictly by the book.'

'Will he?'

'Especially once he knows I sailed home with you.'

Her eyes narrowed. 'Pity you got involved really, wasn't it?' she said quietly. But before he could reply she added, '*Please* Tom...'

'What?'

'Could you stop lecturing me? ... Just for a bit.'

'I'm trying to get you to face the future.'

'I know.'

'Have I upset you?'

She didn't reply, but something raw in her expression touched him, and he made a rash guess. 'It disturbs you, doesn't it?' he said.

'What? Facing up to things?'

'Having a *man* try to help.'

She looked up sharply.

'We're not *all* tarred with Carl's brush, you know... Maybe you'll realise that one day.'

Still she looked. 'What's *that* supposed to mean?' she said at last.

'Well...' he said with a shrug, then plunged on, pushing himself. 'Maybe one day soon, some dishy young chap will swim into your life, and... you'll discover he's exactly what you want and need.' His voice had become a little thick.

'Some dishy young chap?'

Tom swallowed.

She turned again to the distant clouds and squeezed her eyes shut. After a while, however, she opened them again, leant forward and gripped his right wrist, pinning it down to the deck. 'Tom,' she said.

He felt himself freeze.

'Stop it!'

248

'Stop what?'

'Stop being so ruddy thick!' She turned over his hand and examined it.

Ariel gave a bounce and crashed into a wave.

'It's not some dishy young chap that I want,' she added quietly, and let his hand go.

Tom looked down at his open palm. His heart was thumping; he also had a huge premonition of danger. 'Oh,' he said. He looked up, and swallowed. 'But Jane… '

'What?'

'Dear God! … I've been wanting *you*, too!'

'Yes,' she said.

'You *knew?*'

'Yes.'

Tom stared.

'But I thought,' she added, 'you couldn't afford to admit it… And I was afraid.'

'Afraid?'

'Of course.'

'Of what?'

'What d'you think? Of what Carl's done to me.'

Tom caught his breath. 'Are you still afraid?' he asked.

She nodded. 'Yes, very. *Very* much afraid.'

*

After this first beginning nothing further happened, as if by agreement. Tom felt desperately confused, and they got on quietly with the sailing and shipkeeping.

But after she had made lunch Jane said suddenly:

'When we get in to Plymouth, I've got to come ashore as your suspect.'

'That's true,' said Tom.

'Anything else wouldn't be safe for either of us.'

He smiled wanly. 'No,' he said, 'it certainly wouldn't…' He thought some more, but to little effect. 'I'm sorry, Jane. That's true… But I can't get my head round it. I'm in a total muddle.'

She nodded.

'Tearing strips off myself for having been so blind.'

'Mm.'

'But… Before we try to think ahead, can I ask you something?'

'Of course.'

'When did you realise?'

'Realise what?'

'What I was feeling.'

She allowed him a little smile. 'After I'd told you what sort of God-awful person I'd been… That was when I was sure. It had some sort of big effect, didn't it?'

'But you suspected earlier?'

'Just a bit.'

'When?'

'For instance, when you changed your mind and accepted.'

'Oh dear… And when did it start for *you*?'

'For me?'

'When did you start to feel strongly about me… I need to understand.'

'It doesn't matter, Tom.'

'But it does,' he said penitently. 'I need to rub my nose in how stupid I've been… Not when we first met?'

'Oh no,' she said, and laughed. 'Not *that* day… You walked me over to the library. I was scared out of my wits. And I realised you didn't like the clothes I was wearing, for God's sake. It made me mad.'

Tom smiled ruefully. 'And after that?'

She looked doubtful. 'Well, I knew soon enough you were a good and dependable sort of man, and I found enough strength to risk inviting you. And you said no. Oh well, I thought. But then you changed your mind.'

'But when did you know it was *more* than that?'

She hesitated and gave a little sniff. 'Well...' she said. 'Maybe the day you described Beth's death... I just ached. To weep with you, I mean. Can you understand that, Tom? Do you mind?'

'No, I don't mind.'

'But I knew that sooner or later I'd have to tell you my story. I was sure you'd run a mile once you'd heard it. I kept schooling myself to expect nothing.'

*

After supper, as he was washing up, Jane became silent, and he wondered. At last she said, 'Tom.'

'What?'

'I'm still scared you know... Because of Carl.'

'He's dead.'

'I know. Afraid of what he's done to me.'

She said no more, and for quite a while seemed to be thinking, so Tom got on with drying the knives. But then she opened her eyes wider and glanced distractedly around the cabin, as if gathering inspiration for something. Suddenly she said, 'Will you let me try something?'

'What?'

'This will seem completely crazy... Come over here!'

He hung up his cloth, worked his way around the

cabin table and sat next to her.

'Further away.'

He did as he was told.

'Lean back!' He obeyed. 'Now, don't rush me…' She nodded, wriggled forward, laid herself down along the bunk cushion, and gently placed her head on his lap, face away from him. She became completely still.

He could feel her warmth on his thigh. After a little while he found the courage to touch her springy hair. For a second or two she became rigid and scarcely breathed, and he was afraid again. But then, without moving her head, she curled up very gradually like a dormouse, and her tension seemed to be released. She searched for his free hand, held it, and after a while dropped off to sleep, or seemed to. Tom relaxed a little too.

Come unto these yellow sands

When Tom came on watch to relieve Jane at 2 a.m. a thin layer of high cloud had begun to blot out the stars. He settled onto the cockpit seat, the oily slickness of dry waterproof leggings under his hands. He had a sense of suppressed excitement, but no sense at all of what the future might hold, whether they even had a future. What might happen when they arrived in Plymouth remained a blank. His only fixed point was that she needed his patience.

By the time a watery sun crept above the horizon ahead, he still hadn't made much progress in thinking things out. Then, as he was frying bacon and reconstituted dried mushrooms, he heard a muffled wail from her bunk and looked down, concerned.

She struggled up, dishevelled in pyjamas.

'What was that?' he asked.

'What?' Her face was blank.

'You made a noise.' He dumped hot plates onto the cabin table.

'Oh… Bad dream.'

Ariel gave a lurch.

'Can we talk some more, Tom?' she asked.

'Of course.'

'About Carl… I'm sorry.'

'OK.'

'It's my vicious feelings.'

'*What* vicious feelings?'

'When I got that rifle into my hands… The court may decide it wasn't murder—but *I* haven't decided.'

'You had a right to defend yourself.'

She said nothing, and started on her bacon.

'Really screwed you up, hasn't he?' he said gently. He went to the galley to make toast. When it was ready he said: 'It's probably no use asking… This thing, this problem with men. How does Carl come into it? Do you know?'

She frowned. 'It's just revulsion,' she said. 'And anger. Overwhelms me, takes over.'

'Revulsion with him?'

'Yes, yes. But it spills over. To other men, all men… They just *become* Carl.'

'Even men you like?'

'Specially them.'

'Oh… Why?'

'They're good, so I can't have them… The trouble is, Tom, after I shot him, these feelings all got more violent.'

He got up again to make coffee. '*More* violent?'

She looked ready to weep. 'Well, I'd built up my life into something—not good, just something. And he comes barging back into it out of nowhere with that fucking rifle. He's turned me into a man-killer, a monster. He's trapped me worse than before—that's what I can't stand.'

Tom had learnt to be angry with Carl long ago. For the first time, he felt stalked. He sat and put an arm round her shoulder.

But she disengaged herself. 'It's *him*, Tom, really' she said.

'Yes… But maybe it's not possible to win that battle very quickly.'

'God! You say that?'

'Look,' he said. 'We understand each other now. But we've still got a long way to go. Working out how to make headway when things carry us backwards. What Carl is doing to you—to us. And we've got an age gap to span...'

'Bugger the bloody age gap,' she said. She seemed ready to argue on, but was suddenly overtaken by furious, violent tears.

'Jane!'

She pushed him away, leaped up and scrambled on deck, leaving her breakfast.

Tom wanted very much to comfort her. But suddenly, he wasn't certain that he could. He cleared away the food, and then, still unsure what to do, thought he'd better find his bunk to catch up on sleep. But the mournful thrumming of the breeze in *Ariel's* rigging kept him awake, queasy, a hungry anxiety in his chest.

*

He did sleep a little eventually, and emerged from the fore cabin about mid-morning; outside, thin cloud still veiled the sun. Jane was sitting beside the chart table, absorbed in the *Yachtsman's Handbook*.

'I upset you,' he said.

'Not your fault...' She gave him a quick smile, and continued.

'What's that?'

She looked up and passed over the heavy book. It was open at the first aid section on drowning.

'Why?' asked Tom.

'When you saved me,' she said slowly, 'how did you know what to do? From this?'

'First aid course.'

'But did you read this too?'

Tom paused. 'Yes,' he said. 'Once I'd got you breathing, I read it right through.'

'Did you do everything it says in here?'

'I think so… Yes.'

'You got me warm? The way it says? In a sleeping bag?'

Tom nodded.

'Were we naked?'

He hesitated. 'Yes.'

'And your warmth brought me back to life?'

Tom laughed. 'I wouldn't say that. You were coming back to life anyway, but I was afraid it might not last.'

She was still looking closely at him, and he was anxious again.

But she smiled. 'No,' she said, 'Don't be afraid.' She looked oddly at him. 'Knowing helps.'

'Does it?'

'Come here!'

'We ought not to rush,' he said. But he went.

She grasped his hand and forced it up under her sweater, laughed and kissed him hard on the mouth.

They broke apart. Tom looked at her, wondering. She smiled, took his hand, and laughed again. But, gradually, her smile ebbed into thoughtfulness.

'Are you OK?' he asked.

She smiled at him again. 'What d'you think!' she said. She lay back on the bunk cushion, hands behind her head. 'Could you leave me alone for a bit, now?'

'Why?'

'Just leave me.'

'Alright,' he said, confused.

He took himself on deck. The veil of cloud was starting to break, a few blue windows had opened in the west.

*

He felt deserted. *Ariel* was passing through a flotilla of eider ducks, bobbing harlequin-like on ruffled water, each with a black eye on Tom. Gradually they left the eider behind, but the interrogation of those beady eyes remained with him. The breeze had strengthened a little, and after about twenty minutes, it veered a little to the north. With the wind change as his excuse, he climbed down into the cabin to update the log.

She was lying as he'd left her, on the bunk cushion, her face now hidden in the crook of one arm. Tom wanted, very much, to show her some understanding and kindness, but it didn't seem quite the moment. Quietly, but dragging it out, he made his log entry, and at last turned, to climb back on deck.

He heard, then, a hasty rustle behind him, and stopped, his hands on the ladder. He felt her hands slide around his waist from behind. He swung around.

She grasped his upper arms and her eyes searched his intently.

Tom drew back.

'Are you scared?'

'No,' said Tom. But he was: the previous day, when her head had lain in his lap, he'd barely had the courage to touch her hair. He stared at her. She stared back, still grasping at his arms. She compressed her lips very slightly. The intensity in her eyes didn't change.

He couldn't find in them the tenderness of the previous day. But there seemed to him only one way to go. Gently he pulled her to him. He brushed her lips with his, and showered her face with an uncertain baptism of kisses. For a moment she stiffened, but then melted into the moment, sighed, and let him go.

Tom took an uneven breath. 'We're in a shipping lane,' he said.

He climbed on deck again. But the sea was still deserted, a bank of mist rising in the west. He checked the radar alarm and the self-steering. He adjusted the main sheet an inch or two. He stood still for quite a while; but the gentle, warm, firm breeze blew them onward as before—and Tom was blown with it.

He clambered down again. She'd flung her clothes all around the cabin, tumbled both sleeping bags together onto the cabin floor, and was lying there naked, watching him, challenge in her grey eyes.

He peeled off his own clothes. She pulled him down onto her, dragged his face down into her breasts, and they were warm and welcoming; but then, as he cupped her shoulder blades from behind and pressed close to her scarred belly, he knew already that something was wrong. She pulled him tighter, but her arm muscles were knotting, she was turning rigid beneath him. He craned his head back and sought her eyes, but they were lost, who knew where. 'Jane, Jane,' he shouted out, but her belly stiffened itself and her shoulders arched away from him.

Suddenly the rigidity was gone. An angry sob burst from her. She got up on her knees, grabbed his throat and shook him. 'Carl! Fucking Carl!' she shouted, and scratched him hard from shoulder to navel, drawing blood with both hands. In a frenzy she started to punch his head, knuckles into his eyes.

For a very brief moment animal instinct urged Tom to fight back. But there was too much hurt, too much danger: it had to be ended. With a struggle, he got both her wrists clamped in his left hand, and with his right slapped her face hard. There was a dreadful pause. They stared blindly at each other. The radar alarm went off.

Tom swore, and climbed naked on deck. An eastbound tanker was emerging from the mist bank, five miles away, its masts almost in line, an admonitory finger pointing at him. Swearing continually, he clambered down again, struggled into the minimum of clothing, staggered back on deck, and set the steering to manual. He sailed correctly and energetically. Guilt and anger mixed to make him ice-cold, too cold. He'd barely looked down at Jane, but knew she'd been frozen into naked immobility on the floor, the sleeping bag twisted around her, her eyes large and dark, fixed on him, a hectic red weal on one side of her face.

It was twenty minutes before the tanker was safely past. Tom set James back to work, and then climbed down into the cabin. Without looking at her directly he could see that she was dressed, in a thick sweater and jeans, her hair brushed and tied tightly back. She sat very still with her knees drawn up to her chin behind the chart table. The weal on her cheek was fading.

Tom silently found some antiseptic, and patched himself up at the sink. The mirror confirmed that a black eye was coming.

He sat down, exhausted, and looked at her. His anger was melting already, replaced by an ache of sadness. But there seemed nothing he could do.

'That was pretty bloody,' he said, almost to himself. She appeared not to hear.

He made some tea. She drank her mugful silently, barely changing her position behind the chart table. At one point he thought she was about to say something, and looked up expectantly. But she only slowly shook her head.

After a while, she asked in a low voice whether she might lie down on his bunk in the fore cabin. Her hands shook as she hauled herself to her feet and fumbled with the cabin door catch. A wave of guilt and defeat rolled over Tom.

Last sea-sorrow

As they passed the Eddystone at first light of a clear bright morning, Jane put a question.

'Tom,' she said, and coughed. 'If we moor up in Mill Bay Dock, could you take *Ariel* up to Sutton Marina, and keep an eye on her for a while?'

She'd helped him bandage the scratches; her hands had been cool and clinical. 'You poor man,' she'd muttered. Apart from that, she'd barely spoken in the thirty-six hours since the tanker passed. They'd done what sailing was needed, which amounted to little more than keeping an improved lookout as they came up channel, for James and *Ariel* were capable of everything else.

Tom, too, had said nothing. He couldn't blame her. If only she could have shot Carl Easton with a silver bullet. A great deal of hesitation returned to attack him. He considered the difference in their ages, his foolish lack of disciplined consideration. Horizons contracted, common sense mocked him. No fool worse than an old fool.

'I suppose so,' he said doubtfully. 'But won't you be wanting to sail her back to the Blackwater?'

'I'm not sure,' she said.

'Why?'

'I think it may be time to let *Ariel* go.'

Punishing herself, he thought. 'And where did you imagine you'd be, meanwhile?' he asked, cautiously.

'I don't know,' she said. 'I suppose, so far as you and your colleagues are concerned, it would be best to be near Plymouth.'

Tom raised his eyebrows. Her eyes searching out his were both sad and gentle but seemed to carry a warning to ask no more, and he found himself powerless, for the moment, to spell out the realities.

Soon the Eddystone was well behind them, and as the lights fading in the morning glow on Plymouth breakwater grew closer, Jane took charge of her ship as she had done on leaving Newport, but this time requesting no assistance. She spoke to Port Control on Channel 8 to confirm berthing and asked them to alert customs. They passed the breakwater. The small waves inside the Sound sparkled in the early sunshine, and the gentle westerly carried them easily up harbour on a broad reach. The citadel and the Smeaton lighthouse on the Hoe grew gradually larger. At last, Jane tucked *Ariel* into quiet water behind the jetty below Mount Batten, and brought her head to wind. The sails fluttered down, and were neatly secured. The engine was started. Still there was no request to Tom for assistance, and still he said nothing. They rounded Drake's Island. Finally, *Ariel* slid quietly up to the East Quay, stopped, and nuzzled her mooring line. Jane laid out the springs and head ropes, and cut the engine. Then she went off saying she needed to find the Queen's Harbour Master.

He made no attempt to stop her. Once she'd left, however, he went below, dug out his mobile, and called HQ. The explanation of what he needed took a considerable time. At last, having nothing else to do, he began to pack his kit, and when he had finished, sat on deck to wait. Fifteen minutes later a familiar black car drove slowly onto the quay and stopped some distance away, with a gentle squeak of brakes. Iain extricated himself from behind the wheel and raised an arm in greeting; Tom went over and spoke briefly. Then he returned to *Ariel* and Iain got back into the car.

After another ten minutes Jane reappeared, a sheaf of official papers clutched in one hand. She took them below. After hesitating for a while, Tom followed her. She was folding clothes and placing them in a small suitcase.

'What's going on?' he asked, facing her over the cabin table.

'It's not going to work out, is it?' she said. Her cool distance had gone; she did seem very sad.

'How can you say that?' said Tom. 'We can't tell.'

'I've screwed you up.'

'No,' he said. 'You may have screwed yourself up, for a while.'

She looked mournfully at him. 'While we were sailing up the sound I decided.'

'*You* decided? What?'

'I ought to put some space between us.'

Tom opened his mouth to speak, but found nothing to say.

She stretched a hand over the table and covered one of his.

'I've got to, Tom. To be fair.' He felt her fingers give an impulsive twitch.

'That's what you think?'

She gave a sniff and withdrew her hand. 'And I need space and time before I face up to the legal stuff. I shan't go back to Essex, not yet... There's an idea I talked about with Father Michael.'

'*Him*? What idea?'

'A place. A retreat house. Near here.'

263

'In a religious community, you mean?'

'Yes. Just for a while… I shan't need to take much, but we ought to check over *Ariel* before I leave.'

'You can't,' he said quietly. A measure of anger had blotted out the persuasive words he still wanted to find.

'It's for the best, Tom.'

'You *can't* just vanish into retreat.'

'Why not? It's only for a short time.'

'I've got no option, Jane,' he said.

'What?'

'I have to arrest you.'

'Arrest me *now*?'

'You've admitted killing a man. When he was incapacitated and helpless… I have to arrest you on suspicion of murder.'

She looked hard at him, raised her eyebrows.

'We don't need to make a meal of it. But I do need to say the words, and with a witness… OK?'

'Bloody hell, Tom!'

He stood and stuck his head out of the companion way, and a few moments later *Ariel* swayed as Iain stepped aboard and backed down into the cabin.

'This is my colleague, Detective Inspector Iain Gemmill.'

Jane looked blankly at Iain, who placed a briefcase on the cabin table, extracted a typed sheet and passed it to Tom.

Tom, still standing, examined it. He nodded and gave a sharp sniff. 'Jane Allison,' he pronounced clearly and quietly, reading from the paper. 'I arrest you on suspicion of the murder of Carl Easton, otherwise known as Charles West, at sea in international waters on the British vessel *Ariel,* on or about 24th June 2000.' He looked up. 'You do not have to say anything,

264

but it may harm your defence if you do not mention anything that you later rely on in court. Anything you do say may be later given in evidence.' He returned the paper to Iain.

Jane was dumb.

'Do you have anything to say, Dr Allison?' asked Iain.

She swallowed, and looked quickly at Tom, but he remained impassive.

She turned back to Iain. 'Yes,' she said slowly. 'It's true... I fired the rifle... And Carl died... But it was in self-defence.' She looked again at Tom.

Iain was writing it down. He read it back, and she nodded. 'Anything else?' he asked.

'No,' she said.

Iain wrote some more. 'Sign, please,' he said, and pointed.

She did as she was told. Iain put the paper away, closed his briefcase, climbed on deck and returned to the car. Tom sat down.

Jane looked at him. 'So I'm arrested?' she said.

'Iain will take you to headquarters. We can probably arrange bail within a day or two.'

'Won't you be coming too?'

'I'd better make *Ariel* secure first. Then I'll come.' There were tears in his eyes.

'Should I take my suitcase?'

'Yes.'

Before hoisting it on deck she sat beside him on the bunk cushion, took his head in her hands and kissed him gently on the centre of his forehead.

He climbed after her to watch the police car drive away, and sat at first numbed in the sunshine and the same warm breeze that had wafted them so far and so firmly. Castles in the air, he thought, castles in the air... And remembered suddenly, word-perfect from a half-forgotten schoolroom: *The cloud-capp'd towers, the gorgeous palaces, the solemn temples, the great globe itself, yea all which it inherit, shall dissolve; and, like this insubstantial pageant faded, leave not a rack behind.* He shook his head, got slowly to his feet, and went down into the cabin to study his face in the mirror. It seemed to him the heavy face of middle age.

Gradually, however, it occurred to him that the brow, however creased it might seem, had nevertheless just been touched by her lips; and that the blue eyes returning his stare were expressive not of relinquishment but of hurt, a hurt not at all deadened by the opiate of mature resignation. And the mouth, he observed with some astonishment, had set itself already into a dogged line.

Printed in Great Britain
by Amazon